SO-BEQ-991

BOOKS BY CLAIRE COOK

Must Love Dogs (#1)
Must Love Dogs: New Leash on Life (#2)
Must Love Dogs: Fetch You Later (#3)
Must Love Dogs: Bark & Roll Forever (#4)
Must Love Dogs: Who Let the Cats In? (#5)
Must Love Dogs: A Howliday Tail (#6)

Shine On: How To Grow Awesome Instead of Old
Never Too Late: Your Roadmap to Reinvention

The Wildwater Walking Club (#1)
The Wildwater Walking Club: Back on Track (#2)
Best Staged Plans
Seven Year Switch
Summer Blowout
Life's a Beach
Multiple Choice
Time Flies
Wallflower in Bloom
Ready to Fall

"A hilariously original tale about dating and its place in a modern woman's life."—*BookPage*

"Funny and quirky and honest."—*Jane Heller*

"These characters are so engaging I would probably enjoy reading about them sitting around discussing dish soap, but fortunately, the plot here is fresh, heartfelt, and always moving forward—not to mention laugh-out-loud funny."
—*Stephanie Burns, Book Perfume*

"[A] laugh-out-loud novel . . . a light and lively read for anyone who has ever tried to re-enter the dating scene or tried to 'fix up' somebody else."—*Boston Herald*

"If *Must Love Dogs* is any indication of her talents, readers will hope that Claire Cook will be telling breezy stories from the South Shore of Massachusetts for seasons to come."
—*The Washington Post*

"A wry look at contemporary courtship rituals, as well as a warm portrayal of a large Irish-American family."—*St. Louis Post-Dispatch*

"Funny and pitch perfect."—*Chicago Tribune*

Must Love Dogs:

A Howliday Tail (#6)

Claire Cook

Marshbury Beach Books

Marshbury Beach Books
Book Layout: The Book Designer
Author Photo: Stuart Wilson
Cover photo: jentara

Must Love Dogs: A Howliday Tail (#6)/Claire Cook
ISBN: 978-1-942671-23-7

One

So apparently buying the family house also meant inheriting Thanksgiving dinner. I guess John and I should have read between the lines before we signed the purchase and sales agreement.

No surprise, my family took it upon themselves to make sure I knew. Three of my five siblings just happened to show up one day without warning, or even knocking, to take their old seats around the scarred pine trestle table in the kitchen. If there was a gene for boundaries, it had definitely skipped at least this generation of the Hurlihy family.

"But we can't have Thanksgiving here," I tried. "We're under construction." I meant that literally, since my sister Christine's contractor husband Joe and his crew were knee deep in renovating our new-old house. But I meant it figuratively, too, as in John and I were trying to construct a life together, a sub-family of our own.

Not an easy task amidst the insanity of living with my father, who had come with the house, and who had a tendency to hog most of the available air in any given room. Polly, my pregnant and single assistant teacher, had moved in, too, after being traumatized when a recent nor'easter rolled through her waterfront winter rental on the other side of Marshbury. Oh, and we'd rescued a mama feral cat and her four kittens, who were still working things out with John's dog Horatio.

Hosting Thanksgiving on top of all that seemed like something that should happen, say, a week from never.

"We *have* to have dinner here," my sister Christine said. "It wouldn't be Thanksgiving otherwise."

Even though I knew it probably wasn't going to fly, I flashed my most pitiful look. "But I've never cooked a turkey in my entire life. I've never even touched one."

"Sure, you've never touched a turkey," my sister Carol said. "Would you like a list?"

I crossed my arms over my chest. "Ex-husbands don't count."

Carol put her hands on her hips. "Yeah, they do."

"We might want to think this through," my brother Michael said, "considering Sarah's idea of cooking is preheating the oven and wandering away." He grinned our mother's crooked smile, which always made me miss her all over again, even though she'd been gone for more years than I wanted to count.

"All my girls are good cooks, thank the good Lord." Our dad made his entrance across the speckled linoleum floor as if it were an off-off Broadway stage. He raked a wayward clump of white hair from his watery brown eyes, leaned over and patted my hand with one of his beefy paws. "I'll be busy setting up my man cavern by turkey day, God willin'. But if you need any help that won't take more than a minute or two, feel free to give me a holler, Christine."

I slid my hand out from under my father's and patted him back. "Sarah. And if you need any help remembering my name that won't take more than a minute or two, feel free to give *me* a holler."

Eventually my family decided to pick on somebody else, as they almost always did if you waited long enough. I took a moment to wonder when my own particular version of the luck o' the Irish had morphed into a bad case of Murphy's Law. I'd probably be stuck hosting Thanksgiving dinner until Hell froze over. Or at least until I managed to come up with a genius escape strategy.

Until then, survival was my goal.

. . . . .

Time flew, like calendar pages in an old movie, and suddenly it was the day before Thanksgiving.

Back in 1978, President Jimmy Carter had officially proclaimed the second Sunday of September Grandparents Day. Celebrating the importance of grandparents in our lives was a terrific gesture, but beyond providing diehard Hallmark card fans with another trip to the store and the mailbox, it never really took off.

So Bayberry Preschool kept the sentiment and changed the date to make it work with our school calendar, something preschool teachers probably would have suggested way back when if anybody at the White House had thought to consult them.

Today, the half-day before Thanksgiving, was now Grandparents Day at Bayberry. This was Bayberry's sweet and memorable way of honoring the kids' doting grandparents, many of whom traveled far and wide to celebrate Thanksgiving with their adorable grandchildren.

Slightly more calculating was the fact that a few hours of *oohing* and *awwing* over the grandparents often resulted in some serious donations for the school.

As the grandparents arrived, cute turkey stick-on nametags would be distributed. Mail and snail mail addresses would be collected. Once the next day's turkey dinners had been digested and the grandparents were home again, a letter would arrive from Kate Stone, Bayberry's founding director, aka our bitch of a boss. *Wouldn't it be lovely if your grandchildren could learn to read their grandparents' names engraved on a special brick on the new entry courtyard? On an engraved plaque on a dismissal bench? Or why not donate a piece of playground equipment so your precious grandchild could not only read your name but also think of you every time s/he took a spin around the safety-first jungle gym?* A giving pyramid designed by the fundraising committee, printed in full color on heavy paper stock, was tucked in with the letter.

It was genius. And the best part about it was that the more well-heeled and bejeweled grandparents had a tendency to get a little bit competitive. One set of grandparents even donated a chic barn-like addition to the school that served as meeting space, gym, theater, concert hall, indoor playground and fitness court, large art project room, and occasional teacher hideout area. The massive brass plaque just inside the door proclaimed it the Jebediah J. Jones IV and Dr. Aubrey C. Jacobs Family Gateway to Excellence Barn. Everybody else called it the all-purpose room.

The sad part about Grandparents Day was that not every child could produce a grandparent. In each classroom, year in and year out, at least one grandparent-less child dissolved into a puddle of tears by the time early dismissal rolled around.

The other teachers and I had brought up this issue at multiple staff meetings over the years. Kate Stone waved our worries away, visions of potential donations flashing before her eyes.

When pressed, our bitch of a boss would say, "Step out of the box and use your creativity. Turn the day into a lesson in sharing. The students who have grand-parents can simply share them with the others."

Spoken like an administrator who had forgotten her own teaching days. Sharing the crayons was enough of a challenge for preschoolers, especially the day before a holiday when excitement was high and self-control was slim to none.

So this year I'd decided to bring in a ringer, a stand-in grandparent to pass around—my dad. The best thing about this idea was that my father was free on the morning before Thanksgiving. The worst thing about it was that a lifetime of experience had taught me only too well that pretty much anything could happen, and often did, when my father was involved.

The thing about your family is that you never quite stop hoping you can change them into the people you'd prefer them to be.

I wasn't taking any chances, so my plan was to make my father ride to school with me this morning. "Hurry up," I yelled up the staircase. "My boss has zero sense of humor when the preschoolers get to school before the teachers."

Polly passed through the kitchen and gave me a thumbs up on the way out the door, reassuring me that at least one of us would get there before the kids.

My father thudded down the stairs wearing a pink Bark & Roll Forever T-shirt and carrying a handful of business cards with little dog treats tied to them with ribbons. When he wasn't letting his middle daughter drag him to school, my dad drove a pink ice cream truck and passed out the cards for the three women who owned the Bark & Roll Forever dog and cat sitting and boarding business.

"You're not wearing *that* to school," slipped out of my mouth. I flashed back to all the times my mother had said the same thing to me a gazillion years ago. Overly mini miniskirts. Too much green eyeshadow or frosted lipstick. A slightly see-through blouse.

Under his shaggy eyebrows, my dad did his wide-eyed innocent look. "Just using my noggin'. I figure I'll follow you in the ice cream truck, and if things get slow, I can pass out some Nutty Buddys and the kiddos can take turns going for rides with me in the ice cream truck. I'll make it educational, don't you worry. You know, teach 'em how to lay a little rubber, pop a wheelie or three."

"Right," I said. "No liability issues there. I mean it, Dad. March right back up those stairs, change into something grandfatherly, and jump in the car with me. Now."

He came back down wearing a blue T-shirt that said I'M A GRANDPA, WHAT'S YOUR SUPERPOWER?

"Perfect," I said, relieved that he'd chosen this T-shirt over his Thanksgiving sweatshirt with the picture of a roasted turkey on it that said I'M A BREAST MAN. I decided to overlook the fact that he was also wearing a pair of gold suspenders. And his Coast Guard Auxiliary hat.

While I drove us to school, my dad sang a few verses of "I Gotta Be Me" in his long-practiced Sammy Davis Jr. imitation.

I did my best to block him out so I could go over my plans for the day in my head. Turkey placemats never got old, so earlier in the week Polly and I had passed out sheets of 10" by 14" oak tag paper. We helped the kids trace their hands and turn them into turkeys, then let them decorate the rest of their placemats with a tsunami of finger paint.

When they'd finished their own placemats, they made more for their grandparents or for my dad. Polly and I made extras, just in case, and then Polly ran them all through the laminating machine so they'd survive the spills ahead. We'd hand out the placemats just before dismissal, and the kids and their grandparents could use them for Thanksgiving dinner and beyond.

I hit the brakes at a stop sign and turned to give my father my serious look. "Promise me. No wild stuff like pony or airplane rides, and only clean jokes. Actually, no jokes at all, just to be on the safe side. All you have to do is smile and look cute, Dad. And let the kids drag you around by the hand if they need to. And do not, I repeat, do not, hit on any of the grandmothers. Or Polly."

I drove up the driveway to the school, past the clay fish totem pole and the plywood teddy bears.

I pulled into a parking space. My dad flashed me a big grin. "Don't get your knickers all in a bunch, sweetie pie. Have you ever known your dear old daddy to let you down?"

CHAPTER

Two

The grandparents managed to contain themselves, but the kids were bouncing off the walls as they entered the classroom. I would have loved to take everybody out and make them run a few laps around the school to burn off some energy, but I knew my boss would kill me if any grandparents keeled over.

My father stood beside me, four or five kids hanging off him like he was a piece of playground equipment.

Polly crossed the room in our direction.

"There she is," my father said. "The longer I look, the prettier you get, darlin'."

"The longah I look, the prettiah you get, darlin'," four-year-old Julian said with perfect preschool parrotry.

"You can't say that," five-year-old Violet said. "Only Grandpa Billy can say that."

"You're not the boss of me," Julian said.

"I'm the boss of everyone," five-year-old Millicent said.

"That's the spirit, darlin'," my father said. "You keep believing that."

"Knock it off," I whispered to my father.

A striking woman with red lips and silver hair walked toward us. She was wearing perfectly pressed wide-leg slate gray trouser pants and a white silk button-down blouse. One extra button was unbuttoned to show off her chunky silver necklace, as well as some substantial cleavage.

Of course, she ignored me and went right for my dad. "Shelby Byrne, Pandora's grandmother." She held out her hand.

"Billy Boy Hurlihy doesn't shake hands with beautiful women." My father took her hand, brought it to his lips. Then he danced her around a few steps and dipped her, long and low.

I held my breath, hoping that Pandora's grandmother's back was as limber as it looked. It would be a bummer of an incident report to have to write and turn in at the office. *Pandora's grandmother inadvertently injured her back this morning while dipping. Ice was applied and every effort was made to keep her separated from the dipper.*

Fortunately, she returned to vertical with a giggle. "Well, you certainly beat those old fuddy duddies I've met on Rematch.com." She held my father's gaze while she reached into her trouser pocket and handed him a card. "Call me, Billy Boy Hurlihy, and we'll go out on the town. I'm here till Tuesday."

"Will do, darlin', will do." My father reached into his pocket and pulled out a Bark & Roll Forever business card with a dog treat attached. "I might even pick you up in the ice cream truck."

"My turn, Grandpa Billy, my turn," four-year-old Juliette said. She held her hand out to be kissed. The other kids, girls and boys alike, held out their hands to be kissed, too.

I nodded to Polly, waited until she was in position, clapped my hands.

"Okay, everybody. Walking on your tippiest tippy toes, line up in a single file," I yelled. I rearranged clumps of kids and grandparents into a single line behind Polly. I made my dad the caboose, hoping he might get into less trouble at the end of the line.

The turkey hop is a Thanksgiving twist on the bunny hop, and the bunny hop is essentially a conga line. My iPhone was already sitting in the charging dock with speakers I'd finally bought with my own money at the start of the school year, a huge upgrade to our classroom CD player, cassette deck and ancient turntable. I found the upbeat, instrumental version of "The Bunny Hop" on a children's classic dance favorites album I'd downloaded.

I stayed where I was and began demonstrating the movements: a forward jump, a backward jump, a forward jump, then three big jumps forward.

I pushed Play. Polly snaked the line around the classroom as the students and their grandparents all danced and sang along.

Hop your drumstick forward
Hop your wishbone back
Hop your drumstick forward
Hop, hop, hop

Join our new creation
Already a sensation
Do the turkey hop
Turkey, hop, hop, hop

"Stuffing" Polly yelled, the way we'd rehearsed it. "Green beans."

Hop your stuffing forward
Hop your green beans back
Hop your stuffing forward
Hop, hop, hop

Join our new creation
Already a sensation
Do the turkey hop
Turkey, hop, hop, hop

The kids started yelling out their favorite Thanksgiving foods. We kept it going, verse after verse, until a couple of the kids accidentally jumped backward instead of forward, and the turkey hoppers started tumbling over like dominoes. A good preschool teacher knows when to wrap things up fast.

"Circle time," I yelled as I stopped the music. Polly and I gathered everybody together on the big fluorescent orange circle, the heart of our classroom. Most of the grandparents were in pretty good shape and made it to the floor just fine. We got the ones who didn't want to trek all the way down there seated on kiddie chairs, which were so small that they probably weren't much of an upgrade from the floor.

My father, never one to shrink from a challenge, eased his way down until he was seated cross-legged on the circle. Half a dozen kids arranged themselves on his lap. Pandora's grandmother looked like she wanted to join them.

When my dad ran a hand through the shock of white hair that always fell into his eyes, he reminded me of a giant cat grooming himself. Julian ran his hands through his own hair in a perfect imitation.

"You're the bestest toy in this whole wide school," three-year old Josiah said as he gave a big bounce in my father's lap.

"Easy tiger," my father said. "Watch out for the family jewels."

"When my grammy and grampy come to visit, I have to wear underpants," three-year-old Harper said.

Harper's grandparents stared straight ahead and pretended not to hear her.

Josiah gave another bounce on my father's lap. "When my nana and papa come, I'm not allowed to play bongo drums on my peepee and sing babaloo," he said.

"Before you know it you'll be all grown up, young man," my father said, "and you can sing babaloo whenever the mood strikes."

I took a page from Harper's grandparents' book and pretended not to hear my father.

"If you're thankful and you know it, clap your hands," I sang.

The kids jumped right in. "If you're thankful and you know it, clap your hands. If you're thankful and you know it, then you really gotta show it. If you're thankful and you know it, clap your hands."

What I was really thankful for was that I could tweak any song to fit any holiday—it was my superpower as a preschool teacher. We clapped our hands. We stamped our feet. Those of us who could snapped our fingers, and the younger kids faked it. We laughed out loud.

When circle time was over, we had mini pumpkin muffins for snack, and then the kids were free to choose their own activities. They rolled out floor mats or found seats at short tables to work independently. Shapes and colors and smell matching games, counting games, fine motor activities, letter tracing, sand play.

I stood for a moment watching Griffin's grandmother read a book to him in our reading boat. When she turned the last page, she caught my eye and smiled. Griffin was sound asleep, his thumb in his mouth, a corner of one of the fluffy pillows clutched in his other hand.

"Griffin's such a sweet little boy," I said, thinking it best not to point out that his only fatal flaw was that he wasn't quite as toilet trained as his parents had led us to believe he was.

"Just you wait," his grandmother said. "Being a grand is the best thing ever. People tell you it's because you can spoil them rotten for a few hours and then give them back to their parents. But that's not really it. The biggest gift of having grandchildren is that it's a do over. You get to be a child again. I could spend another five hours playing at that sand table over there."

I smiled. "Feel free. Just lock up when you leave."

She smiled back. "Of course, that's ages and ages away for you. How old are your children?"

"I don't have any," I said in a voice I didn't quite recognize.

She waved a hand in front of her face. "You have plenty of time."

Not really, I wanted to say. *I'm actually on borrowed time and quickly approaching it's not going to happen territory.*

Griffin's grandmother headed for the sand table. I stared out the window, watching fall leaves twirl through the air, defying gravity, only to give up and flutter to the ground.

Polly and I passed out the Thanksgiving placemats, herded kids and grands outside.

My father grabbed Polly by both hands and started dancing her between the freshly trimmed boxwood ducks that lined the walkway. She laughed and pushed him away.

I looped my arm through my father's, dragged him over to the dismissal area, where I thought I might have half a chance of keeping him out of trouble.

My bitch of a boss turned and gave us a long look. Back when I was growing up, we used to call that look a hairy eyeball.

"Who's the broad with the broomstick up her rear end?" my father stage-whispered to me.

"Da-*ad*." I dug my fingers into my father's arm. "You know that's my boss. Come on, please don't get me in trouble."

"Look." My dad pointed over my shoulder.

By the time I realized I'd fallen for the oldest trick in the book, he'd managed to slip out from my death grip and was heading straight for my bitch of a boss. He scooped her up in his arms, gave her a spin around one of the dismissal benches. Then he dropped her off where he'd picked her up, like it was a bus stop.

Amazingly, Kate Stone seemed to be laughing. She might even have been flirting.

My father kissed her hand and came back to join me.

"Let me know when you're up for a raise," he said. "I'll take her for a longer twirl and get her in the mood to say yes."

Ethan, the new teacher, brought his class out to sit next to ours on the dismissal benches. Ethan said something to Polly, and she said something back to him, their heads close together. The two of them laughed.

Beside me, my dad crossed his arms over his chest and gave Ethan his famous stink eye.

"I don't like the cut of his jib," my father said.

Three

Before I knew it, I was stumbling down the stairs of the house I'd grown up in, on my pre-dawn Thanksgiving turkey mission. In a lifetime spent doing my best to avoid the perils of domesticity, this was by far my biggest challenge yet.

I managed to locate the kitchen and open the ancient refrigerator. I identified the turkey right away, all twenty-eight pounds of it. An old Roseanne Barr line popped into my head: "Here I am at 5 o'clock in the morning, stuffing breadcrumbs up a dead bird's butt."

Not to get all competitive, but when it came to early rising on Thanksgiving, I had Roseanne beat by almost an hour.

A text popped into my phone. Even though it was from my sister Carol, I found my reading glasses and read it anyway:

> *Do not, I repeat, DO NOT, cook the stuffing inside the turkey. It's an invitation to salmonella.*

My bossy big sister thought pretty much everything was an invitation to salmonella, but I decided to listen to her anyway. Mostly because this cancelled out the hand-up-the-turkey-butt issue.

I took a deep breath, reassured myself that I had the Turkey Hotline number on speed dial. Not only that but just in the nick of time the Turkey Hotline had also gone digital, backing up their telephone outreach with both Twitter and text capabilities. Over fifty turkey experts with nimble fingers were at the ready.

I was good to go.

. . . . .

"Hey," John whispered. "Happy first Thanksgiving together."

I jerked awake, yanked my head off the kitchen table, delicately wiped a smidgen of drool from one corner of my mouth.

"Why didn't you wake me up so I could help?" he said.

I turned my morning breath away so his kiss landed on my cheek.

"Did you save the giblets for the gravy?" he said.

Giblets. My foggy brain sputtered as it tried to remember what the word meant.

"Damn," I said. I jumped up, slid across the kitchen floor in my fuzzy faux-rabbit slippers, a gift from one of my students. I grabbed the potholders and wrestled the mammoth beast to the stove top. Then I opened drawer after drawer until I found a pair of barbeque tongs.

John took a step toward the turkey and me, as if one or both of us needed to be saved. I narrowed my eyes. He took a step back.

The kitchen door swung open again. Polly tiptoed into the kitchen with an armful of empty cat food dishes. She took one look at me and kept tiptoeing.

I reached inside the turkey with the tongs, feeling oddly like a gynecologist brandishing a metal speculum. I found the plastic pouch and hurled it into the kitchen sink.

"Try the other end," John said.

"Eww," I said. But he was right. I flipped a smaller plastic pouch into the chipped porcelain sink.

When I looked up, Polly and John were staring at me.

I pointed the business end of the barbeque tongs at them. "If either one of you tells me this turkey is contaminated, I will take you out. We'll never find a replacement turkey in time."

They kept staring.

"Fine," I said. "We'll buy a turkey pot pie and cut it into equal slivers. And the story of my epic turkey fail will be immortalized into family history, told and retold at every Thanksgiving for the rest of my life. With my luck, my family will think it makes a good St. Patrick's Day story, too. And let's not forget the instantaneous family Facebook post competition."

John's thumbs pranced away on his phone. He looked up. "The Food and Drug Administration site says that if the plastic packaging containing the giblets has changed shape in any way during cooking, do not use either the turkey or the giblets because harmful chemicals from the packaging may have penetrated the meat."

I leaned over the sink for a closer look. "How exactly are we supposed to tell what shape the packaging was to begin with?"

Polly leaned in beside me. "I think they mean if the packaging has started to melt. I have total pregnancy nose, and I don't smell any melted plastic at all."

John came over to check things out for himself. "Looks fine to me."

"Crisis averted." I blew out a puff of air. "Fingers crossed it's all smooth sailing from here."

John and Polly nodded encouragingly, as if wishing might make it so.

Polly had borrowed the turkey cookie cutter from our classroom. I watched her shape canned turkey paté dog and cat food into the perfect Thanksgiving breakfast feast.

"Genius," I said. "You're so creative."

Polly smiled. "Thanks." She was barely awake and she was glowing already, her pink cheeks making her freckles pop. Strands of tinsel gray lit up her auburn hair. Her baby bump looked cute and unintimidating, more like a fashion accessory than something that encased a real-life person-to-be. I liked Polly. But if I was really honest with myself, I'd probably like her a lot more if I was pregnant, too.

John fed Horatio in the kitchen, while Polly and I carried the feline paté turkeys into the former family room, which was now the official cat room.

I turned the cut-glass doorknob, bumped the old door open with my hip. The four kittens, boys all—Sunshine, Squiggy, Oreo, and The Great Catsby—made a wobbly dash for us, mewing away. Pebbles, the mama cat, climbed up to the safety of the bookshelf, her emerald eyes sparkling. I stepped over the kittens, stayed low, slid Pebbles' dish to the other end of her shelf. She waited until I moved away again, then dug in.

Polly placed four small dishes on the big plastic boot tray we'd repurposed as a feeding station. The kittens jammed their tiny paws and noses into the cat food, managed to get a little bit into their mouths. Once Pebbles had finished her food, she'd come down from the bookshelf and clean up their leftovers. Then she'd stretch out on the floor, and the kittens would all line up for a group nursing session.

Already we knew the routine by heart.

· · · · ·

John's dog Horatio was a cross between a Yorkie and a runaway greyhound, but he'd somehow come out looking like a tall, disheveled dachshund. If John had to choose between the two of us, he wouldn't. He'd find a way to keep us both.

Horatio hesitated in the doorway. Pebbles eyed him. Horatio plopped down on the threshold. The two of them seemed to have worked out the exact distance they needed between them to coexist peacefully. Maybe if I watched carefully, I might learn something that would help me out with my family.

John stood still for a moment, as if he might stretch out on the floor beside Horatio. Then he joined Polly and me on the old plaid sofa. We were an odd threesome, all in our bathrobes on Thanksgiving morning. The man I hoped I'd spend the rest of my life with. The teaching assistant I'd hired because even though she had absolutely no experience with children, she was such a train wreck I couldn't stop thinking that if the situation were reversed, I hoped she'd hire me.

And me, the woman who could never quite figure out how the rest of the people in the world managed to look like they were living their lives with such effortless grace. It felt like everyone but me had gotten the memo, the how-to-thrive instruction manual.

Then there was the fact that Polly had managed to get pregnant but hadn't found the guy to complete the happily-ever-after package. I'd found the guy but couldn't seem to get pregnant. John had found me, and against all odds, he didn't seem to think that was a bad thing. If you smushed all three of us together, you could probably reconfigure us as the perfect couple.

We all yawned, one after another, like a wave at a baseball game.

"Are you sure I won't be in the way for Thanksgiving dinner?" Polly said. "I could go hang out at Burger King or something, and you could save me some leftovers."

"Don't be ridiculous," I said. "Half my family likes you better than they like me already. Plus, if anybody gets to hang out at Burger King during Thanksgiving dinner, it should be me."

I, I heard my dead mother say. *It should be I.*

Growing up, my mother always corrected our grammar, especially when we answered the phone.

May I please speak to Sarah? Or Carol. Or Johnny.

This is her, we'd say. Or him.

She! He! Hands on her hips, my mother would await our revisions. *This is s/he,* we'd mumble into the receiver.

I'd lost the sound of my mother's voice shortly after she died. But I could still hear her correcting me.

"It should be I," I whispered. Fortunately, the live people on either side of me didn't appear to notice.

"I'd like to propose," John said, "that we keep the animals locked in this room for the duration of Thanksgiving dinner."

"Ha," I said. "Like locked doors have ever worked with my family. Once we locked my brother Michael in the basement with a padlock after he stole some of our Easter candy. And he just climbed out the window and snuck up behind us. It scared the bejeebers out of us, as my brothers used to say."

John bit his lower lip. He seemed to be doing that a lot since we'd moved in to my childhood home.

"Then maybe," he said, "we could print out a list of unsafe Thanksgiving foods for animals and post it somewhere central."

I rolled my eyes as diplomatically as I could. "Sure. Or perhaps we could recite the list after grace just to make sure they don't miss it."

John dug in his bathrobe pocket for his phone. "It says here that the bones and skin are the worst, but even too much turkey meat can cause diarrhea, vomiting, and dehydration in both dogs and cats."

"Let's not forget about salmonella," I said. "Although if we do, my sister Carol will be only too happy to remind us."

John stayed glued to his phone. "Onion and garlic, as well as all other members of the allium family, are toxic for dogs and cats. Chocolate's out, too, of course. Unsweetened canned pumpkin is actually good for them though. As long as the cans are BPA-free."

"Great," I said. "There's still time to ditch the turkey and just open some cans of pumpkin and pass them around. Because I have to tell you that Mother Teresa has been lapping our Thanksgiving plates since early puppyhood, so this is not going to go over well with her."

Mother Teresa was my brother Michael's Saint Bernard. His wife Phoebe wasn't too crazy about the name, but the rest of us applauded it, since it appealed to our immature, lapsed Catholic sensibilities.

"Hmm," John said. "I suppose we could keep the cats and Horatio in here, and let Mother Teresa out long enough for a quick lap around the table. Pun intended."

I smiled at him. John's dorky sense of humor was part of his charm. I felt that little jolt I always did when my eyes caught his. His Heath Bar eyes were his best feature, a circle of toffee surrounded by a larger circle of chocolate. You could get lost in those eyes.

"But," I said, "the kittens are supposed to be handled by humans as much as possible to socialize them. I mean, my family doesn't come in handy all that often, so I think we should put them to work."

"No offense," John said, "but your family's interpretation of 'as much as possible' might turn into a bit of a mob scene."

"I could drive over to Bayberry," Polly said, "and borrow the bathroom pass from our classroom. That way they can take turns."

I laughed. "Maybe we could just give my family numbers and herd them in two at a time for kitty handling. We could hose them down first to make sure they're not harboring any poison food particles."

"Just in case you think I'm kidding," John said. "I'm serious."

I leaned sideways, touched my head to his. "I know you think you are. It's one of your many endearing qualities."

Four

"Enough with the flapdoodle and fiddle-faddle," my father said as he walked into the cat room carrying a big pink plastic flamingo.

"Where did you find Pink?" I asked. "I thought Christine took her home when we rescued her from the dumpster." I turned to Polly. "Long story, but basically when we were getting the garage and the secret room cleaned out so they could be renovated for my dad's man cave, a few valuable family treasures needed rescuing."

It was John's turn to roll his eyes.

"Nothing in this house goes anywhere unless I sign off on it," my father said. "No siree Bob."

"Sarah," I said.

When my father gave the flamingo a twirl in front of the kittens, I had to admit Pink was pretty light on her single metal foot. I once read that flamingoes are seriously flirty birds that have over 130 sexy moves to attract a mate. If I had a single sexy move that had attracted John, I'd be hard pressed to name it. I wondered if plastic flamingoes gave lessons. Maybe Pink could start with me, and then we could write a sexy moves blog together.

I'd also read that flamingoes are monogamous, but only for a single mating season. I didn't think either John or I were the least bit flamingo-ish, but I had to admit reading that still gave me pause. Could we make our human mating season last a lifetime?

Oreo, the bravest kitten of the bunch, went into attack mode and stalked Pink across the floor. He swatted at her metal stake with one tiny paw. The other kittens followed.

"That's enough, young mousers." My father swung Pink away from the kittens, tucked her under one arm like a football. "So here's the plan: I stick the flamingo in that big pot of christ-and-the-mums, or whatever the heck they are, next to the front door. That's our signal that everybody is welcome to stop by for dessert and a wee Thanksgiving sip or two. Just make sure we hide the fancy pants stuff under the kitchen sink so they don't drink us out of house and cocktails."

John and Polly leaned forward in tandem and each scooped up two kittens, which was apparently my signal that I was on my own here.

I cleared my throat. "We have a full house for Thanksgiving already. Besides, how will everybody know what Pink sticking out of the mums even means?"

My father winked, never a good sign. "Sugar Butt enlightened me that an open door and a pink flamingo out front means come on by, y'all. I knew you wouldn't go for the open-door part, what with all these felines meowing all over the house—"

"Maybe in parts of the South that's what it means," I said, "but a pink flamingo doesn't exactly scream open house in New England. How about a tasteful little garden flag that says WELCOME—you could add it to your Christmas list. Wait, you talked to Sugar Butt?" Sugar Butt was my father's second worst girlfriend. Or maybe the third worst. In any case, it was definitely not a relationship we were encouraging.

"Don't look at me." My father raised his shaggy white eyebrows skyward. "I simply put that secular phone you kids insisted on buying me in my pocket. And lo and behold, when I sat down, Sugar Butt was on the other end."

I let out a long-suffering sigh. "You pocket dialed her, Dad. We keep telling you—either enable locking on the phone the way we showed you, or keep it out of your pocket."

My father gave Pink another twirl. "So then it hit me that I could email my entire thingamabob, too."

"Contact list," I said.

"That, too. What with all the strays around, what's a few more at the tail end of turkey day? And after we let dessert settle for a spell, all the blessed souls who flamingled in can have the honor of flamingling me up to my new man cavern."

I had to hand it to my father, he had a definite talent for making everyone else do all the work. Maybe I could help him put together an online tutorial, and we could split the profits.

"Once you get moved in to your man cave, Billy," John said, "do you think we could hang on to your friend's canned ham trailer until the upstairs renovations are finished? We'd be willing to rent it from him, of course."

"I've already put in a good word for you with my buddy Ernie," my father said as he tangoed the flamingo across the room. "He doesn't have anything planned for the trailer until springtime. Just keep the floor swept and make sure the beer's stocked before he picks it up again. And don't turn on the microwave and overhead light at the same time."

"Great," I said.

"I can sleep in the trailer," Polly said. It might have been my imagination, but she seemed to lose some of her glow as she said it.

I shook my head. "You will not. Joe and his crew aren't going to start work on the next phase until Monday, so we've got the whole weekend to figure out the sleeping arrangements. There's one bedroom upstairs that won't be touched, and we can always put a bed in this room. So between that and the trailer, we should have more than enough room."

John had rented out his Boston condo through an executive rental program. My ex-husband's realtor wife had sold my tiny Marshbury ranchburger practically overnight without being asked. John and I had spent our fair share of time looking at houses with nonexistent peek-thru ocean views and promising typos like *a huge dick for entertaining.* Nothing we saw came close to the 1890 Victorian that my father was rattling around in alone. Surprisingly, buying the house was John's idea.

So, in the end, against my better judgment, we bought the house from my father and agreed to renovate it to work for all of us. My father deposited money from the sale, enough for the next twenty years, into a bank account set up to automatically transfer rent to John and me on the first of the month. If my dad was still alive and kicking after that, he got to live with us rent free. I fully expected him to take that as a challenge and live to be at least a hundred and one.

My father settled Pink into his cracked leatherette recliner. He put a record on the old turntable.

He reached out his hand to Polly. "Don't think I've forgotten about you for a moment, darlin'."

Polly blushed, but she passed the kittens she was holding over to me. I breathed in their new kitten smell while I still could. Pebbles, the mama cat, was a beautiful tri-colored calico with black and ginger spots that looked like beach pebbles on her sandy white fur. Two of the kittens, Squiggy and Oreo, were black and white, and the other two, Sunshine and The Great Catsby, were ginger and white. Catsby climbed off my lap and began to scale my arm in the direction of my shoulder.

Frank Sinatra broke into a scratchy version of "The Way You Look Tonight." It was an odd song choice for a tango. A tango was an odd dance for Thanksgiving morning. But there was nothing odder than watching my womanizing widower father dancing with my single and pregnant teaching assistant.

When my father danced Polly across the floor of the den-slash-playroom-slash-cat room, she was almost as light on her feet as Pink.

CHAPTER

Five

My father stuck Pink in the flower pot next to the front door and then drifted back to the trailer. Polly peeled and cut the butternut squash and helped me set the table and then wandered upstairs. John peeled the potatoes and did whatever you do with giblets and then went off to take Horatio for a walk.

Some of the many and myriad online sources I'd consulted questioned the necessity of basting a turkey while it roasted. But I wasn't taking any chances. Plus, I figured that even if basting didn't make the turkey taste better, the extra effort would make me feel better.

So once the bird started giving off its juices, I set the timer on my phone to go off every half hour. For backup, I twisted the vintage kitchen timer until it reached the thirty-minute mark.

I visualized my whole family being razzle-dazzled by my culinary feat. I kept my focus. I snapped the ends off a big family's worth of green beans. I took the pies we'd baked yesterday out of the refrigerator. Before they went in the oven, I'd distressed the frozen crusts with the back of a fork so they'd look homemade rather than store bought. Now I gave them a few gentle karate chops with a knife just for added faux authenticity.

My phone and the kitchen timer went off simultaneously.

"See," I said to the empty kitchen. "We've got this."

I found my mother's old turkey baster with the faded turquoise handle, grabbed two worn potholders.

Maybe it was my lack of sleep that did it. I grasped the oven handle and pulled up. Then I remembered how to open an oven and pulled out.

The entire oven door came off in my hands.

If you've never held a vintage oven door in one pot-holdered hand, you have no idea how heavy they are. I grabbed the handle with my other hand for backup.

I thought for a moment, considering my options.

Then I aimed the metal latches that were now sticking out of the door at the oven, which seemed like a reasonable thing to do.

After that I pushed. The latches slid into the front of the oven a little way and then came right back out.

I backed up a few steps to get some momentum going. I rammed the door against the oven with all my strength. It didn't stay on.

I tried tilting the door to one side and then to the other. I tried aiming the latches at the oven from above and then from below. The oven door remained unattached to the oven, like a couple at the end of a bad first date.

A bead of sweat rolled down my torso, maybe from the unexpected workout. Or maybe because the heat coming out of the open oven was turning the kitchen into a sauna. My sister Carol's voice popped into my head, warning me about the dangers of salmonella if I let the turkey temperature drop too much.

After taking a moment to ponder whether or not using the camp stove in the canned ham trailer in the backyard might be an option, I decided it would probably only fit a drumstick or two.

I pressed the oven door against the gaping hole, wondered if I could keep holding it for about three and a half more hours or until somebody showed up to take a shift.

My forearms started to ache. When I couldn't take it anymore, I held on with one hand long enough to reach for my phone. Carol answered on the first ring.

"Sorry," she said when I filled her in. "But we've already got a turkey in the oven over here."

I heard myself gasp. "Why are *you* cooking a turkey? *I'm* cooking the turkey."

Carol laughed. "I think you just answered your own question."

"Funny," I said. "So funny I forgot to laugh."

"Don't bother calling Christine," Carol said. "Her oven is otherwise occupied, too."

"I hate you both," I said.

After I hung up on Carol, I thought about calling my brothers, decided I couldn't handle it if they were cooking turkeys, too.

I called the Turkey Hotline.

"Seriously?" I said after the Turkey Hotline person finished talking. "People's oven doors fall off all the time on Thanksgiving? You have no idea how much better that makes me feel."

. . . . .

So much for getting a long weekend off from school. Polly held the door open, while I burst into the teachers' room at Bayberry Preschool carrying the turkey. I'd followed the Turkey Hotline's instructions to the letter, double-wrapping the turkey and pan in foil to hold the warmth in, wrapping an old winter jacket around that, blasting the heat in the car as I transported the turkey to a new oven as fast as I could.

Lorna and Gloria were sitting at the long rectangular table. They were two of my favorite teachers and partners in crime—Lorna because she always said the things I'd never dare even think, and Gloria because she was one of those preschool teachers who mothered everybody and made you want to crawl into her lap with your blankie and start sucking your thumb.

"There better not be a turkey in that oven," I said.

"Like I cook," Lorna said.

"Happy Thanksgiving to you, too, honey," Gloria said.

Just in case my technique was still faulty, I let Polly open the oven door. I shoved the turkey in, slammed the door shut, turned on the oven with lightning speed.

Polly and I took seats across from Lorna and Gloria.

"Don't ask," I said once I'd caught my breath.

"No explanation needed," Lorna said. "It's actually a great way to get out of having to mess up your own oven. I call Christmas."

Polly laughed.

I shook my head. "Cute. What the hell are you two doing here anyway? Or did that bitch of a boss of ours erase Thanksgiving from your list of paid holidays?"

Lorna vibrated her lips, managing to sound exactly like the horse on that old TV show *Mr. Ed.* "Mattress Man's parents are here. I had to take a break before my head exploded." Mattress Man was Lorna's husband. His nickname was based not on more amorous activities, but on the fact that he spent most of his life in bed with the remote. I didn't get the attraction, but I wasn't married to him, so I didn't have to.

Gloria ran a hand through her frizzy hair and smiled her toothy smile. "I was out dropping off for the food bank turkey drive, and I saw Lorna's car heading up to the school when I went by."

"Do they need any help?" Polly said. "I should have thought to volunteer for something like that."

"They're fine," Gloria said. "Just take care of yourself and that sweet little baby in your belly, honey."

I flashed back to last Thanksgiving. At that point, I'd already met and managed to screw things up with

John. After a lifetime of Thanksgivings spent with my family, I decided to break away from the pack and volunteer to serve dinner at a church on Cape Cod. Especially since Dolly, my father's worst girlfriend of them all, had weaseled her way in to cook our family turkey.

I joined a huge group of volunteers feeding the handful of people who showed up to eat. I had a conversation with an old woman named Mrs. Wallace who wore heavy gold jewelry, lipstick that had mostly missed her lips, and reminded me that as sad and lonely as I was, it could be worse one day.

You could look at it that I'd come a long way, baby, since last Thanksgiving. Or you could look at it that I wasn't out of the woods yet. I blinked my eyes to make the flashback go away.

The teachers' room door swung open. Ethan, the new teacher, walked in. He had the lean torso and sun-streaked hair of a surfer. He walked with a limp he'd acquired when he totaled his car after his life as an indie filmmaker imploded. Kate Stone, our bitch of a boss, was his godmother, and she was the only one who'd been willing to give him a chance. Already I knew that he had the makings of a good teacher. The kids were lucky to have him.

"Hey," Ethan said. "Happy Thanksgiving."

Polly's glow turned into a serious blush. I'd read just enough Nancy Drew books in my formative years to know that this was no accidental meeting. Maybe she'd texted him before we jumped into the car with the turkey. Polly, not Nancy.

Ethan was trying to work things out with his girl-friend. A single and pregnant teacher friend was not necessarily the best way to make this happen. Still, even though the connection between Polly and Ethan didn't fit easily into a category, it was unmistakable.

Lorna slid her chair away from the table. "I guess I'll head home. The sooner we eat, the sooner I can shove my in-laws out the front door."

"I'll walk out with you, honey," Gloria said.

After they left, I handed Polly the turkey baster. "Would you mind hanging around here and keeping an eye on the turkey? That way I can run home for a while and get some more stuff done."

"Sure," Polly said.

"I'll stay and keep Polly company," Ethan said, as if I'd had even a sliver of doubt.

Before I'd high-tailed it out the door with the turkey, I'd sent John a quick text. I didn't want him to get back from his walk and think that the holiday pressure had gotten to me and I was making a run for it.

"Notice anything?" he said the moment I walked into our new old kitchen.

My eyes went right to it. "You fixed the oven door!"

Horatio wagged his tail. I would've wagged mine, too, if I had one.

"My hero," I said. "I knew you'd come in handy one of these days. How'd you do it?"

"YouTube. Three videos. Not only am I an expert at oven doors now, but I can fix toilets and do brain surgery at the same time."

"Good strategizing," I said. "We might need all three before the day is finished."

John opened the oven door and shut it again. "So, it turns out it's all about the latches. When you pull off the oven door, the latches are locked in the wrong position. Essentially, you find a hollow pipe and put it over each latch in turn, and then you use the pipe as a lever to pull the latch back until it locks in an angled position again."

"Impressive," I said. "I always wondered how you did brain surgery." I sidled up to John and gave him a kiss. A real one, like I didn't have the weight of hosting Thanksgiving sitting on my shoulders.

When we came up for air, he gave me *the look*.

"Don't even think about it," I said. "You have potatoes to mash."

His face fell. "Really? We've got the house to ourselves. And it might be a good thing to find out if we can still remember how to make love without an agenda."

John and I had decided to take trying to get pregnant temporarily off our To Do list until the renovations were finished. I'd ditched my digital ovulation kit and stopped peeing on sticks. We'd put off trying to decide when to make an appointment with a fertility specialist.

In the four-legged department, John had decided Horatio needed another dog to hang out with, as well as to balance all the cats that had come into our life. But we'd also made the decision not to increase our canine family until we were safely post-renovation and the dust had settled.

We'd even tabled John's marriage proposal for a while. I was afraid any wedding we planned would only bring back memories of our first weddings, of our starter marriages that had both crashed and burned. I had enough Irish worldview in me to think that happiness in this life was something to be downplayed so you didn't jinx it. Waving another set of wedding rings around was like asking for lightning to strike twice.

I had to admit it felt pretty good to take a brief time-out from all of it.

John reached his arms around me and started massaging the holiday stress from the back of my neck.

"Good try," I said, "but you know the second we get our clothes off, someone will show up early. Probably even my entire family."

We kissed again, long and leisurely, like we had a lifetime of kissing ahead of us. I wondered if we could get away with handing my family takeout bags and sending them on their merry way when they showed up for dinner. And then we could get back to this kiss.

"Do I get a raincheck for later?" John whispered.

I gave him a quick kiss on the ticklish spot behind his right ear. "Absolutely."

· · · · ·

My siblings and their families came in through the kitchen door, dumping desserts—pumpkin pie, cranberry cobbler, Boston cream pie, whoopie pies—on the kitchen counter. They carried side dishes—grilled Brussels sprouts with bacon and pecans, parmesan peas, smashed cauliflower, maple walnut sweet potatoes, apple and cranberry stuffing with sausage—straight to the dining room.

The turkey cracks started immediately.

"Hey, Sarah," my brother Michael said. "Was that you I saw earlier on the side of the road scoopin' up some roadkill?"

"Don't worry," Billy Jr. said. "I already called to check—Boston Market's open till six."

"I've got a can of tuna in my back pocket just in case," Carol's husband Dennis said.

That reminded me I'd forgotten to put out our prized vintage Chicken of the Sea salt and pepper shakers. The shakers were two little ceramic fish—tuna, I presumed, loosely interpreted—one yellow, one turquoise, each maybe three inches long by two inches tall. My grandmother on my mother's side had saved her Chicken of the Sea labels religiously until she'd collected enough to buy the set. When we visited her at her walk-up apartment in Holyoke, the smell of old wood greeted us in the foyer, and we raced up three flights of stairs for the privilege of shaking those tiny fish first.

Later, spurred by a *Brady Bunch* episode where the kids decide to cash in their S&H Green Stamps—the Brady girls want to buy a sewing machine and the Brady boys want a boat—we helped our mother paste stamps into Green Stamps Quick Saver books. Each page held 50 stamps, and we were sure we'd have an

Admiral 17-inch Solid State Color TV in no time. But 150 books of Green Stamps proved to be too much delayed gratification for the Hurlihy kids, so we settled on a Pillow Top Vinyl Hassock for 5½ books. We fought over the sticky russet-colored square for a week or two, then forgot all about it.

I found the salt and pepper fish in the third cabinet I tried. I shook some salt over my left shoulder for good luck. Shook some over my right just in case I'd remembered the wrong shoulder. I made a place for the tiny treasures in the hodgepodge of dishes on the dining room table.

"Where did you end up cooking the turkey anyway?" Christine asked when I got back to the kitchen.

"Teachers' room at school," I said. "Not that it's any of your beeswax."

"Just tell me it didn't fall out of the car on the way," Carol said.

A wave of laughter broke over the kitchen.

"Ohmigod," I said when I could talk again. I turned to loop in John and Polly. "So, one year we were driving to our dad's parents' house in Worcester, and for some reason we were bringing the cooked turkey with us—"

"We were all jammed into that old station wagon with the fake wood strips on the sides," Michael said.

"Watch it, sonny boy," our dad said. "I'll have you know that was real wood on those panels."

"Right," Carol said. "From a rare Alpine plastic tree."

"God, I wish I had that station wagon now," Michael said.

Michael's wife Phoebe crossed her eyes.

"No seatbelts, of course," I said. "And I was holding the turkey on my lap."

"You were not," Christine said. "I was holding the turkey."

"Don't be ridiculous," Carol said. "I was holding the turkey, and after a while my thighs started burning like I had a tower of pizza boxes on my lap. Johnny said he'd hold it, but he and Billy Jr. were in the way back. So I turned to hand the turkey to Michael, just for a minute while I got on my knees so I could pass it back—"

Christine jumped in fast. "And somehow the car door opened, and the turkey flew out!"

"It wasn't *my* fault," Michael said. "Somebody's bony knees were digging into my thigh, and then suddenly I had a lap full of stuffing."

"Never, ever," I said in my best Carol imitation, "cook the stuffing in the turkey. It's an invitation to salmonella and back-seat ejection."

Carol gave me a dirty look, but everybody else cracked up.

"So, what happened?" John asked. I couldn't detect any judgment in his voice, but I could still tell he was waiting to find out exactly what level of barbarian we were.

"We pulled over to the side of the road—" Billy Jr. said.

"And Dad handed the beer between his knees to Mom," Carol said. She gave her seventeen-year-old daughter Siobhan a quick glance. "It was a different time back then."

Siobhan rolled her eyes.

"Then Dad jumped out of the car," Christine said. "He grabbed the turkey, danced it around in a circle, put it back in the roasting pan—"

Our father slapped his thigh. "And then I hightailed it back to the car, lickety split, as the crowds cheered."

"I think I remember crowds cheering," Michael said. "Or maybe it was horns honking."

"Did you actually eat the turkey?" Polly asked.

"Of course, we did, darlin'," our dad said. "I'm no psychometrist, but in my opinion the five-second rule was in full play."

. . . . .

There were so many of us that it was impossible to really tell who was there and who wasn't until we were all seated. The adults squished in elbow to elbow around the long dining room table, made longer by yanking both sides in opposite directions and pulling up two leaves hidden underneath. A sofa and a wing chair squeezed in with the dining room chairs, since we'd relocated them from the front parlor to make room for John's two vintage pinball machines.

The kids were arranged around an assortment of card tables that abutted one end of the dining room table to form a T. Dining room chairs mingled randomly with kitchen chairs, folding chairs, two old wooden highchairs with the trays removed, and a couple of backless wooden stools.

"Hey," Michael said. "Where's Johnny?"

Of the six of us, my brother Johnny was the only one we didn't see on a regular basis. He lived just two towns away, but he had a corporate job that required lots of traveling, which was either true or just an excuse not to see us on a regular basis. His wife Kim had some kind of corporate job, too, and they spent more than their share of holidays with her family in Pennsylvania. When they did grace us with their presence, they were always sneaking off to check email and texts on their phones. Johnny had been the first of the bunch to get married. He and Kim had kids right away, and their youngest had just gone off to college.

"Maybe he got a better offer?" Christine said.

"Five will get you ten," Billy Jr. said.

"Bite your tongue," my father said. "Thanksgiving is a blessed day in this family's life. Our Johnny boy will be here, you mark my word." He waited the perfect beat, then waggled his shaggy white eyebrows. "And with any luck at all we'll have finished his share by then!"

"That'll teach him!" my five-year-old nephew Sean yelled from the kiddie section. He'd been working with a speech therapist I'd helped Christine find. I took a moment to appreciate how much better his enunciation was getting and to send a thumbs-up in Christine's direction.

"Let's get this show on the road," my sister Carol said. "I've been starving myself all week for a slice of apple pie slathered in ice cream."

"The apple pie is totally from scratch," I lied, "even the crust. I worked hard on that pie."

"*You* made the apple pie?" Carol said. "I'm so not wasting my carbs then."

My father pushed back his chair and stood at the head of the table. He cleared his throat dramatically. "If you wish to make an apple pie truly from scratch, you must first invent the universe."

"Carl Sagan," John said.

"Are you sure?" Christine said. "Carl Sagan's not Irish, Dad."

"You have no proof of that," my father said.

"Was that grace?" my niece Siobhan said. "Some of us would like to take out our phones again in this lifetime."

"Hold your horses," my father said. He raised his glass. "'Here's to alcohol, the rose-colored glasses of life.'"

Carol blew out a blast of air. "Jesus, Dad. Come on, it's freakin' Thanksgiving."

"I'll have you know that's F. Scott Fitzgerald," our father said. "He's no slouch, our Francis. And as Irish as the day is long."

Our dad peered out from under his eyebrows at his grandchildren. "Do any of you young whippersnappers want to make a confabulation in the grace department?"

"My tummy's a rumblin'," my nephew Ian said. "So let's stop this mumblin'."

"Amen," the kiddie table yelled.

"Father, Son, and Holy Ghost," my nephew Trevor said. "If you eat the fastest, you get the most."

"Yay, God," the younger generation yelled. For an encore, they pounded the table with their fists and stamped their feet.

"Settle down," Carol and Dennis said in tandem.

Our dad held his wine glass high. We all held up our glasses—wine for the adults, milk for the kids and Polly.

Our father looked straight at Polly as he recited:

> Wine comes in at the mouth
> And love comes in at the eye;
> That's all we shall know for truth
> Before we grow old and die.
> I lift the glass to my mouth,
> I look at you, and I sigh.

CHAPTER

Seven

"William Butler Yeats!" I yelled like I was a contestant on a game show.

Apparently I was the only contestant. Everybody else was staring at Polly, whose glow was definitely heading into blush territory again.

I raised my glass higher to divert their attention. "Happy Thanksgiving!" I tried.

They kept staring at Polly.

"Sláinte!" I roared, which is the Irish equivalent of cheers, though it actually means *health* and sounds like slurring *it's a lawn chair* really fast.

That finally snapped everyone out of it. "Sláinte!" they yelled. We clanked glasses all around.

Our dad reached over to the sideboard for his electric knife with the harvest gold handle. He took it out only three times a year—Thanksgiving, Christmas, and Easter—and it never failed to put him in a good mood.

He slid the turkey platter a little closer. He revved the motor and executed a few show-off air slices to warm up. He sliced my perfectly done first turkey.

"This bird is the cat's meow," my father said.

"That's good, right?" I said. Not that I was needy or anything.

"You might want to hold off on the praise," Michael said, "until we see how many of us are still alive and kickin' tomorrow."

We circulated dish after dish around the table. A glass of milk tipped over, causing a minor flood in the kiddie section. Carol jumped up, grabbed a pile of paper napkins from the sideboard.

As kids, we'd made igloos with our Thanksgiving dinners. We mounded the mashed potatoes and shingled them with carefully cut pieces of turkey. We dribbled the gravy evenly over the entire dwelling, then scraped it off in the shape of doors and windows.

Our parents played along. They would judge our creations, giving us each a different award. Best House in a Blizzard, Most Likely to Be Eaten First. And just before we'd dig in and actually eat, my father would bestow a final award.

"Before we conclude this evening's festivities by eating ourselves out of house and home," he'd say, pausing for a laugh, "I'd like to announce the winner of the Loveliest of the Lovely Love of My Life Perfect

Wife award. And the winner is Marjorie Hurlihy, the best gosh darn wife I've had all year."

"She's the only wife you've had all year," we'd yell.

"Criminy. You've got me there."

As the flashback faded away, I missed my mother all over again. Not just the everyday dull ache of missing her, but the gut-grabbing, heart-wrenching kind that could still sneak up on me.

I tilted my head back, blinked so the tears wouldn't spill out.

I held up my glass, swallowed the sob stuck in my throat. "To Mom."

"To Mom," my brothers and sisters said.

"To Grammy," the kiddie table said.

Our dad put down his fork. He took out his pocket handkerchief and wiped first one eye, then the other. "I talked to her just last night like I always do. She can't wait to see me moved in to my man cavern, by the by. She said to wish you all a day to remember. And she wrapped up by saying, 'Billy, you make sure those precious children and grandchildren of ours don't forget how to build a good Thanksgiving igloo. I can help you judge from up here by the pearly gates if you need me.'"

"Jesus, Dad," Billy Jr. said as he dabbed at his eyes with his napkin. "You're killing me here."

"Igloo contest!" Christine said when she finished wiping her eyes.

"Timed," Carol said. "Five minutes only."

"Winner winner turkey dinner," Michael said.

"But we already have a turkey dinner," one of the kids said.

I held up my preschool teacher's watch with the big analog face. "Ready . . . set . . ."

"Go!" the whole dining room yelled.

Adults and children alike began mounding their potatoes into igloos and shingling them with turkey and fixings. I jumped up, grabbed the huge platter of mashed potatoes John had made and headed for the kiddie table. Maeve and Sydney had both just turned three and were the youngest members of the Hurlihy family, so I spooned up massive scoops of potato and plopped them on the middle of their plates to even out the playing field. I put the platter down so the bigger kids could get more if they needed it.

By the time I sat down at my own place again, I'd decided to use parmesan peas to trim the doors and the windows of my igloo, and pecan halves to shingle the roof. I leaned in front of John to ask Polly to pass the peas, please.

The dining room hummed with creativity. Maybe if more people took the time to have mashed potato igloo competitions during Thanksgiving dinner, there might be fewer knock-down, drag-out family fights about politics or sports or old wounds from childhood.

We were almost like a Norman Rockwell painting. That one where the polite, humble, idyllic family with impeccable manners is gathered around a perfectly set table. And this woman in a white frilly apron is lowering a flawlessly cooked turkey to the exact center of the table. Okay, I wasn't exactly wearing a frilly white apron, but still, I'd cooked a pretty damn flawless turkey despite some formidable challenges.

"Smash cake!" Maeve yelled from the kiddie section. She lifted one chubby hand high and brought it down hard on her igloo-in-process.

"Smash cake!" Sydney yelled. She brought her chubby hand down even harder on her own igloo-to-be.

Globs of mashed potato flew everywhere. John wiped a potato splotch off the lens of his glasses.

"Damn," Christine said. "I knew we never should have let them have smash cakes at their birthday parties."

"Damn," Maeve said. "Damn, damn, *damn*."

"Thanks for that," Carol said.

"What the hell's a smash cake?" Billy Jr. said.

"Hell," Sydney said. "Hell, hell, *hell*."

"Thanks for that," Christine's husband Joe said.

"Smash cakes," Carol said, "started out as tiny cakes given to one-year-olds at their first birthday parties so they could make a mess without trashing the main cake. But now sometimes smash cakes can be great big piñata-like cakes filled with candy or other treats. I just ordered one for a 50th birthday party I planned for a client filled with—never mind." She cleared her throat. "In short, they're a thing."

I don't know what came over me. Maybe it was getting up too early. Maybe it was post-traumatic oven-door stress.

"Smash cake!" I yelled.

I lifted my hand up high and brought it down on my Thanksgiving igloo. When my palm made impact, warm gravy and mashed potato oozed between my fingers. I liked it.

"Smash cake!" everybody else yelled, even the in-laws, even John and Polly. Many igloo particles flew.

"Good gravy," our dad said. It was unclear whether it was just an expression or he was complimenting John's giblet gravy.

Laughter followed, that crazy out of control kind of laughter that hurts your stomach after a while and doesn't happen nearly enough once you're not a kid anymore. When one of us wound down, somebody else would get us going again.

We licked our fingers. We licked the palms of our hands. We rebuilt our igloos and polished them off by eating with actual forks.

My brother Johnny appeared like a vision in the doorway to the dining room. He looked around at the detritus spotting the tablecloth, our faces, our hair.

"Mom would be so proud," he said.

"I'll have you know," our father said, "your mother was entirely onboard for this. It might have even been her idea."

"Whoa, bro," Michael said. "What the heck is that you're wearing?"

Christine leaned sideways to get a better look. "Is that an African dashiki?"

"With Celtic designs on it?" Carol said. "I'm confused. But if you have to wear it, I'd like to think it's at least an intentional mashup."

Johnny turned slightly, just enough that we could all see that he was wearing a suede man purse over one shoulder. Decorated with a peace sign made from metal brads pounded through the fabric. And fringe. Long fringe.

Our eyes went to his hair, which was pulled back in a man bun. We gasped.

On the floor beside Johnny was a tie-dyed backpack. There might have been some embroidery going on, too. As brightly colored as it was, it was clearly a serious backpack. Massive, the type that had padded straps and an aluminum frame bar. The kind you'd buy if you were planning to go somewhere for a long time. Like the Flower Power cruise I'd read about, where you could kick back and relax while cruising the Caribbean and being entertained by the likes of Herman's Hermits, The Turtles, The Hollies, Canned Heat, and anybody else they could find who was still alive.

"Groovy," Billy Jr. said.

"Far freakin' out," Carol said.

"The Grateful Dead called," Michael said. "They said they'll swing by in an hour to pick you up for tour."

"Peace out, Uncle Johnny," Siobhan said.

"Who are you?" I said. "And what have you done with my brother Johnny?"

As if we didn't have enough to try to wrap our collective heads around, the doorbell rang. We heard the heavy oak front door creak open.

A gaggle of 40-to-forever women paraded in to stand behind Johnny. They were balancing desserts on palms and holding bottles of wine in party bags. Some of them looked familiar, for better or worse, some I'd

never laid eyes on. Polly and I gave Pandora's grandmother a little wave.

"Well, Begosh and Begorrah,"my father said.
"Aren't you lovely ladies a sight to make an old man
young. And just in time for dessert and a wee sip before
you give me a hand moving into my man cavern."

I took the opportunity to exit the dining room and
walk casually to the front porch.

A pink plastic flamingo really stands out against the
front of a white 1890 Victorian with black shutters and
a wraparound porch. I pulled Pink out of the pot of
chrysanthemums, shook the potting soil off her metal
stake. I took her for a walk around the yard, looking
around for a good place to stash her.

The turquoise canned ham trailer in the backyard
seemed to be calling out for a pink flamingo.

"Here you go," I said to Pink as I poked her into the
soil beside the little trailer door. "Don't cause any
trouble back here, okay?"

CHAPTER

The Thanksgiving sign I'd made for the cat room door said DON'T FEED THE ANIMALS (AND THAT MEANS YOU!) in big bold letters.

Michael opened the door slightly more than a crack so that Mother Teresa could squeeze out.

Horatio tried to slip out behind her. "Sorry, boy," I said as I grabbed him by his fancy collar. "No plate lapping for you this year. But we'll work on you-know-who for next year, I promise."

"Clean up on aisle fourteen," I yelled after Michael and Mother Teresa as they disappeared in the direction of the dining room.

I shut the cat room door. I made a beeline for the kitchen and dumped the pile of dirty plates I was carrying on the kitchen counter. I began filling tiny dishes with cat food. John came out, placed his pile of dirty dishes next to mine, started spooning dog food into Horatio's monogrammed stainless-steel dish.

I reached over to pick some stray food out of John's hair. "So, your mashed potatoes were a big hit."

"Your family is certifiable," he said. "And don't think for a moment that I've forgotten who initiated that food fight."

"That was not a food fight in any way, shape or form," I said. "The Hurlihy family is far too sophisticated for food fights."

John picked some food out of my hair.

I smiled. "It's like we're chimpanzees eating each other's lice."

John grinned. "Thank you for that lovely image. I have to admit your family's Thanksgiving is a lot more fun than mine is. Right now, my parents are having turkey Lean Cuisines and cranberry juice on their his-and-her TV tables, watching their favorite television shows and asking each other what just happened—"

"You said your sister was going there for Thanksgiving."

"My sister and her family are probably sitting in the dining room by themselves, wondering why the hell they drove all the way to Tampa."

"They are not," I said.

"Okay, it's not quite that bad." John shrugged. "The truth is I think my parents have always been kind of a self-contained unit. I mean, they love their kids and their grandkids, but they don't really need us. What they love most is their routine—grocery shopping on senior-discount Wednesdays, a walk on the beach on Friday mornings, their bird-watching group on the first Thursday of the month, an all-day jigsaw puzzle on Sundays. It throws them off when they have to deviate from their schedule, even for holidays."

After a big fight not that long ago, I'd followed John to Tampa and met his parents briefly. They seemed nice. Okay, nice-ish. Okay, kind of boring.

"Promise me," I said, "we'll never end up like that."

John leaned in for a kiss. "Falling into a rut while living in this house with your father is not even in the realm of possibility."

Polly and some other women cut through the kitchen carrying what looked like pieces of a bed. A platform bed. A round platform bed. A red vinyl round platform bed.

"It even has LED lights," one of the women said.

"Of course it does," I said.

Billy Jr. and his wife Moira came through the kitchen next carrying a rolled and shrink-wrapped mattress. Maeve and Sydney brought up the rear, giggling and trying to balance king-size pillows on their heads.

"Where's Dad?" I said.

"Supervising," Billy Jr. said.

While there was a break in the traffic, John and I made a run for the cat room. I placed Pebbles' dish on her shelf. John put Horatio's dish near the entrance to the room. The kittens were sleeping together, curled into a single ball of fluffy fur. As soon as we put their tiny bowls on the repurposed boot tray, they rolled away from one another and staggered toward the cat food, mewing away.

John put his arm around me as we sat on the couch. I rested my head on his shoulder while we watched our brood eat. I could have watched them forever.

"The only thing missing is dessert," I said. "But if one of us tries to sneak into the dining room, someone might see us and put us to work."

John considered this. "Do you think there will be leftovers if we just wait it out? I mean, everyone has to leave eventually, right?"

"You never know," I said. "That round bed looked like it could hold a lot of people."

The door creaked open. Carol came in holding a bottle of wine and some wine glasses. Johnny followed with an entire Boston cream pie and a handful of forks.

"Sit," Carol said. Horatio sat.

"Not you," she said. "The other one."

Johnny sat. He reached over and put the Boston cream pie on the coffee table, handed us each a fork.

Carol poured wine all around, gulped some down. I handed her a kitten.

Johnny twirled his glass, took a sip, stared straight ahead. I handed him a kitten, grabbed the other two for John and me.

"You need to find homes for some of these kittens," Carol said. "And not mine."

"They already have a home," I said.

Carol looked back and forth between Johnny and me a few times, then aimed a searing gaze in my direction.

"*What?*" I said, in the exact same wimpy voice I'd been using with my big sister since childhood.

"So," Carol said. "What are you going to do to keep Dad and that assistant teacher of yours apart?"

"Me?" I said. "Why should *I* have to do anything? Dad and Polly are both adults. Nothing's going on between them. I have no idea what you're talking about."

Carol looked at me while she took a long slow sip of wine. "Sarah, Sarah, Sarah."

I forced myself to hold her gaze. "That's my name, don't wear it out."

"Dad's clearly gaga over her."

I rolled my eyes. "Like that's something new. You can hardly pick Polly out from the après-dinner harem Pink summoned. I mean, maybe they can all move in, and we can get our own reality show." I paused for a breath. "He'll say the whole thing was Mom's idea—you know he's still completely convinced she's pimping for him from Heaven."

"You have to nip it in the bud," Carol said. "Otherwise Dad will be doing his knight in shining armor rescuing a damsel in distress thing. Before we know it, Polly will be our new stepmother, they'll be out on the town, and we'll be changing the diapers."

I knew there had to be a more intelligent response, but I couldn't seem to wrap my head around it. So I put my fingers in my ears long enough to sing, "Lalalalalala."

"Wowza, a new stepmother," Johnny said. "Heavy."

"Heavy?" Carol said. "*Heavy?* You don't say heavy."

"He ain't heavy, he's my brother," I sang. My pitch was a little bit off, but I totally nailed the tune. At least I thought I did.

Carol narrowed her eyes at Johnny. "What happened to all the corporate gobbledygook you're always spouting? You know, differentiating value? Strategic theme areas? Backward compatible? Future proof?"

If Johnny heard her, he didn't let on. He kept one hand on the kitten while he shoveled a massive chunk of Boston cream pie into his mouth, washed it down with some wine. "So which one is Polly anyway?"

As if on cue, there was a soft knock on the door.

Horatio barked. Pebbles growled low in her throat. "Come in," the rest of us sang.

Polly poked her head in an inch or so. "Sorry, I didn't mean to interrupt. I just wanted to check to see if any of them needed feeding . . ."

When Johnny grinned, he looked almost like his old self. "I do. You could snag me another dessert or three."

"Don't listen to him," I said to Polly. I narrowed my eyes at Johnny. "She meant the other animals."

"Okay, then," Polly said. "Well, I guess I'll be hanging out at Burger King if you're looking for me."

"Don't be ridiculous," I said. "Get in here. You know my sister Carol, and this is my brother Johnny."

John and I scrunched over so Polly could fit on the couch with us. Johnny said hi and handed Polly a fork. She took a polite little bite of Boston cream pie. Her other hand rested protectively on her baby bump.

"When are you due?" Carol asked.

"April," Polly said.

Carol nodded. "Is the father in the picture?"

"Knock it off, Carol," I said. "Now."

"That's okay," Polly said. "The baby's mine. There is no father."

Carol raised her eyebrows. "Immaculate conception? We were brought up just Catholic enough to believe it."

Polly shrugged. "Something like that."

Silence hung in the room like a wet beach towel. The truth, which my older sister would never, ever drag out of me no matter how hard she tried, was that Polly's ex-husband was the father of her baby.

Said ex had left Polly for another woman, after talking Polly into not having kids because he didn't think it was fair to the kids he'd already had with his first wife.

Eventually Polly had decided that she did want kids after all. She lured her ex into post-breakup sex. He had three kids with his first wife and another one with his third wife. So Polly figured the least he could do for his second wife was to save her a trip to the sperm bank. *He's an asshole*, I remembered Polly telling me, *but he's got good genes.*

I'd asked her if he knew she was pregnant.

He doesn't know, she'd said. *He'll never know, he wouldn't be the least bit interested even if he did know, and his name will not be on the birth certificate. End of story.*

Back in the cat room, nobody was saying anything. Not only that, but those of us who weren't pregnant were running out of wine.

"I like your shirt," I said to Johnny, just for a conversation starter.

Johnny looked down at his shirt, or Celtic dashiki, or whatever it was. "It blew my mind when I saw it. This tree of life represents the idea of something rooted to the ground and striving to the heavens at the same time. And like wow, man, the endless cycle of regeneration. We live, we croak, we're reborn. I get blissed out just by the awe overload."

He closed his eyes, maybe demonstrating his blissed-out state, then opened them again. "The Celtic knots that surround the tree of life have no beginning or end, which symbolizes the timeless nature of our spirit. Those Celtic knots are totally bitchin'."

"What is your problem?" Carol said. "I mean, the last person who said bitchin' was a freakin' Valley Girl."

"Don't blow your cool, sis." Johnny balanced the kitten on his knee. He dug his fork into the Boston cream pie, scooped a big bite into his mouth. "Life's way too short."

We chewed in silence as the sugar rush kicked in. A Boston cream pie is basically a yellow cake with custard globbed between the layers and chocolate frosting on top. It's really a cake, but everybody pretends it's okay to call it a pie. The old Parker House Hotel in Boston claims to have created it back in the day. I'm not sure I buy that either, since one would think that a professional chef would have had the good sense to call a cake a cake. As a preschool teacher, these are the things that drive you crazy. I mean, if the adults don't use the correct words, how can we expect the kids to learn them?

"Okay, big bro," Carol said. "Time's up. Out with it."

Johnny shrugged. "She boogied. The old lady boogied."

"Could it possibly be because you called her an old lady?" I said.

"I, for one," Carol said, "am finding all this hippie talk confusing. Do you mean Kim went out dancing, or she took off?"

I heard a funny sound, and when I followed it to my brother, he was crying.

In our family, you didn't hug someone who was crying, especially if it was your brother. You gave him his space.

I reached out one hand and laid it carefully on Johnny's forearm.

He looked at me through tear-filled eyes.

"Okay if I crash for a while?" he said.

"Of course," I said. "Just to clarify, you mean stay here, right?"

CHAPTER

Nine

"What was I supposed to say?" I said to John.

Carol and I had settled Johnny into the space my father had just vacated, the bedroom that had been my parents' room. John and I were alone in my childhood bedroom again. We could still hear people clomping around downstairs.

"My dad left his old bed behind," I added. "So it's not like it's that big a deal."

John and I were sitting side-by-side on the edge of the king-size bed we'd bought to replace the twin beds my sister Christine and I had slept on while we were growing up. The new bed took up most of the space in the room. Because nothing else would fit, we each had a pile of books on our side to serve as temporary bedside tables.

Maybe I could start a home improvement blog and write a post about bedside table alternatives for tight spaces. Except then I'd have to come up with another idea so I could write a second post, and I couldn't really think of one. Come to think of it, using the books for bedside tables had been John's idea. Scratch that blog.

We heard a rousing cheer from my father's new digs.

"Sounds like we're missing the first toast in the new man cave," I said.

John crossed his arms over his chest. "It's ridiculous. You have four other siblings who could have taken him in. We're in the middle of a major renovation, we've got a house full of animals, Polly's staying here. And we've got your father, which is no small thing, even if he's theoretically moved into a separate space. And, might I remind you, I'm trying to work *remote* through all this."

"Relax," I said. "Maybe Johnny will only be here for the weekend. He and Kim probably just had a stupid little fight. I'm sure he'll tell us the whole story tomorrow after he gets a good night's sleep."

John didn't say anything. A vision of Johnny's massive backpack flashed before my eyes. I tried to imagine how many changes of clothes it could hold.

"Okay," I said. "Worst case scenario, my brother stays for a little while. So let's try to figure out how we could make the sleeping arrangements work."

My father's new space took over the entire garage, as well as the room above it, which we called the secret room. The secret room was the only place worth sneaking a boy into when I was growing up. You accessed it by going through the little square postage stamp of a mudroom, unlatching a tongue-and-groove wooden door, and climbing up a rickety old staircase.

Every surface of the room had been covered in the same century-old knotty pine planks, darkened by time to a deep caramel. Walls turned into ceiling and met in a point overhead, providing a small central area where you could stand up straight. The only electricity had come from an old brown extension cord running through a hole cut in the ceiling of the garage.

I had a moment of silence for the secret room, all gone now except for the ghosts of our semi-wild teenage adventures. In its place was a new two-story self-contained abode that would host more adventures than I cared to think about for my father and his red vinyl round bed with the LED-lights.

Right now, my dad still had to enter and exit through the door in the mudroom we'd used, but once the new garage was built, he'd have a private entrance from there as well.

The renovations had been John's vision. I had to admit I still had a hard time seeing the house I'd grown up in as anything other than the house I'd grown up in.

"I know you've told me a million times," I said. "But just explain again how this next part of the makeover will work."

John actually smiled. He loved to talk about reinventing our new old house.

He didn't even have to stand up to reach for the plans sitting on one of the two tiny bureaus we'd been able to squish into the room. After he pulled the rubber band off the plans, he unrolled them and held them open so we both could see. He marked a spot with one finger, then pointed at the wall beside me.

"This is where the existing wall will come down between this room and the one next door—"

"The boys' room," I said.

"Right." He pointed to the cold blue lines of the plans again. "And that will give us space for a walk-in closet here, and for an en suite bathroom that will back up to the existing bathroom. And these two other bedrooms will remain intact. One will become a shared office—with built-in storage right there and a double desk along that wall."

"Right," I said. "And then the other room, my parent's bedroom, currently inhabited by my brother-turned-hippie, can be a guestroom, or you know—" I remembered we were on a baby-talk timeout, so I stopped myself before I mentioned what else this room might be used for.

"So . . . where were we?" John said as he found his place on the plans. "Okay, then this room at the end, the one that opens into the long screened-in balcony—"

"The sleeping porch."

"Right. The sleeping porch stays, but we'll put in new energy efficient double French doors leading out to it. And the room next to it will become our separate living space. Since the living room fireplace is directly below, they'll open up the chimney behind the plaster and put in a vented gas fireplace."

John tapped his finger like it was a magic wand. "Mantel here. Television over it. Nice couch here. A couple of comfy chairs here and here. It'll be cozy, but we'll have a place to get away whenever we need it."

"And we'll definitely need it," I said. "Don't forget to tell me about the moat filled with crocodiles again. The one that will give us clear boundaries and make us feel that buying this house wasn't the most bat-shit crazy idea two relatively sane people ever came up with."

John pointed. "Well, it's not quite a moat, but our space will have this new door at the top of the main staircase. And when we build the new garage, we'll have a private staircase going up from that as well."

"The word private," I said, "never made it onto my family's vocabulary list."

John turned the page, tucked it carefully behind the others. "I told Joe to install the biggest locks he can find."

"Good." I sighed. "The part I love the most is that the heart of the home pretty much stays the same. And that it'll be accessible from our space, my dad's space, and also to the rest of my family from both the front and the kitchen doors. If we get really lucky, they won't even notice the door at the top of the stairs."

John shrugged. "I suppose it won't much matter if everybody's staying up here with us anyway. First Polly, then Johnny, then the rest of them. Maybe we can just line up a row of mattresses in the hallway."

"Stop," I said. "The last thing I need is for you to get all grouchy on me. Let's just take a minute and figure this out."

John rubbed a finger back and forth across his lower lip. What had started out as slightly, adorably chapped seemed to be moving in the direction of one seriously stressed-out lip. I wondered if I should start handing John a tube of Chapstick every time he started to rub it, the way I handed my students a tissue whenever they started to pick their noses.

"What if you and I move into the trailer in the backyard?" John said. "Leave everybody in here to fend for themselves. You know how much I love those canned ham trailers. We could pretend we're camping."

I'd spent a few nights sleeping in that trailer when John had dragged me off to canine camp before the start of the school year. We'd had a big fight, and when I found out that my father and the trailer just happened to have followed us to camp, I packed up in a huff and relocated. I'd slept on the trailer's tiny dinette that converted to a bed of sorts. Watching the sun rise through the pompoms on the café curtains while I tried to roll over without giving myself a bloody nose with my knees was not an experience I cared to repeat.

"What about our four-legged friends?" I said. "The kittens and Horatio would probably be fine in the trailer, but Pebbles is just starting to get comfortable in the cat room. Plus, there's not exactly much elbow room in there for all of us, not to mention the kitty litter and the pet dishes and the food. And all the rest of the paraphernalia."

"I didn't factor in any of that," John said. "I guess I was thinking the cats could stay where they are, and Horatio could either stay with us or bunk in with your dad if he preferred." He rubbed his lower lip a few more times. "Okay, what if Polly sleeps in the trailer? Didn't she already offer to stay out there?"

I yawned. "Did you see how pale she got when she said that? She's definitely not over being rescued from her rental in that nor'easter. The last thing she needs is to be all by herself in a tiny trailer that rocks and rolls on a windy night. I think she'll feel safer in the house."

John yawned. "Okay, then. Johnny gets the trailer. Polly stays where she is—"

I yawned again. "She can't. She's in Carol's old room, which will become the office, at least I think it will. My parents' room is the farthest room away from the construction dust—I think that's the safest place for her."

"And I was hoping that's where we could sleep," John said.

"I don't think I could sleep there," I said. "I haven't set foot in that room since we went through my mother's things after she died. Sometimes I can even feel her presence when I walk by the closed door. Carol promised she'd help me set it up as a guestroom once we get through the renovations, but until then—"

John put his arm around me, kissed the top of my head.

He yawned again. "I think we're running out of rooms. So where exactly are you and I going to sleep?"

"I'll show you." I was so tired that it took every ounce of strength I had to stand up again. I reached out a hand to John, helped him up.

The old maple treads creaked as we clunked our way down the center staircase. My father and a group of women were playing pinball on John's prized pinball machines.

I looked at John to see if that bothered him. He shrugged, like a preschooler who still wasn't crazy about the idea but was learning to share his toys.

The kitchen was in pretty good shape. The dishwasher was running, and the dishes that couldn't fit were rinsed and stacked neatly on the counter. Somebody had even emptied the trash and put in a fresh bag.

We dished out food for the cats, and John grabbed a treat for Horatio.

When I opened the fridge, a nice stash of leftovers had been neatly wrapped in plastic wrap and left behind. Hosting Thanksgiving dinner definitely had an upside.

I pulled out the apple pie I'd made, fed a forkful to John.

"Mmm," he said in his polite voice after he finished chewing.

I took a small bite. I'd never admit it to Carol, but she was right. This pie was so not worth the carbs. I grabbed John and me each a whoopie pie instead. I liked a good whoopie pie as much as the next person, but once again, it wasn't really a pie. It was more of a small cake or a cookie or even a big fat soft Oreo. For the life of me I couldn't understand why people had to make the world so unnecessarily complicated.

I loaded up my share of the cat dishes. We paraded our way to the cat room. John and I fed Pebbles and the kittens. John gave Horatio his treat. I handed John his whoopie pie.

"So," I said. "You're looking at our new love shack beginning Sunday night."

"Seriously?" John said. We assessed the room. Five cats, one dog, food dishes, litterboxes, toys, a plaid sofa, an old TV. Knotty pine walls and built-in shelving. Somebody must have moved my father's ancient cracked recliner up to his man cave, because there was a gaping hole where it used to be.

"Okay, so it's a bit cozy." I shrugged. "But it'll just be for a little while."

Ten

John and I made love as soon as we woke up. Trying not to wake Horatio, who was snoring away in his bed on the floor. Trying not to wake Polly, who was asleep in Carol's old room. Trying not to wake Johnny, who was asleep in my parents' old room.

All things considered, it went pretty well.

We pulled up the covers, wiggled our way into cuddle position.

John kissed me on the shoulder. "I think I'll ask Joe about adding some insulation to the walls of our new bedroom suite."

"As much as he can fit," I said. "Maybe he can squish some under the floorboards, too. And don't forget the ceiling—you never know who might be lurking around up in the attic."

"Good point. What I'd like to create is a soundproof, cocoon-like sanctuary, so quiet that when we're in there it feels like we're the only ones in the house."

I sighed. "I can't believe we only have two more nights in this bedroom before it's going to disappear and become a completely new room. Two more sleeps, as my sisters and brothers and I used to say when we were counting down to something."

John glanced over at the wobbly pile of old books on his side of the bed, nudged his alarm clock over to a slightly less precarious position on the top book. "I have to admit I'm looking forward to an actual bedside table again. With a lamp." The only light in the room was a gooseneck floor lamp that turned on with the switch just inside the door. Which meant that somebody had to walk over to turn it off again and then roam blindly back to bed. My shins throbbed just thinking about it.

I let out another sigh. "It's not that I can't wait for our fancy-schmancy new master suite, but it's still bittersweet. Half my childhood was spent in one half of this room, pretending that my sister Christine wasn't in the other half."

John sniffed dramatically. "Smells like teen spirit."

"Ha. More like teen angst. I've blocked out most of it, but I can still vaguely remember years and years of anxiety, sort of a chronic, generalized dread that every time I moved a muscle I was going to screw things up. Wrong hair, wrong outfit. The something stupid that would come out of my mouth every time I talked to a boy."

John shrugged. "I still feel that way sometimes."

"Aww," I said. "I think you do great when you talk to boys."

"Cute." John laced the fingers of one hand through mine. "Did you know," he said, "that the phrase 'smells like teen spirit' was scrawled on the wall of Kurt Cobain's apartment by a friend of his then-girlfriend, because apparently his girlfriend was a big fan of Teen Spirit deodorant?"

"Gee, what don't you know?" I said.

"I went through a brief phase of wanting to be a rock historian. Before I tried making a living building wooden boats and refinishing vintage pinball machines, and ultimately made the fiscally responsible choice to become an accountant again."

"I used to wear Teen Spirit deodorant. Teen Spirit Pink Crush. It made me smell like baby powder and berries, at least I hoped it did."

"Right Guard all the way," John said. "My mother bought the big economy aerosol spray can of Right Guard Super Dry Antiperspirant and left it in the upstairs bathroom for all of us to use." He made his voice sound like the old commercial. "If you're still getting wet, start getting tough."

"Ohmigod," I said. "I thought it was bad enough that I had to share with my sisters. I can't believe you had to share your deodorant with your *whole family.* That's the saddest story I've ever heard."

"It's okay," John said in the most pathetic little voice he could muster. "She sends me my own can for Christmas now."

I would have laughed longer, but I really needed to pee. "Hey," I said as I kicked the covers off. "Do you think buying this house will turn out to be a bad idea? You know, all the things we can't control? All the memories I can't shake? All the people we can't keep from showing up to stay here?"

"It's a beautiful house," John said. "We'll be fine. I mean, how much worse can it get?"

. . . . .

John made coffee and cooked breakfast while I filled dishes with food for Horatio and Pebbles and the kittens. Then we all ate together in the cat room.

The animals dug right in. The humans balanced our plates on our laps and ate with a tad more restraint. John had made actual omelets, with bacon and broccoli and cheddar cheese and green onions. I would have just zapped some Thanksgiving leftovers. I took a moment to marvel at the possibility of a lifetime of upgraded meals. I mean, how lucky can you get? Sure, there were more compelling reasons than cooking expertise for falling in love with someone. But it was definitely a nice perk.

"We're going to have to stop calling this the cat room once we move in," John said.

"I already renamed it," I said. "Remember? The love shack?"

"Right." John took it all in, settled his gaze on the litterbox. "It doesn't get much more romantic than this."

When we finished eating, I grabbed an empty wine bottle somebody had missed during last night's clean-up patrol.

"Run away with me," I sang into it. It was my best Norah Jones imitation, which I had to admit wasn't all that good. I was pretty sure I'd botched the lyrics, too. *Get away with me? Sneak away with me? Come away with me?*

John didn't seem to mind. "Sure. As long as it includes a substantial walk and Horatio's invited, too."

"Horatio's invited, and it absolutely includes a walk," I said. "But that's all you're getting out of me."

. . . . .

Not many cars were on the road on the morning after Thanksgiving. But extra cars seemed to be clumped in the driveways we passed, signs of grown-up children visiting their parents for the weekend. Gold and burgundy chrysanthemums were clustered outside doorways and tucked into window boxes. By the end of the weekend, they'd be replaced with greenery—pine and boxwood and spruce. And Marshbury would twinkle with Christmas lights, most a tasteful white.

Living near a beach is like always having a sandbox to play in. As soon as we pulled into the beach parking lot, Horatio's tail began wagging a mile a minute. We all jumped out of my car. John and I zipped up our jackets.

The ocean wind whipped my hair around and around, making me feel much better about the fact that

I hadn't bothered to brush it before we left. I breathed in the sharp salt air and immediately felt more alive. I knew there were so many other beautiful places to live—lakes and mountains and deserts and even the urban patchwork of a city. But for me, there was no more magical place in the world than a little beach town.

"Look," I said.

At the top of the boardwalk, a wood and wire beach fence meandered, protecting the graceful sand dunes from footsteps. Midway along the fence, a signpost sprouted up from the ground. The sign that had once been attached to it was long gone, maybe washed out to sea in a hurricane.

Hanging from the top of the sign post was a Christmas wreath. The base of the wreath was made out of branches. Leathery green leaves were arranged on top of the branches. A circle of cranberry-colored berries topped the green leaves. Three dried starfish dangled in the open-air center of the wreath, the distant blue of the ocean behind them making them pop. A big rawhide dog bone with a red bow decorated one side of the wreath, and tiny plastic-wrapped candy canes hung here and there.

I reached into my pocket, took out a handful of Horatio's dog treats, tucked three of them into the wreath.

Horatio let out a polite whine.

"I saved you plenty, honey." I threw a treat up in the air for him. Horatio caught it before it hit the sand.

We stepped over the band of dried seaweed and assorted stones and sea glass and shells and foam and feathers and tiny carcasses and driftwood and too many pieces of plastic and who knows what else. This strip was actually called the wrack line, but everybody I knew called it the high tide line.

The three of us worked our way down to the packed wet sand and began walking the length of the beach. John let Horatio stretch his retractable leash as far as it would go. Horatio dashed and dipped, stopping occasionally to dig in the sand.

Dogs weren't allowed to set paw on Marshbury beaches between 9 A.M. and 6 P.M. from the Friday before Memorial Day through the Monday of Labor Day weekend. But after Labor Day, canines ruled the Marshbury beaches.

Technically the dogs were supposed to be attached at all times to leashes held by the humans who accompanied them. But by this time of year, owners often let the rules slide long enough for their dogs to enjoy a quick burst of delicious freedom.

We passed a pair of burly Newfoundlands swimming in the frigid water, their owners high and dry on the sand.

"It's not fair to Horatio," John said. "If he has to follow the rules, why shouldn't they?"

"So, let him off the leash," I said. "I think the fine for the first offense is only twenty-five dollars."

John picked up his pace to catch up to Horatio. "It's against the law. And if Horatio gets caught, it probably stays on his record permanently."

"Ha." I took a big skip to catch up to John. "You sound like one of my preschool parents. They're always

trying to get me to change my parent-teacher
conference reports so their three-year-old's lack of
interest in blocks doesn't end up on his permanent
record and keep him from getting into Harvard."

"You're missing the point," John said.

A spectacular dog whizzed by us, heading straight
for the water. We all turned to get a better look, even
Horatio.

The dog was large and brown with a fluffy topknot
and wiry curls covering its body. "Is that a standard
poodle?" I asked.

John shook his head. "I think it's an Irish Water
Spaniel. You didn't happen to notice whether or not it
had webbed feet, did you? That's a sure sign."

"Can't say that I did. I'll try to be more observant in
the future."

We started walking again.

"An Irish Water Spaniel," John said, "is on my short
list for our new dog."

"My father would certainly approve of the Irish
part," I said. "Wait. Ix-nay on the og-day talk.
Remember? It's on our short list of forbidden subjects
until after the renovation."

John shrugged. "Okay then, I won't mention that I
ultimately ruled out Irish Water Spaniels because they
have a strong prey instinct and can't be definitively
trusted without supervision around children and
smaller pets."

"The kittens and I thank you for that."

"But," John said, "I found some other interesting breeds to look into down the road: Affenpinscher, Löwchen, Brussels Griffon, Coton de Tulear."

"Too chichi for me," I said. "There's no way I want a dog that would make us dress for dinner before we could feed it."

I thought it was a pretty good line, but John didn't even crack a smile.

"It's just," he said, "that since Horatio's lineage is a mixed bag, I was thinking it might be interesting to choose a dog based on breed characteristics. What about a Boston Terrier? Easily trained. Highly intelligent. Great manners—its nickname is even the American Gentleman. They're a little bit territorial, but I think Horatio could win one over."

"Uh-uh-uh," I said. "Not until after the renovation dust has settled."

Eleven

I looped my arm through John's and steered him back up to the top of the beach. Horatio galloped along beside us.

"Ta-dah," I said. "Another amazing Marshbury holiday beach custom."

A scraggly scrub pine, probably a first cousin of Charlie Brown's Christmas tree, stood in a little clearing surrounded by clumps of autumn-colored sea grass.

A hand-strung popcorn garland was draped across its spindly green branches. Pinecones spread with peanut butter and rolled in birdseed alternated with brightly colored ball ornaments and more little candy canes.

I tucked a few of Horatio's treats into the branches, threw one to Horatio.

"It's like something out of another time," John said. "Is there a committee in charge of decorating it?"

"Nope," I said. "As far as I know, the decorating is all spontaneous. It's been going on for as long as I can remember. Beginning the day after Thanksgiving, everybody just adds a little something to the tree. Or takes something, like if your dog needs a treat or you're in the mood for a candy cane. I think what I love most is that it's all about generosity. And leaving a little bit of holiday magic for the next person who walks by."

"Nice way to put it."

"Thanks. Of course, the seagulls will swoop down and fly off with that popcorn garland any minute, but people will keep replenishing everything between now and New Year's Day."

"What happens after that?"

I shrugged. "It goes back to being a flip-flop tree. For the rest of the year, whenever a single flip-flop drops out of somebody's rolled-up towel, or people leave whole pairs behind, someone hangs them on this tree. By the end of the summer, it's like a found art flip-flop sculpture that pretty much screams Life's a Beach."

"That's one hard-working little tree," John said.

"Yeah," I said. "I like the flip-flop tree better than the other flip-flop custom, where people kick them off at the end of the boardwalk before they step down to the sand, and pick them up again when they leave the beach. One summer, my sister Carol figured out we could upgrade our flip-flops—I think we still called them thongs back then. You know, wear our crappiest pair to the beach and then casually pick up a fancier pair on the way out. My mother caught on in no time. It was all Carol's idea, but she ratted me out anyway."

"What happened?"

All these years later, I could almost feel myself blush. "Our mom made us write apology letters for each pair we'd stolen, in our best cursive and signing our full names and everything. Then we had to scotch tape the letters to the straps of the flip-flops and leave them at the base of the boardwalk. Plus, we had to go to Confession and put our entire allowance in the collection basket at church that week."

"Your mother didn't mess around," John said.

"She sure didn't." I smiled. "Even my father behaved around her, at least most of the time."

We heard the faint but perky strains of "It's a Small World" coming from the beach parking lot.

"Speak of the devil," I said. "I'd know the sound of that ice cream truck anywhere."

. . . . .

By the time we made it to the parking lot, a gang of dogs was racing toward the pink ice cream truck, their leash-carrying owners hot on their heels.

"Hey, Dad," I yelled. "Need any help?"

"Hunky dory at this end," he yelled back as he opened the door. My father, wearing his hot pink Bark

& Roll Forever fleece over a matching T-shirt, jumped out, nimble as ever, and swung the backdoor open.

When we caught up to him, he was already pulling out a hot pink carpet runner and some metal poles with thick pink cords attached to them. John and I helped him roll out the carpet, which was sprinkled randomly with black paw prints, so that it created a path to the service window. We set up a row of cords anchored to metal posts on either side of the carpet.

My father ran his hand through his hair. "Just a quick stop here today. The ladies are all booked up at Bark & Roll headquarters for the holiday weekend and want me on poop patrol. I let them know I don't do doo-doo for just anybody. Truth be told I barely changed a diaper back in the day when you kiddos were knee-high to a grasshopper. And we were blood relatives."

My dad climbed up on a stool, unlatched the service counter from the side of the truck, pulled it down until it was horizontal to the ground. Then he swung out a stop sign-shaped sign so you could read BARK & ROLL FOREVER from both sides.

"The original letters underneath say DON'T SKID ON A KID," I whispered to John.

"Smart upgrade," he whispered back.

My dad climbed into the truck again, leaned out the service window.

He winked at Horatio, threw him a treat. "Homer doesn't wait in line," he said in case anyone might have an objection. For some reason, my father had decided to change John's dog's name. Horatio didn't mind answering to both names, and even John appeared to be getting used to it.

"Hold your horses, pooches," my father said to the rest of the canine crowd. He reached into a basket and grabbed a handful of dog treat cards. "Find someone who can read and has opposable thumbs to untie the ribbon on one of these babies for you, and we'll be in business."

Eventually the humans caught up and my dad started handing out cards and treats while he talked up Bark & Roll Forever. He joked. He flirted, no surprise.

An unleashed dog I'd never seen before came out of nowhere. It was so scruffy and scrawny that it looked like it might be related to the beachy little Christmas tree we'd just visited. Horatio yipped with delight, and the two of them started rolling around on the sand-covered parking lot like long-lost littermates.

"Horatio, come." John yanked at Horatio's leash, trying unsuccessfully to pull him away from the other dog.

I reached into my pocket, scooped up the rest of Horatio's treats. I held them out in my open palm. The dog darted over to me and woofed them down with lightning speed.

I gave the dog's matted fur a few strokes. It licked my hand, maybe to get the last crumbs, maybe just to reward nice with nice.

When I looked over, John had already dragged Horatio halfway to my car. The unkempt dog watched them with sad eyes, then darted off to find a place at the back of the treat line.

"What a smart dog," I said to John when I caught up to them at the car.

John looked up from brushing sand off Horatio. "I can't believe the owners let it run around off-leash like that. I just hope its shots are up to date." For the second time this morning, he reminded me of one of the Bayberry parents. And not in a good way.

"So, what?" I said, "You're afraid that because it touched Horatio, it might have given him cooties? Unlike one of those la-di-da dogs you were talking about, like a Highchen, or whatever it was."

"A Löwchen," John said. "With a diaeresis over the O. That's two dots, in case you were wondering."

I stared straight ahead while we drove back to our new old house. *That's two dots, in case you were wondering,* I said to myself over and over again. Of course, I knew what a diaeresis was. At least I was pretty sure I would have been able to pick it out in a multiple-choice question. And I definitely knew what two dots meant.

"It's also called an umlaut," John said.

I didn't say anything.

"The two dots," he said. "Not the dog."

"You're a freakin' umlaut," I said, whatever that meant. "And no offense, but you're really getting on my nerves."

. . . . .

As soon as we walked into the house, John disappeared with Horatio, probably to give him a cootie bubble bath. Or take one himself.

My brother Johnny was sitting at the kitchen table, his head buried in his hands.

"Hey," I said. "The beach was beautiful."

"Who was askin'?" he said to his hands. Nice talk for a hippie.

For lack of a better idea, I stared at the top of his head.

"Is that hat made out of hemp?" I said.

"Could be," he said. He lifted his head up a little and gave the hat a pat, as if he might be able to tell by the feel. The hat was kind of a crunchy skull cap— crocheted, dirt-colored, slouchy looking, with a small peace sign that looked like it was made out of some kind of bone stitched over his right temple.

"Got any java around here?" he finally said.

"Yeah," I said. "On the counter, next to the coffee maker."

He didn't move a muscle. I should have waited him out, but I really needed another cup myself. So I played Suzy Homemaker and got a pot of coffee going.

While it was brewing, I opened the fridge and grabbed myself a slice of turkey.

My brother held out a hand, so I gave him a drumstick.

He sat up straight and took a big bite. I sat down across from him. We looked over each other's shoulders while we chewed.

"Nobody was here when I woke up," he said. "Not you and John. Not Dad. Not even Poppy."

"Polly," I said.

He shrugged. "Bummer way to start the day. Alone again."

"Naturally," I sang, thinking a little Gilbert O'Sullivan blast from the past might lighten things up.

Johnny took another bite of his drumstick, wiped his mouth with the back of his hand. I jumped up to go grab him a napkin, good sister that I was.

"Where are you going?" he said.

I turned to look at him. "Um, to get you a napkin?"

He nodded. "Just don't split again without telling me, okay?"

I handed him the napkin, took a long sip of coffee. "Really?"

He nodded. "I don't remember how to be my myself. Plus, I don't have wheels."

A quick picture of skateboard wheels glued to the bottom of his feet flashed before my eyes, even though I knew he meant he didn't have a car.

"How'd you get here then?"

"Lyft." He shook his head. "Thought I'd never make it. The driver was a dead ringer for Mr. Magoo. Younger, but he had those same round Coke-bottle glasses and didn't go over twenty-five the whole way. Finally dropped me off down the street because he was afraid he wouldn't be able to find his way back out to the highway if he didn't turn around right there. And, get this, when I climbed out of the car, he had the balls to tell me to be sure to give him a good review."

At least my brother still remembered how to talk beyond the occasional hippie word.

"Where's your car?" I asked.

"I told her to take it," he said. "Take the *F*-ing car, take the *F*-ing house, take *F*-ing everything."

I was seriously bad at this kind of conversation. I tried to remember what Johnny had said to me back when Kevin and I first split up. Maybe I could recycle it and use it on him.

I thought for a moment. And then it hit me. When my own marriage had shattered to pieces, when my entire world had collapsed, my brother Johnny never said a word.

Twelve

As soon I finished feeding the cats, I stretched out on the floor with all four kittens on my lap and called my sister Carol.

"It's the brother thing," she said. "In this family, they're held to a completely different standard than the sisters."

"You know," I said, "now that you mention it, I've barely heard from Michael since he and Phoebe started getting along again."

"Exactly. That's how it works. When the boys' lives are falling apart, the girls hover all over them. Let them whimper on our shoulders. Make sure they get haircuts and have birthday cakes and keep the drunk-dialing to a bare minimum. By the time the girls need something, they've checked out again."

I rubbed Oreo's belly while I let this sink in. When Oreo started attacking my hand with his new razor-sharp little teeth, I substituted a stuffed mouse so he wouldn't get the idea that chomping on hands was okay.

"I hope," Carol was saying, "you at least got the scoop from Johnny about what happened between him and Kim. And you also found out how that ridiculous hippie talk got started. He's not old enough to relive his hippie days. He was barely out of diapers back then."

"Sorry," I said. "I didn't wait around for the whole story. Polly came back from wherever she'd been, and the two of them started talking. I saw my chance, so I slipped away to call you."

"Okay, then," my big sister said. "Here's the plan. We call Billy Jr. and Michael and lay it on thick about how much Johnny needs them. We guilt-trip them into doing the first line of support, when Johnny's in full wallow mode. Then we step in later when he's ready to listen to some kick-butt sisterly advice. It'll save us a lot of time and aggravation that way."

"Sounds good." I leaned back against the couch to get more comfortable. Sunshine climbed up my arm, pounced on a clump of my hair, started chewing on it. I grabbed a stuffed frog and redirected him.

"Ooh, I know," I said. "We can get them to move Johnny out to the trailer while they're listening to him wallow and then—"

"Wait. You're putting Johnny in the *trailer?*" She made it sound worse than putting Baby in the corner in *Dirty Dancing.*

"Joe starts work on the next phase of the renovation Monday." I rolled a ping pong ball across the floor for Squiggy and Catsby to chase. "John and I are sleeping in the cat room, so don't you dare try to make me feel guilty."

"Dad's friend's teeny-tiny canned ham trailer?" Carol said, like there might be more than one trailer in our backyard.

"Yeah," I said. "Unless you'd rather have Johnny stay at your house?"

"The trailer's great. I mean, Dad probably even left some beer out there."

. . . . .

John looked up from playing fetch with Horatio on the side lawn.

"Sorry I called you an umlaut," I said.

He nodded. "Apology accepted. Sorry I acted like one."

"That's okay. But next time you get stressed out about Horatio, try not to question the depth or breadth of my vocabulary, okay?"

He nodded again. "I'll work on that."

"Thanks." I leaned in for an official making up kiss. "Okay, moving on. Have you seen Polly?"

"She and Johnny drove off in her car a little while ago."

"That's great," I said. "Nice of her to take a Johnny shift. Hey, you know what I was just thinking? What if we got our stuff all moved down to the love shack today instead of waiting till Sunday? My other brothers are coming over to move Johnny out to the trailer, which will free up my parent's old room for Polly, so she could move, too."

"Good idea," John said. "Once we get everybody relocated, we might even be able to knock down some walls before Joe and his crew get here on Monday."

"Somebody's been watching too much HGTV," I sang.

"It doesn't look that hard." John's Heath Bar eyes were shining. "Especially if Joe would let us borrow a couple of those big mullets."

"Mallets," I said.

John raised his eyebrows. "I gave you that."

"Thanks," I said. "And I deserved it."

. . . . .

John and I managed to get the king-size bed frame taken apart. We figured it wasn't worth the hassle of putting the bed frame back together again for such a short stint, so we stacked the pieces up against one wall in the front parlor, making sure we kept them a safe distance from John's prized vintage pinball machines.

We crammed the two small bureaus into one end of the dining room, made sure the drawers were facing out so we could get to our clothes. Then we put the mattress on the floor of the former cat room, set up our rickety book piles on either side. We were afraid the teething kittens would chew through the cords of our alarm clocks, so we decided to rough it and use the alarms on our phones instead.

We jammed as many of our hanging clothes as we could into the front closet. We hung some more on the shower curtain rod in the downstairs bathroom. The rest we draped across the dining room table.

Our new old house was heated by oil. The inside temperature fluctuated between extreme hot flashes from the steam radiators and icy cooling off periods. As soon as John and I started sweating from all the relocation exertion, we'd cycle into another round of goosebumps.

We'd just circled out to the kitchen for a water break when my sister Christine walked in. She was carrying a sledgehammer, which was apparently what we really needed to take down a wall. As opposed to a mullet.

"Holy moly," she said. "This thing is heavy. And I can't believe you and Carol called the boys instead of me. I could have gotten the whole story out of Johnny with one hand tied behind my back."

I shrugged. "I think they're out in the trailer with him if you want to jump in."

"Maybe I'll wait a little while. Let them break him down first so he'll be ready to talk." Christine opened the fridge, grabbed a slice of turkey.

"Hey," I said. "Get your mitts off that. You cook your own turkey, you don't get my leftovers."

Christine chewed a few times, then opened her mouth so I could see what was left of my turkey.

"Oh, grow up," I said.

"You grow up," she said.

It turned out John and I were wrong about both the mullets and the mallets. Joe walked in carrying another sledgehammer, plus something smaller that looked like an ordinary hammer to me, as well as what I was pretty sure was a crowbar. I took a moment to wonder why tools didn't come with their names labeled on them in big easy-to-read letters. It seemed to me that it would be a lot easier to dive into the DIY frenzy if you knew exactly what weapon of destruction you were holding in your hot little hands.

"Thanks for coming over," John said.

"Listen," Joe said. "I'll get you started, because all I need is another set of homeowners screwing things up by trying to save some time and money and costing us more of both. But the truth is, if you can manage to do it right, we'll get in and out of here a lot faster, which will mean savings all around."

"Thanks," I said. "I think."

"That's what we were hoping for," John said. "The saving time and money part, not the screwing up part."

"Don't make me regret it," Joe said. "And as soon as I get you going, I'm out of here. There's no way in hell I'm working Thanksgiving weekend."

· · · · ·

All four of us put on the safety glasses Joe had brought with him.

Christine and I crossed our eyes at each other, cracked ourselves up.

"We look like mad scientists," I said.

Christine held up her phone. "Come on, you guys. Let's take a selfie together."

"Chris." Behind his safety glasses, Joe narrowed his eyes.

"Fine," Christine said. "Be a jerk."

She tilted her head until it touched mine, hit the button on her phone.

"I'll email it to you," she said. "Carol will be so pissed she's not in it."

I doubted that. And I certainly wasn't going to forward it to Carol to find out. My sister Christine is seventeen months younger than I am and happily married, at least most of the time, with two kids who are more perfect than not. It drove her absolutely crazy that all family information filtered through Carol first. As far as I could tell, Carol's position as the family know-it-all was the only thing Christine had ever wanted that she couldn't get.

Joe knocked on the wall between my room and the boys' room in a few different places, his ear close to the wall. He made a few marks on the wall, then threaded his thick carpenter's pencil through his curly brown hair and tucked it behind one ear.

That pencil was the perfect size for preschoolers to grip, like the pencil version of a jumbo crayon. I started to ask Joe where I could order some for my class. Took one look at his face and decided I'd wait and make Christine find out for me later.

"Okay," Joe said. "In a house this old, we're looking at quarter-inch wood lath strips nailed horizontally across the wall studs. Three-coat plaster is applied on top of the lath, typically a total of 7/8-inch thick. Which gives us walls that are an inch thick, give or take, versus the usual ½-inch thickness of today's drywall."

John was hanging on every word. "Do you know what this old plaster is made out of?"

Joe stroked the wall with one palm. "In this neck of the woods, it would have been lime-based plaster, generally made up of lime putty, sand, and horsehair—or some other kind of hair—to reinforce it."

John stroked the wall, too. "Amazing to think that horsehair from almost 130 years ago is still in those walls."

Christine and I both neighed spontaneously. Joe and John ignored us.

Joe nodded. "An old-time plasterer I know told me they used horsehair to reinforce the plaster here on the coast because the only sand available was beach sand, which has lots of salt and broken-down particles from the ocean mixed in with it, so it doesn't hold up well over time. No idea if he really knew what he was talking about, or if he was just spouting off."

Christine took another selfie, this one a solo shot, standing in the middle of the room that had once been half hers.

Joe held up the sledgehammer like it was a dinner fork. "Who wants the honor of breaking through?"

John looked at me. "Ladies first."

I managed to swing the sledgehammer a couple inches in each direction at about knee height.

When we used to play catch as kids, my brothers tried to coach me so I didn't throw like a girl. I still threw like a girl, and I definitely swung a sledgehammer like one. Maybe even like a toddler.

I kept swinging. I might have made a slight dent in the wall. This whole thing looked a lot more fun on HGTV.

"Somebody hand me that mullet," I finally said.

John traded the sledgehammer for a hammer, and between the two of us we managed to open up a big enough hole in the plaster to see the old wood lath behind.

Joe took the sledgehammer from John. John took the hammer from me.

"Come on," Christine said. "Let's go check on the other boys."

Thirteen

"I'll meet you out in the trailer," I said to Christine once we were in the upstairs hallway. "I just want to check on Polly and see if I can help her move out of Carol's old room. She doesn't have much stuff, so it won't take long."

"Where's she going?" Christine smoothed both hands over her hair, as if watching us break through the plaster might have messed up her shiny brown bob.

"Nowhere," I said. "She's just relocating to Mom and Dad's old room."

Christine's jaw actually dropped. "What? You're making Johnny stay out in the backyard in a trailer, and you're letting a *stranger* sleep in Mom and Dad's room?"

I felt Polly's presence at the foot of the stairs before I saw her. She turned, took a step, turned again, disappeared. A moment later, I heard the door to the cat room close softly.

"Whoopsies," Christine said.

"*Whoopsies?* How old are you?" I shook my head. "I can't believe you did that."

"What?" she said. "I just asked a simple question. It's not my fault she was listening."

"Go," I said. "I can't even look at you right now."

"Fine." Christine stomped down the stairs.

I waited until the stomping stopped. Then I walked downstairs, opened the door to the cat room.

Polly was sitting on the couch, her lap filled with kittens, tears streaming down her cheeks. Pebbles watched us from her bookshelf, her emerald eyes glittering. I remembered Ethan telling me that in some cultures cats are considered to be mystical creatures, and the fairy world is watching us through their eyes. I took a moment to throw a pleading look to Pebbles, or the fairies, or the patron saint of lapsed Catholics, or whoever was minding the shop. *Just don't let me screw this up.*

I sat down beside Polly. "I'm sorry that happened."

Polly sniffed. "It's just these damn pregnancy hormones. Everything makes me cry. I took a walk down by the town pier this morning, and a bunch of ducks were swimming around. I guess they were diving for their breakfast, but it looked like they were doing handstands in the water. You know, all these cute little fluffy white duck butts sticking up in the air." She took a raggedy breath. "It was so beautiful."

And then she burst into tears.

I moved the kittens off Polly's lap and down to the floor. I patted her back like she was a baby. I handed her a tissue.

"I'd like to promise you," I said, "that no one in my family will ever say something like that again. But I have no control over them. In fact, if I tell them not to do something, it usually backfires. I think they're just genetically predisposed to saying stupid things. What did we used to call it in high school—having diarrhea of the mouth?"

Polly wiped her eyes, blew her nose. "I can stay somewhere else. I just need a little bit of time to figure out where."

Polly was an only child and her much older parents were both dead. She'd grown up a few towns away. When her husband left her for another woman, she'd given up her middle-management job on the other side of the country and moved back. I didn't get the feeling that she'd kept in touch with any of her old friends. And even if she had, what do you do, private message them on Facebook? *Hey, I'm ba-ack. Want to have coffee sometime? By the way, I'm single and pregnant, and no, I don't want to talk about it.*

"Don't be ridiculous," I said. "You're staying here. As long as you want, but at least until after the baby is born and you've got the hang of being a new mom. And until my family has driven you so completely bonkers that you can't wait another minute to get out of here."

Polly smiled, wiped her eyes again. "At least let me move into the trailer. I'll be fine out there. It's just—"

"Knock it off," I said. "You're not staying in the trailer."

I jumped up. "Come on, let's get your stuff moved."

Polly followed me up the stairs. I waited and let her open the door to my sister Carol's old room.

The bed was neatly made, something Carol had certainly never done back when she was living in there. All the baby hand-me-downs Gloria, our teacher friend from Bayberry, had given to Polly—car seat, changing table, basinet, clothes, toys—were stacked against the walls.

"Wow," I said. "I'd forgotten how tiny this room is. It always seemed bigger to me growing up because I was so thoroughly pissed off that Carol had her own room and I didn't."

I picked up a bag of baby clothes in each hand. "There's still room in the attic—do you want to move some of the baby stuff up there?"

"Thanks, but I like looking at it. It makes me feel like this baby is really happening, you know?" Polly grabbed her purse, her pillow, the car seat.

I pushed open the door to my parents' old room. I took in their beautiful rich cherry wood bedroom set. The framed watercolor of the Marshbury lighthouse at sunrise hanging over the bed. The Irish lace curtains covering the windows, curtains that my mother used to wash by hand and hang on the clothesline to dry on a hot summer day.

"You're actually doing me a favor by staying here." I leaned back against the doorframe. "Since my mother died, I've had a really hard time walking into this room. It just makes me miss her so much, you know? Anyway, I think it will help to start thinking of it as your room. And my mother would have loved the idea of a baby in here." I pointed through the arched entry that led to a sitting area on one side of the room. "We can set that up with the baby stuff. It's perfect for a nursery."

Tears rolled down Polly's cheeks. "See, it's like I'm a waterworks display." She sniffed. "I'm sorry I never got to meet your mom."

I wiped my own eyes. "She would have been crazy about you. And she would have done a much better job of taking care of you than I'm doing."

"Cut it out." Polly handed me a tissue from the box on the bedside table. "You hired me for a job I was completely unqualified for, you helped rescue me in a storm, you offered me a place to stay. I can't imagine anybody else in the world who would have done all that for me."

I gave her a quick hug. "Do you still miss your parents?"

Polly tucked the car seat into a corner of the sitting area. "I miss the idea of them, I think. They did the best they could, but the truth is that by the time they managed to have me, they didn't quite know what to do with me. My whole childhood I kept wanting to yell, *Here I am, see me!* But I didn't quite have the nerve, you know?"

I tucked the bags of baby clothes in next to the car seat, while I let that sink in. What if by the time John and I managed to have a baby, we didn't know quite what to do with it either? And we were too set in our ways to figure it out?

I gave Polly another quick hug. "Come on, let's get to work."

We dragged everything out of Carol's room and found a place for it in the new room. I'd already stripped off the sheets Johnny had slept on, so I found another set in the hallway linen closet, and Polly and I made the bed together.

As we were stuffing pillows into the pillowcases, Polly's phone rang.

She froze.

"Go ahead," I said. "Answer it. We're just about done in here anyway."

She gave her pillow a punch, threw it on the bed.

"That's okay," she said. "I can call back later."

. . . . .

Christine was sitting at the kitchen table, eating another hunk of my turkey. She was also drinking a glass of what my father called John's fancy pants wine.

"Help yourself," I said.

"Thanks," she said. "Don't mind if I do."

Since Christine had already opened the bottle, I figured I might as well pour my own glass.

"Sorry about Polly," Christine said. "Do you want me to go upstairs and apologize?"

I shook my head. "I don't think she needs the drama. Just be nice to her from now on, okay?"

Christine nodded, took another sip of wine.

I tried swirling the wine around in my glass like they did in the movies. It crashed over the side like a wave at high tide and landed in a puddle on my jeans. I rubbed it in even though it was red wine, tried to remember if we had any stain stick in the laundry room.

"Graceful," Christine said.

"Thank you," I said. "I work hard at it."

"Do you think Carol's right about Dad and Polly?"

"Of course not," I said. "You know Dad—he pretty much flirts with every female he comes across. And Polly is just trying to survive right now. Plus, she's pregnant. And our age."

"Here's to Carol not knowing what she's talking about." Christine clinked her glass to mine. "I love it when she's wrong."

Apparently Johnny's hippie backpack had only made it as far as the kitchen door. After Christine and I finished our wine, I hoisted it up and slung it over one shoulder.

"Jeez Louise," I said as we walked across the yard. "This thing weighs a ton and a half."

Two women of indeterminate age were loitering outside the trailer. Maybe they'd seen Pink stuck into the ground and taken it as an invitation. The women were illuminated by tiny white lights strung above the entrance to the trailer. It would have been nice if someone had taken the decorating bull by the horns and they were Christmas lights. But as far as I could tell the lights had come with the trailer, and the trailer had been in the yard since the end of summer, making the lights officially multi-seasonal.

The two women were eyeing each other. They were both holding casseroles.

"Have you seen Billy?" one of them yelled. "I have a little something I want to drop off for him." She held up the casserole. "Shepherd's pie made with Thanksgiving leftovers."

The other woman held up her casserole. "Seafood lasagna." *Take that*, the tone of her voice implied.

Our father's dating escapades may have been responsible for varying levels of discomfort in his six adult children, but he'd yet to connect with a woman who hadn't contributed at least one casserole to sustain him against the ravages of widowerhood. Even the women who owned Bark & Roll Forever paid him in casseroles they acquired by bartering with a friend who had a catering business.

One of the upsides about buying the family house was that I no longer had to drive across town to shop my father's refrigerator. The casseroles came with the house. I loved the way they filled the freezer. The way there was always something for dinner if you didn't mind waiting long enough for it to thaw and cook. The way those casseroles kept me from looking like I was slacking and John was doing most of the cooking.

"Hi," I said. "I'm Sarah. If you go all the way around to the other side of the house and in through the mudroom door, you'll find my father's new place. I don't think he's there right now, but make yourself at home if you want to wait."

"Hi, I'm Christine," my sister said.

I held out my hands before Christine got any big ideas about taking a casserole home with her.

"I can take those for you if you want," I said. "I'll put them right in the fridge for my father."

The women introduced themselves. I smiled but let their names slide in one ear and out the other. The truth was I didn't bother to retain anything about the women in my father's life until at least the fifth date. Or after the third casserole, whichever came first.

The shepherd's pie lady took a moment to write a note on the back of a receipt and tuck it into the fold of the foil. The other woman had already taped a card and a big blue bow to her seafood lasagna.

They handed the casseroles over to me. I forced myself to remain dignified, as opposed to jumping up and down and cheering.

"Thanks so much," I yelled as they walked away. "We worry about our dad getting enough to eat."

Fourteen

I got both casseroles safely tucked away with the others in the house. Then I ran back and picked up my brother Johnny's mammoth tie-dyed backpack again. My sister Christine was just standing there doing nothing, so I turned the doorknob with one hand, while I gracefully kicked open the trailer door with the other.

My three brothers looked up. They were jammed into the trailer's little dinette like giant sardines, each with a bottle of Sam Adams in front of him on the teensy tabletop.

"You want a hand with that?" my brother Johnny said.

"Yeah." I sighed and gave the backpack a martyr-like shift on my shoulder.

All three of them started clapping.

Christine burst out laughing.

"Find some new material, you guys." I let Johnny's backpack fall to the floor. "That joke wasn't funny the first time I heard it, like a century or so ago."

"So what's up?" Christine said. "Are we interrupting anything good?"

Billy Jr. took a gulp of his beer, burped. "Just shootin' the shit."

Michael took a gulp of his beer, burped louder. "Yeah, you know. How about those Patriots and all that."

Johnny stared straight ahead.

By the looks of things, my brothers would be sitting here all night, or at least until they were out of beer and burps, without even touching on why Johnny was impersonating a hippie, not to mention why he'd left home in the first place.

I had a couple options. I could turn around and walk out the door. Leave Christine in charge. But then, in all fairness, I should go back upstairs and offer to help John and Joe demolish walls again. And the truth was that the bloom was off the renovation rose. From now on, I'd stick to watching home improvement shows on TV.

I could call my sister Carol. But then I'd have to wait for her to drive over here. It was getting late. I was tired. Even a mattress on the floor of the cat room was starting to sound good to me.

Before I had time to make a decision, my father opened the trailer door and stuck his head in. In my family, when one person showed up somewhere, another was sure to follow, as if there was some natural law of synchronicity. I should have asked him what took him so long.

But of course, my dad had his own opening line. "I have the distinct impression that my very own family is smack-dab in the middle of a party to which I was not invited."

"Yeah," Billy Jr. said. "Looks like you caught us in the act." He took another sip of his beer. "Long time no see. How's it going since yesterday, Dad?"

"Can't complain. Can't complain at all, Billy Boy. I was just pulling the ice cream truck into the driveway, happened to notice the extra cars in the nick of time to hit the brakes."

Our dad watched as Johnny took a long, sad sip of beer. "Hey, what's your tale, nightingale?"

Johnny didn't say a word.

My father disappeared out the trailer door for a minute. He came back with Pink hoisted over his head, dirt from her metal stake sprinkling the trailer floor.

"Pack up, kiddos," our dad said. "This shindig is moving up in the world and over to my man cavern. Just follow the pink flamingo."

. . . . .

Our father stuck Pink in the pot of dead geraniums outside the mudroom door to help direct future traffic. The women bearing casseroles hadn't waited around for him, so we had his new man cave all to ourselves. He stood for a moment, jingling the change in his pocket, then settled into his cracked brown recliner. The rest of us got comfortable on the floor or took a seat along the outer edges of his round red bed.

Billy Jr. passed out what was left of the beer from the trailer fridge. Christine and I got a beer to share, which balanced out the fact that we'd each already polished off a glass of John's wine.

"Slainté," we all said as we held up our bottles, Christine's and my hands overlapping.

Christine tried to grab the bottle from me, but I was too fast for her. Since I was older, I thought it only fair that I take the first sip before I handed it over. And so I did.

"The place looks great already, Dad," I said.

He nodded. "It's on its way, darlin', it's on its way. As long as you kiddos don't forget about that 90-inch television set you promised me for Christmas."

"90-inch?" Michael said. "No way. We told you 27."

"Don't kid a kidder," our dad said. "And no matter what the ladies in the supermarket say about size doesn't matter, the truth of the matter is we all like to be able see what we're looking at."

"Don't anybody touch that one," Billy Jr. said. "Just let it roll right by."

"Back to my Christmas list," our dad said. "Make sure you don't forget that new recliner you promised me either. This one has a tendency to get stuck in the way-back position—in a pinch I've been known to resort to rolling over one of the arms to get out. And if you're having a particularly good year in the moolah department, I do believe a minibar over in that corner would add to the overall deviance."

We all looked around. "Don't you think you should move the bed upstairs to the bedroom, Dad?" Christine said.

We were sitting in the former garage, which was a large open living area, with a kitchenette with an island at one end and a guest bath tucked in on the other end. An open staircase led up to the former secret room, where two dormers had been added to create a large master bedroom and bath.

Our dad leaned back in his recliner and crossed his legs. "It would be a sorry state of affairs if any visitors happened to miss the bed." He clapped his hands twice. The LED lights circling the bed lit up. We watched them flash white to red to orange to blue to purple.

"Like, wow," Johnny said. "How to trigger a flashback."

"I thought those lights only clapped on and off," Michael said. "I didn't know you could make them change colors."

"You're darn tootin' they change colors," our dad said. "And you should see the lights on my new throne upstairs, so make sure you check out that baby before you leave. I stocked up on toilet paper when I moved in, so don't you worry about that."

We all nodded.

Our father shook his head in wonder. "No need to even clap in the necessarium. There's a built-in motion detector that senses your body heat or some such thing when you approach the facilities. It turns on the light, and then shuts it off again when you walk away. Makes a great nightlight, too, in case your night vision doesn't happen to be what it used to be. Changes the water in the crapper bowl to sixteen LED colors, if you can imagine that."

"Might be even more colors than that," Michael said, "if you factor in how they mix with piss yellow."

"Language," our father said.

"Yeah," Christine said. "Don't be a sasshole, Mikey."

"Sasshole." Billy Jr. shook his head. "That's forking ridiculous."

"Put a cork in it. Now." Our dad gave us his stern face. "Never forget for a minute that while Billy Boy Hurlihy is still alive and kickin', not one of you is too old to have your mouth washed out with a bar of Irish Spring."

. . . . .

I was just dozing off when John finally came into the cat room, which I had to admit I still thought of as the cat room. Apparently, the love shack thing wasn't going to stick.

"Hey," I said. "How'd it go with the demolition?"

I rolled over, propped myself up on one elbow. "I was afraid if I went upstairs to check on you, Joe would realize what time it was and leave. So instead I drove Christine to Carol's house to pick up the kids and then dropped them all off at home."

John lowered himself to the other side of the mattress on the floor. He smelled like sandalwood soap and Tom's of Maine peppermint toothpaste, mixed with a dollop of sweat.

"Joe and I demoed the snot out of those walls," he said.

I smiled. "I can't believe you said snot. You're such a bad, bad boy."

"I know, right?" John leaned over for a kiss. "Joe kept saying he was going to quit, but we kept going and going. He called to have a new dumpster dropped off tomorrow, so if you and I can get those rooms cleared of debris, Joe and his crew will be able to jump right in first thing Monday morning."

"That's great." I yawned. "As soon as I get a good night's sleep, I'll be all over it."

John yawned back. "How did it go at your end?"

"Animals all fed and watered and accounted for. I borrowed an extra nightlight from Christine so we don't step on any kittens in the dark."

"Good thinking."

"And my dad's madly in love with the LED lights on his new bed and toilet. He's ramped up his Christmas TV request to a 90-inch. And Billy and Michael were useless. Basically, they just hung around and left as soon as the beer was gone."

"How did it go with Johnny? Did he tell everybody what's going on?"

"Nope. When Christine and I left, he was still pouting away in his hemp hat. Maybe after a cozy night's sleep in the trailer, he'll be ready to talk. I mean, nothing in my family ever stays a secret for long."

John rolled over, pulled up the covers. "He's not out in the trailer. I passed him on the way in here. He's curled up on the living room couch with a pile of throw pillows under his head and an afghan pulled up to his chin."

"Great," I said. "Do you think I can pretend you didn't tell me that? Just until tomorrow. Then I'll be all over that, too."

"Why not?" John said. A minute later he was snoring softly.

I tossed and I turned. Slowly, just in case any kittens had managed to scale the mattress.

It wasn't my job to worry about Johnny. If he wanted to sleep on the couch, he was a grownup and he could sleep on the couch. Back when Kevin and I had broken up, I could have been sleeping in the streets for all my brother Johnny knew. For all he cared.

I took out my hurt feelings and polished them until they were shiny and pathetic. Once you get going on something like that, it's kind of like picking a scab, or trying to eat the proverbial one potato chip. So I kept it up, sifting through half-forgotten memories, binging on old injuries.

I went over the entire ancient history timeline of my relationship with my brother Johnny. When we were little kids, he was actually pretty mean to me. When I thought about it, I could distinctly remember him making fun of me in front of his friends. Once, he pointed out my new pimple to the entire school bus. He called me ugly to my face. Other than that, he ignored me, the biggest hurt of all.

Once I became a relatively mature adult, I'd mostly forgotten about all that old stuff. But my brother Johnny and I never really talked. Because there were six of us, we had the luxury of spinning off into subgroups. Little cliques formed and reformed, with some of us temporarily included and others left out. There was a well-established family grapevine, so even if you didn't hear it from the horse's mouth, you still eventually heard everything.

Time flies. We all get older and older still. And without really noticing, the years could slip by and you could suddenly realize that you had no idea who one of your siblings was. To be completely honest, you weren't even sure if you cared.

Especially because at this particular crazy point in your life, you had enough on your plate without taking on one more thing. Especially a brother who didn't come close to deserving it.

I dozed, woke up. Dozed some more.

Finally I kicked off the stupid covers. I tiptoed out of the cat room, making sure none of the animals wandered out with me. I made a pit stop at the bathroom, circled out to the kitchen, poured a glass of tap water, guzzled it down.

I tiptoed into the living room, tried to figure out whether Johnny was awake or asleep.

I couldn't tell, so I sat in the armchair across from the couch. I figured that even if he was asleep, on some kind of karmic level I should get points for sitting here.

He groaned. "What's up?"

"You were such an idiot to me when we were growing up," I said. "You were mean. Really, really mean."

He groaned again. "How about you wait another thirty years or so to lay it on me. And until then we both try to catch some Zs."

I wanted to knock the smug right out of him. And his man bun.

"Go kick rocks," I said. "Barefoot.

"Not my bag," I heard him say to my back as I stomped toward the cat room.

A pajama-clad figure coming down the center staircase scared me almost to death.

"Dad?" I said. My heart was beating a mile a minute. "What were you doing upstairs in the middle of the night?"

"Hmm," he said. "At first gander, I'd have to say I might well have been sleepwalking."

My father stuck his hands out straight in front of him, fake-closed his eyes, kept walking.

Fifteen

The Monday after the long Thanksgiving weekend is always a tough day for preschoolers. Not to mention their teachers.

Polly was leaning back against the far wall of our classroom, her crossed arms resting on the shelf of her baby bump. One of the bright orange starfish she'd painted on the wall looked like it was dancing on top of her auburn hair. Either that or I seriously needed another cup of coffee.

"Low expectations," I said. "Our goal is to get through the day with a minimum of Band-Aids, tears, puking, and pooping that doesn't involve full contact with the toilet bowl."

"Got it," Polly said. "What about the kids?"

"Yeah, whatever," I said.

Polly wandered out to the hallway to stand by the cubbies and greet the students as they arrived. I crossed the room to our reading boat, started rearranging the pillows. The reading boat was the pride and joy of our classroom. Polly had surprised me with it right after I'd hired her. Ethan had recently been hired at Bayberry, too, and she'd asked him if he had any idea where she could find a boat. He just happened to have a non-seaworthy one in his storage unit from his indie film-making days.

The two of them had put their heads and creativity together. As a result, an entire small fiberglass boat was now tucked into the far corner of the room. Nautical-striped pillows cushioned the bottom. The stern was fitted out with a low bookshelf, a smaller bookshelf tucked into the bow. READ READ READ YOUR BOOKS GENTLY THROUGH YOUR LIFE was stenciled in big block letters on one side of the boat. The other side said MERRILY MERRILY MERRILY MERRILY READING IS A DREAM.

The reading boat was by far the coolest thing in the room. Whenever I looked at it, I wanted to crawl in and get comfy, crack open a book, be a kid again.

"My eyes have a hundred bazillion sleeps sticking them closed," Depp said as he staggered into the classroom.

"*My* eyes have *twenty* hundred bazillion sleeps sticking them closed," Juliette said from the sand table.

For preschoolers, knowing that twenty hundred bazillion is way more than a hundred bazillion is some pretty advanced math.

The students kept stumbling in and eventually everybody arrived. We gathered on the circle, each of the students coming in for a landing on the dot that marked their place without any major collisions. The kids took turns sharing their Thanksgiving stories, the football games they went to (my team won!), how big their turkeys were (this big!), how far they had to drive (a million miles!), what the best dessert was (pilgrim cupcakes!), what a great time they had (my mommy's more fun when she drinks lots of wine!).

We all stood up. Polly and I got the kids sorted into groups of two, facing each other. We started singing a rousing rendition of "A Sailor Went to Sea," making patty-cake motions and then triple high-fiving when we came to each repetition of words.

> A sailor went to sea, sea, sea,
> To see what he could see, see, see.
> But all that he could see, see, see
> Was the bottom of the deep blue sea, sea, sea.

It was an oldie but goodie, and always a crowd pleaser with the preschool set.

I couldn't draw like Polly or build things like Ethan, but one of the things I loved best about being a teacher was making up fun things on the spot.

I added some other movements to our triple high-fives:

> A sailor went to shake, shake, shake,
> To see what he could shake, shake, shake.

But all that he could shake, shake, shake
Was the bottom of the deep blue shake, shake,
shake.
Sea, sea, sea.

A sailor went to wiggle, wiggle, wiggle,
To see what he could wiggle, wiggle, wiggle,
But all that he could wiggle, wiggle, wiggle,
Was the bottom of the deep blue wiggle, wiggle,
wiggle.
Shake, shake, shake.
Sea, sea, sea.

A sailor went to jump, jump, jump,
To see what he could jump, jump, jump.
But all that he could jump, jump, jump
Was the bottom of the deep blue jump, jump, jump.
Wiggle, wiggle, wiggle.
Shake, shake, shake.
Sea, sea, sea.

The kids started yelling out other ideas—hop, skip, spin—and we patty-caked and patty-caked until our list of movements got so long that even Polly and I could no longer keep it straight.

After that we helped the students choose individual work. Griffin headed for our reading boat, grabbed a book and a pillow. His eyes suddenly filled with tears and his lower lip quivered. "I can't read!" he yelled. Then he fell immediately to sleep.

Jaden threw the dice at the penny-counting game. "Come on, work with me, pennies," he yelled.

Pandora sat down at the smell-matching game and took a sniff from the first tiny bottle. "Is that Chanel No. 5?" she asked me.

I took a sniff, too. "Smells like preschool spirit," I said.

Pandora tilted her head and gave me a funny look.

"Never mind," I said. "It's lavender. Now see if you can find the other bottle that smells just like this one."

Pandora sniffed the tiny bottles—pumpkin pie spice, vanilla, lemon, pine needles, peppermint—then held one up triumphantly. "Lavender No. 5!" she yelled.

Polly had come up with the genius idea of gluing brightly colored pompoms on the non-business ends of dry erase markers. The pompoms were instantly transformed into the most awesome erasers ever. The kids wrote their names over and over again on our whiteboard, just for the joy of erasing them and doing it all over again.

We moved on to snack and recess, and then to dismissal for the half-day students. The full-day students still didn't look fully awake, so after lunch Polly and I went easy on them.

It was a gorgeous late-November afternoon, what we used to call an Indian summer day back before that became politically incorrect. Polly and I gave the students each a little wicker basket. We walked around the school grounds, swinging the baskets and singing "A Tisket A Tasket" at the top of our lungs.

I made up new words to that song, too, changing *I wrote a letter to my love* to *I found some leaves with my friends.* I mean, really, what preschooler needed to be singing about writing love letters and losing them? They had their whole rest of their lives to worry about that stuff. While we sang, the kids collected autumn leaves and pinecones and dried wildflowers and seed pods and anything else that looked interesting and would fit in their baskets.

The kids found seats at the picnic tables on the edge of the playground. Polly and I handed out big sheets of paper and tiny paper cups filled with paste and a popsicle stick for smearing it. The kids pasted away to their hearts' content, creating found object collages that at least one parent would be sure to complain made a mess of her fancy SUV on the drive home.

I didn't care.

The students weighted their masterpieces down with small rocks so they wouldn't blow away while they dried. We all sat in a circle on a nearby patch of grass for one more activity, taking advantage of this scrumptious weather, because before we knew it, it would be gone until spring.

I took out a bag of pinecones and passed them around. Making pinecone birdfeeders was one of my favorite activities to do with my students. We used to make them with peanut butter, back before Bayberry had become peanut-free due to the explosion of nut allergies. Now we used suet. Suet is animal fat, which you can buy from the butcher. Or you can cheat like I do and buy it from the bird-food aisle in the big box store.

Polly cut foot-long pieces of twine while I gave them out, then we helped the kids tie their twine to one end of the pinecone, two to three rows below the wider end of the cone and tucked in behind the scales so they didn't slip off. Then we tied a loop on the other end so their birdfeeders would be able to hang from a tree or even a plant hook.

We shared spatulas and little tubs of suet, and the kids smeared their pinecones with the suet. Only one student, Liam, tasted the suet this time around, which was a major improvement over last year. Polly redirected the spatula so quickly that it was almost as if it hadn't happened.

I thought for a moment, decided I really didn't feel like writing the incident report: *While making bird-feeders in school today, Liam inadvertently sampled the animal fat. It was not to his liking, so very little was consumed, but please do keep an eye out for potential symptoms.* I mean, half the Bayberry families were on low carb diets anyway, and suet and bone broth were practically the same thing. Right?

I'd filled a shallow plastic storage box with birdseed. The kids took turns rolling their pinecones around and around in the birdseed. Polly and I helped them slide their finished birdfeeders into zip-lock bags, so that no SUVs would be harmed on the homeward ride.

Sixteen

Polly and I were sitting in our student-less classroom, making our own pinecone birdfeeders with the rest of the suet and birdseed. Instead of carefully using a spatula for the suet the way we'd instructed the kids, we were going at it with our hands full throttle.

"I bet this stuff is really good for dry skin," Polly said as she rubbed her suet-covered hands together. "And it's so much more dignified than playing with the Play-Doh."

"Plus, we might as well use it up," I said. "Not that I'm a suet expert, but I'm pretty sure it doesn't keep that long."

A vision of my father descending the stairs last night flashed before my eyes. "Hey, I just have to ask you. My father hasn't been pestering you, has he?"

Polly waited a beat before she answered. "Of course not. He's adorable."

I watched her, shrugged. "Okay then, three good things that happened today."

Polly found our classroom notebook and managed to pick up a pen without it slipping out of her greasy hand. "One, there was a noticeable absence of name-calling today, even at recess."

I nodded. "Always a good thing."

"Two," Polly continued. "Josiah didn't play bongo drums on his privates and sing bababoo once today."

"Babaloo," I said. "You know, like Ricky Ricardo used to sing when he played the bongos on *I Love Lucy*? Anyway, that's definitely a good thing. I always think the other kids didn't even notice, but then it turns out that they were only waiting until they get home to try it out at the dinner table."

Polly worked her slippery fingers to a better grip on her pen. "And three—"

Lorna poked her head through our doorway. "If I'm late for the staff meeting, then you two are going to be seriously late. Which will really help me out a lot, so thanks for that."

Lorna disappeared. Polly and I looked at each other.

I shook my head. "What kind of *animal* schedules a teachers' meeting on the Monday after Thanksgiving?"

Polly and I race-walked through the hallways, wiping our hands with scratchy institutional paper towels, birdseed trailing behind us.

I glanced over my shoulder. "Well, at least we won't have any trouble finding our way back to the classroom again."

We caught up to Lorna outside the all-purpose room. I thought we had enough speed going that we might even pass her, but she gave us a quick smirk and beat us through the door.

Polly stepped back to let me walk in before her.

"You go first," I whispered. "She's far less likely to yell at a pregnant woman. At least I think she is."

We entered the room with our heads down, like two middle schoolers who were afraid they were going to get a detention for being late to class.

We paused. The only two empty chairs were in the front row. Wouldn't you think teachers, of all people, would fill up the first row first? Studies have shown, again and again, that where you sit in a room can have a major effect not only on your engagement, but on how you're perceived by the person in charge, and even on how much you learn.

But although they certainly knew better, teachers always ran for that back row.

Kate Stone stood at the front of the all-purpose room, all business. She was wearing one of the handful of batik-print tunics she'd been rotating for at least a decade, this one the color of overripe beets, over a long black skirt and Birkenstock sandals. Dangly earrings poked through her thin brown hair, which was streaked with coarser strands of gray.

Polly and I slid into seats directly under our bitch of a boss's nostrils. We reached into our canvas teacher bags for notebooks and pens.

A flurry of birdseed peppered the area in front of our feet, black sunflower seeds coming in for a landing on the wood floor, smaller round seeds I couldn't identify skittering to almost touch Kate Stone's Birkenstocks.

Polly and I choked back giggles.

When our bitch of a boss crossed her arms over her chest, the sleeves of her tunic made bat wings. She cleared her throat pointedly.

"Now that we're all *finally* here," she said. "I'd like to remind you about Bayberry's expectations for our third-year students."

She followed the length of her nose to look directly at Polly and me. "The final year of preschool does not consist of entire afternoons spent skipping around to the tune of 'A Tisket A Tasket.' Bayberry students are not only expected to be ready for kindergarten, but to shine brightly when they get there."

I wanted to jump to my feet. I wanted to tell Kate Stone to her face that we'd given our students exactly what they needed this afternoon. A day to recover from the exhaustion of Thanksgiving weekend, a day to enjoy the autumn beauty before it slipped away to winter. We'd accomplish more on the yang of those hard skills tomorrow by giving the kids the yin of the laid-back day they needed today. That we all needed today.

Sure, it was critical that the kids learned basic colors and geometric shapes. That they could write their names while holding their writing instrument with the appropriate-three finger grasp, identify upper and lower-case letters, recognize numerals, count objects, rhyme, tell stories. And more, so much more.

And they would. It was my job, and I took those kindergarten-readiness skills seriously. I was a good teacher.

But in the scheme of things, one of the most important things my students might take away from their time at Bayberry was how to make a damn pine cone birdfeeder. Who knew, they might decide to make one every year, year after year after year, for the rest of their lives. And wouldn't the world be a better place if we all took the time to make an occasional pine cone birdfeeder?

"Sarah?" Kate Stone seemed to be saying off in some foggy distance.

And the bummer was that I was the only Sarah in the room.

I blinked myself back to the meeting.

Beside Kate Stone was an enormous pad of white paper attached to a tubular steel display stand. She pulled a purple marker from the pocket of her batik tunic and uncapped it with her teeth. Still using only her teeth, she placed the cap on the marker's non-writing end.

The whole time she was looking right at me.

I gulped. At this point in my career, I'd been through most of my bitch of a boss's stupid team-building exercises at least twenty gazillion times, so I took a wild guess.

"Dedication," I said. "Enthusiasm."

There was dead silence. And then the entire room burst out laughing.

"On that note," Kate Stone said. "I'd say Sarah has just volunteered to be in charge of this year's Bayberry holiday performance. Ethan, you'll be co-chair."

. . . . .

"Shit, shit, shit," I said.

We were sitting around the long rectangular kiddie table in my classroom. I reached under my bra strap discreetly, removed a sunflower seed that had somehow become lodged there.

Polly scooped some of the remaining suet out of the tub, rubbed her hands together, passed the tub to Lorna. Lorna scooped some suet, passed the tub to Gloria. Gloria scooped and passed it to Ethan, then Ethan scooped and passed it to his teaching assistant June. June was my former assistant. I liked her a lot, despite the fact that she was ridiculously young and blond and beautiful.

They all rubbed their hands together and looked at me.

"You know," Lorna said, "if we marketed this stuff as high-end hand lotion, we could quit this stupid job and not have to worry about the holiday performance."

"Great idea, honey." Gloria held a finger up to her nose. "We might just have to do a teensy bit of work on the smell first."

There were two events in the yearly calendar that could turn the teacher coerced into chairing them into a star. Either that or cause her to crash and burn in front of the entire Bayberry community. One was the holiday performance, and the other was graduation.

Kate Stone had put me in charge of last spring's graduation. I'd worked my fingers to the bone. For weeks, the graduates-to-be had watched caterpillars spin silken cocoons and waited for them to gradually emerge as butterflies. Once the butterflies appeared, the kids took turns adding sugar water to tiny cups with eyedroppers and soaking flowers in it to feed them.

Thanks to my brilliant timing, the butterflies were fluttering around in their butterfly gazebo on graduation day, locked and loaded and stashed out of sight in the shade of a grove of pine trees. When the time was right, Gloria picked up her ukulele and began playing "Fly Me to the Moon." Lorna and I ceremoniously placed the butterfly gazebo in front of the graduation podium. The butterflies soared magically over the crowd.

And then one by one, they started dropping like flies.

It was so bad that Kate Stone told the parents that the school psychologist would be available all weekend. We'd actually had to find a bar a few towns away to drink our end-of-the-school-year pomegranate martinis.

I blinked the horrific memory away. "Don't any of you dare say the *B* word."

June's china doll blue eyes filled with tears. "I still dream about the carnage. And I still remember their names. There was Tinkerbelle and Wings and Flutter and Flopsy and Justin Bieber and—"

"Get a grip," I said as I handed her a tissue.

"In summation," Lorna said, "particularly for our two new colleagues who missed the graduation debacle, you've got a lot riding on this holiday performance."

"Thanks for the understatement." I cleared my throat. "Okay, the biggest obstacle I see is that it's all been done before. I mean, how can we come up with a holiday performance that's fresh and fun, while keeping it politically and religiously correct, inclusive, heart-warming—"

"And all the rest of that crap," Lorna said.

I nodded. "Exactly. And let's not forget that we have to make each and every Bayberry parent think that their child is the real star of the show." I scratched my head with both hands, as if I might dig my way to a good idea. I took a moment to consider the possibility of suet as a deep hair conditioner that might go viral, forced myself to stay focused.

"I mean, just take me out to pasture and shoot me now," I finally said.

"Just a thought," Ethan said, "but I made something new for our classroom that we might be able to use as a jumping off point."

I was already wiping the suet off my hands.

"Halleluiah," I said. "Lead the way."

Seventeen

Ethan's classroom looked exactly like the set of a Disney movie. Three-dimensional flowers climbed one wall and reached for a sparkly painted sun smiling down from the ceiling. Styrofoam clouds circled the sun like big puffy pillows. On the far side of the room, black chalkboard paint sliced through the length of two walls and a snippet of ceiling, transforming day to night. Randomly placed stick-on stars actually glowed against the dark paint. The Big Dipper hung from the ceiling. Next to it, a hanging cow jumped over a hanging moon.

The last time I'd been here, a reading nook had been tucked into the nighttime corner. It was partitioned off by a sturdy plywood divider that looked exactly like an open book, complete with a blank line so the kids could fill in the book's title, as well as another line to add their own name as the author.

The open book had been replaced with a plywood Egyptian pyramid. It was maybe six-feet tall, with a square base and four triangular sides. It was painted white and covered with chocolate brown hieroglyphics. Two square openings allowed the kids to climb in one side and out the other. I peeked inside to see a fluffy floor pillow, a pile of books, a flashlight.

"Good job, Ethan honey," Gloria said. "Many people would have mistakenly built a tetrahedron pyramid that has a base and three sides, all congruent, instead of an authentic Egyptian pyramid."

June sighed. "Teacher nerd talk is everything." She flicked her hair, creating a wave of shimmering blond.

"I don't mess around." Ethan threw his shoulders back, gave his chest a couple of Tarzan beats.

Ethan and Polly exchanged looks. I could tell by the way Polly was grinning that she'd already seen the pyramid. Maybe she'd even painted the hieroglyphics on it. Maybe every time Polly disappeared in her car, she was meeting Ethan at Bayberry. Maybe it was none of my business.

"It's incredible," I said.

"Thanks," Ethan said. "Okay, just throwing this out there, but maybe the theme of the holiday performance could be celebrations around the world. A little bit of Christmas and Hanukah and Kwanza and whatever, plus other things that are more secular and multicultural. We could put a big red bow on top of the pyramid—"

"And what," Lorna said, "try to pass it off as an Egyptian Christmas tree?"

"Stop," I said, as if that might work with Lorna. "I know, we can play The Bangles' 'Walk Like an Egyptian,' and the kids can do a line dance in one door of the pyramid and out the other."

We all immediately broke out our "Walk Like an Egyptian" dance moves.

"See," Ethan said. "We've got this."

"Not so fast," I said. "If we use the extended dance mix of the song, that should kill five minutes, maybe even six. Now all we have to do is figure out how to fill the rest of the time."

"*We?*" Lorna said.

· · · · ·

The cheesy smell of seafood lasagna bubbling away greeted me when I opened the door.

My brother Johnny was slouched over the scratched pine kitchen trestle table. His hemp hat was gone, the better to show off his man bun.

"Whoa," I said. "Did you put that casserole in the oven all by yourself?"

"Negative," he mumbled to the table. "Prince Charming did. But I watched."

"You can't call him Prince Charming," I said. "Only I can call him Prince Charming."

Men's voices rumbled above us like thunder. The popping sound of a nail gun broke out.

"Home sweet home," I said. I opened the dishwasher, rooted around for clean dishes to fill for the animals.

Johnny was still staring at the table.

"So how was your day?" I said, heavy on the flippant.

"Groovy," he said. "Nothing like a grown man getting driven to and from work in a pink ice cream truck by his daddy."

I took a moment to enjoy the image of our father pulling into Johnny's corporate headquarters, the ice cream truck clinking "Pop Goes the Weasel."

My brother sighed. We might not have had much in common, but we definitely both had the martyr thing down cold.

"So do something about it," I said. "Like maybe go pick up your freakin' car."

"Now why didn't I think of that?" he said.

"Jerk," I said. I plopped food in the dishes, piled them up in the crook my arms."

I was on my way to the cat room when I heard him mumble something to my back.

I gave Horatio his food near the threshold, put Pebbles' dish on her bookshelf, lined up the kittens' dishes in a row on the boot tray. They all dug in.

"Bon appetit, you guys," I said. "I'll be back in a flash for playtime."

I closed the door behind me and retraced my steps to the kitchen. My brother hadn't moved a muscle.

"What did you say?" I said.

"Poppy's taking me to get my car," he mumbled to the table.

"Her name is Polly," I said.

"I call her Poppy," he said. "She likes it."

"She likes it," I said.

I sat down at the kitchen table, taking my childhood seat, just like Johnny had taken his.

"So," I said. "You're going to show up at your house to pick up your car with a pretty, pregnant woman. How do you think that's going to fly with Kim?"

He lifted his head off the table. "What's that got to do with anything?"

Polly opened the kitchen door, closed it behind her. She took one look at us, froze.

I pushed my chair back.

"Have a nice trip," I said.

. . . . .

It was practically dark by the time John and I got to the beach to hang the pine cone birdfeeders I'd made on the beachy little Christmas tree. Horatio raced ahead, stretching his retractable leash as far as it would go.

John and I held our available hands, swinging them back and forth to the sound of the waves crashing.

"When I stayed overnight at your condo," I said, "sometimes I used to pretend that the sound of the traffic was the ocean."

"I'm sure the short-term executive rental company who's handling it could find a way to get that into the pitch materials. *Distant ocean sounds* or something like that."

"Yeah," I said. "Like those peek-through ocean views we almost fell for a couple of times when we were house hunting."

"Sometimes," John said, "when I wake up in the middle of the night now, it's so quiet I can't get back to sleep. I guess I got used to that sound."

"I bet there's an app for that," I said. "You know, traffic sounds to lull you softly to sleep."

The beachy version of Charlie Brown's Christmas tree came into view.

The scruffy dog we'd seen last time was standing up on its hind legs in the fleeting light, sliding a ribbon-tied dog treat off one spindly tree branch with its teeth.

"Aww," I said. "How cute."

The dog turned at the sound of my voice, gulped down the treat. When it saw Horatio, it began wagging its tail a mile a minute. Horatio got low, wagged his tail back.

The scruffy dog and Horatio dashed toward each other like long-lost friends.

"No," John yelled as he retracted Horatio's leash. "Go away," he added in a really mean voice in the other dog's direction.

The scruffy dog backed away, cowering. Then he turned and ran.

We stood in front of the tree. It was weighed down with candy canes and popcorn garlands and double the amount of ornaments that had been here last time. It still had more dog treats on it.

John pulled a flashlight out of his back pocket and shined it on the tree. I reached into the plastic bag I was holding. I pulled out the pine cone birdfeeders I'd made. One by one I hung them on the tree.

It should have been a beautiful moment, maybe even the start of a new yearly tradition for us. The beach to ourselves. The crash of midnight blue waves in the distance as the dark closed in on us. Decorating the most beautiful little Christmas tree in the world.

"How could you?" I said.

To his credit, John didn't pretend not to know what I was talking about. "I don't want that dog near Horatio. It could have been anywhere. It might be sick. There's a leash law."

"I thought I knew you," I said softly.

I started walking back toward the car in the near dark, sinking into the crisp dry sand, tripping over the occasional piece of shadowy driftwood.

"Stop," John said behind me. "Did I say anything when you just let your brother and your pregnant guest ride off into the sunset together? You don't think that was your job to go with him?"

When I whipped my head around, I thought it might keep circling and circling like Linda Blair's head in *The Exorcist.*

"I can't believe you just said that," I said. "Did you even talk to your sister on Thanksgiving?"

"I would have if she were staying with us," John said.

Under the light of the flashlight, Horatio looked back and forth between us anxiously. In a minute he'd be down on the sand, covering his head with his paws.

Still, I couldn't seem to stop myself. "Right. Easy for you to say, since she'll never be staying with us. Your parents probably won't even visit."

John reached down to pet Horatio reassuringly. "Since you've already managed to fill every available nook and cranny, there wouldn't be room for them anyway."

We walked to the parking lot in silence. John's flashlight beam was waving back and forth in front of our feet. It reminded me of one of those guys with the orange batons trying to keep a plane from crashing into the runway. Or into another plane. Maybe John and I were two separate planes heading right for each other. A single beam crisscrossing in front of us to keep it from happening seemed woefully inadequate.

When we got to John's car, instead of unlocking it, he leaned back against the hood. He pulled out his phone, typed in his password. He searched, tapped in a number.

"I'd like to report an unleashed dog running around at North Beach," he said. "This is the second time I've seen it. Unleashed."

"I can't believe you just did that," I said as he put his phone back in his pocket.

John shrugged. "There's a leash law. Plus, it's for the dog's own good. A coyote could get it."

"That's not what you're worried about," I said. "You're worried about Horatio getting dog cooties."

"It shouldn't be loose," John said. "And Marshbury Animal Shelter is a no-kill shelter."

"Great," I said. "Maybe I'll move in there."

I took off across the parking lot, swinging my arms, gulping down the damp night air. Maybe I'd just keep walking. Find a new little beach town where I didn't know a soul. I'd meet a guy who was more like me, a guy who wasn't a dog snob, a guy who would never talk me into buying my family house.

I mean, just when you're finally, belatedly starting to figure out who you are and what you want your life to be, to maybe actually even grow up at long, long last, what in the world would possess a person to buy her family house? How could you figure out who you were without your family if said family was always under foot?

Just as I reached the road, John's car pulled up beside me.

He rolled down the window. "Come on, get in."

I kept walking toward the soft glow of a streetlight.

He crawled along beside me.

"It's not that far," I said. "I want to walk. Go."

We could barely see each other.

John handed me the flashlight.

I didn't even say thank-you.

Eighteen

Ethan and I sat across from each other in the teachers' room, each with a notebook in front of us, ready to brainstorm. Mine was a college-lined composition book, Ethan's an unlined spiral sketch-book.

A beam of late afternoon sun coming in through the room's only window landed right on Ethan's surfer-boy hair. Not so much like a halo, but more like he should be in an ad for Sun In. Did they still make Sun In?

"Obviously, this co-chair deal is all new to me," Ethan said, "so what if you go first?"

"How about this," I said. "We have the kids in one class all in reindeer antlers. And we let them dance and sing to a medley of 'Up on the Housetop,' and 'He'll Be Coming Round the Mountain,' except we change that to the tried and true preschool version, 'He'll Be Coming Down the Chimney.' I'll tweak the lyrics, make them a little bit more fun. We'll recruit Gloria and her pitch pipe to keep everybody relatively on key."

Ethan nodded. "I can build a plywood chimney, three-sided with an open back. We can ask Polly to paint it to look like red bricks, and then we can glue cotton balls around the top to make fake snow. We can set up a little stepladder behind it that the audience won't be able to see. That way the kids can look out over the top and it will look like they're inside the chimney."

"Yeah, yeah," I said. "The kids can take turns climbing up a couple of steps, doing something cute to give their parents a video moment, and then climbing back down. We'll put lots of foam on the floor around the ladder. And we'll have the assistant with the quickest reflexes hiding back there with the kids so we don't take any chances."

Ethan turned to a fresh page, sketched away.

He swiveled the notebook around and showed me his perfect preschool chimney.

"Unbelievable," I said. "You're just so talented."

"Polly can draw circles around me," he said. "You don't know where she took off to so fast today, do you?"

I shrugged. "I think she was probably just trying to get some space from me so she could breathe."

"Everything okay?" When Ethan tilted his head, he lost the sunbeam and his hair turned ordinary again.

I crossed my arms over my chest. "You know, living and working together is a lot. Not to mention major construction at the house, so it's been like playing musical bedrooms. Many animals, even more family. No privacy. And let's not forget global warming and Mercury in retrograde."

Ethan didn't say anything.

"Why?" I said. "Do you think something's wrong with Polly? Is there anything I should know?"

He turned to a fresh page in his notebook and started drawing what looked like a checkerboard. He scribbled in some of the boxes like he was looking for a way to win the game, or maybe it was a puzzle he was trying to solve.

He looked up. "I'd feel better if Polly moved in with me."

A curtain of silence fell between us. It was dark and velvety and almost palpable, like we could reach out and touch it if we dared.

"And how would your girlfriend feel?" I finally said.

He began to cover his drawing with big overlapping Xs.

"So, what," I said. "You'd keep Polly hidden up in the attic? Let her come down when the coast is clear?"

"Life," Ethan said, "is just too damn complicated."

"Agreed." I blew out a puff of air. "And I, for one, really suck at it."

We both nodded, lost in our thoughts.

"I think the best thing we can do for Polly," I said, "is not to bring any drama into her life right now. You know, just keep things simple and quiet and uneventful, at least until she has the baby and gets her feet under her again. I'm not saying things aren't crazy at my house, but Polly's safe there. And she's got a big bedroom with plenty of space for the baby once it's born."

Ethan turned to a fresh page, started filling it with a honeycomb pattern, like drawing a sturdy beehive might be the first step toward building a durable life.

"I can see that, I guess." He looked up. "You'll let me know if I can do anything?"

"Yeah," I said. "I will. Listen, I know it's not my business, and I'm the last person who's qualified to give relationship advice of any kind, believe me, but maybe you should use this time to figure things out with your former wife, current girlfriend, or whatever she is."

Right after we'd met, Ethan had told me that when his career as an indie filmmaker had imploded, he'd also blown up a marriage to a woman he'd loved with all his heart, and that by the time he'd wrecked his car, blowing up his leg wasn't even that big a deal.

"Figuring things out was the plan," Ethan said. He was drawing arrows now, each one pointing off in another direction. "But I think the problem is that the Curse of Knowledge has come into play. You know, once you know something, it's impossible to imagine what it's like not to know it."

"Which means?"

"Which means she knows what I'm like at my worst. And I don't think she can forget it long enough to believe that it's never going to happen again."

"What are you going to do?" I asked.

Maybe if Ethan went first and figured out his relationship, I might get some new insights that would help me navigate things with John. Like getting a bonus clue. Not that I'd ever met Ethan's ex, and not that Ethan and John were anything alike. But maybe all relationships flourished or floundered because of the same basic things. And I'd really love to figure out exactly what those things were.

When Ethan leaned back and stretched out his damaged leg, he was back in the sunbeam again.

"I have no idea how it will all play out," he said. "Sometimes I think it's like there's this tree dying in a pot in the living room. You know it's dying, but you've had it for so long and you're really attached to it and you can't imagine what it would be like not to have it. And then you stop watering it. You forget, or you just get lazy. But you know damn well that the minute you throw it out, all you're going to think about is how amazing it used to be, and you'll be kicking yourself that you didn't put the time and energy in to keep it that way."

"If I have one regret about my former marriage," I said, "it's that when things were first falling apart, I didn't try harder to save it. But hindsight 20/20, I think there's also a point that you can't look back. You've got to focus on moving forward. You know, fish or cut bait."

Ethan nodded. "Shit or get off the pot."

"Insert overused cringe-worthy expression here," I said.

Ethan stared out the teachers' room window, sketched, stared out the window, sketched some more.

I found a fresh page in my own notebook, started playing around with an idea for "Five Little Icicles."

Five little icicles
Hanging on the door
One broke off
And then there were four

Four little icicles
Dangling from the tree
One fell off
And then there were three

I turned the notebook around so Ethan could read it.

"You get the idea," I said. "The kids from one of the classes could dress all in white, with strands of tinsel taped all over them. Maybe we could attach some of those plastic icicle ornaments to cheap plastic tiaras, too. They'd do it as more of a chant than a song, and they're be reinforcing their counting skills at the same time."

"Sounds good to me," Ethan said. "I've got an old door in my storage unit we could use. And I could find a big tree branch somewhere, cut off any small branches that might poke the kids."

I nodded. "Obviously, we'd keep the song going until the icicles are all gone, and then bring them all back for a happy ending. I'll keep working on it."

"Great. Hey, and thanks for listening," Ethan said as he turned to a new page and began sketching. "I'll keep working on my own happy ending, too. You know, figuring how to deal with that tree semi-dying in the pot and all that."

I glanced over at Ethan's notebook, tilted my head to look at the massive tree he'd drawn.

"Not that it necessarily means anything," I said. "But that tree you just drew looks like something out of *Little Shop of Horrors*. Just saying."

. . . . .

John looked up from his laptop when I walked into the kitchen.

"Hey," I said.

"Listen," he said.

"Wait," I said.

"What?" he said.

"Never mind," I said. I dumped my teacher bag on the floor, opened the dishwasher, started pulling out dishes for the animals.

John's car wasn't even in the driveway when I'd finished walking home from the beach last night. I'd brushed my teeth and washed my face quickly, changed into a sleep T-shirt, crawled under the covers in the cat room with a book. Realized it wasn't even 7 PM yet, but stayed there anyway. When I tiptoed out to the kitchen to get more animal food a few hours later, I heard the Addams Family theme song coming from one of John's prized pinball machines in the front parlor. I didn't even look in.

Now John pushed his chair back from the table. He picked up my bag, put it on the kitchen table.

"If I wanted that on the table," I said sweetly, "I would have put it there."

John watched as I opened the pet food cupboard.

"Horatio's already been fed," John said. "In fact, he's been overfed a lot lately. Over fifty percent of the dogs and cats in this country are clinically overweight, so it's something to be aware of. I was thinking I could create an Excel sheet so we can keep track. You know, that way we can check off the feedings. And the snacks."

"Sure," I said. "Either that or maybe I can feed my animals, and you can feed yours."

Nineteen

The kitchen door swung open, saving me from whatever John was about to say.

My sister Carol never knocks. She doesn't say hi or how's it going either. She just starts talking while she walks right into the house, as if she's simply picking up where she left off last time.

This time around she was also shaking a copy of *The Marshbury Mirror*, the local weekly newspaper.

"You're not going to believe this," she said. She unhooked her reading glasses from the front of her jacket and put them on, opened the newspaper, refolded it. "All that time we spent getting Dad up to speed online, and now he's backsliding. This paper doesn't even have a dating section anymore, so his ad's in the For Sale section, right between an ad for a mostly intact outdoor nativity scene with everything but the baby Jesus, and one for a litter of purebred Great Dames."

"Dad would be all over that one," I said. "He's a huge fan of dames, great and otherwise."

"Listen to this," my big sister said. "*Free mattress to good home. Must have references. Former owner, a charming gentleman of a certain age who loves dogs, moonlit strolls, and long meandering bicycle rides, to visit occasionally.*"

I shook my head, took a moment to be thankful that my father wasn't hitting on Polly. Not exclusively anyway. "Well, at least he's keeping himself busy. That's important at his age, you know. You rest, you rust and all that."

"Don't be ridiculous," Carol said. "You probably wouldn't even notice it online, but that ad is *local.* And in print. It makes Dad sound like some kind of pervert."

"Did I hear dessert?" our father said as the kitchen door swung open again. "Sure, I'll have some. You kiddos know I'm not one to turn down any kind of dessert."

John finished filling the animal dishes, headed off in the direction of the cat room.

I took a casserole out of the freezer, put it in the oven. With all the upheaval around here, we weren't exactly going for nightly sit-down dinners with candles and cloth napkins, especially since John's and my clothes had completely taken over the dining room table.

One of us would stick a casserole in the oven, and everybody would scoop some out when they were hungry. Sometimes people sat at the kitchen table to eat it. Sometimes they took their food to their rooms. The last person to eat would put the leftovers in the fridge.

"Have a seat, Dad," Carol said.

Our dad grabbed his chair at the head of the kitchen table, turned it around and straddled it. "Long day in the ice cream truck. Be a good girl, Christine, and—"

"Carol," my big sister said.

"Just making sure you're awake, honey. Now, about that beer."

Carol opened the fridge, grabbed a bottle.

Our dad shook his head. "Irish I had a Schlitz," he sang in his best baritone.

Carol put the craft beer bottle from the new local brewery back, handed over a tall can of Schlitz. She gave our father a chance to take a long sip, then slipped the newspaper in front of him. "You want to explain this?"

Our dad slapped his thigh. "Good one, if I do say so myself. Between you and me and the lamppost, you need some originality to stay in the game at my age. I'm no sidekick, but I can tell you the ladies will be falling all over themselves when they get a load of this one."

I'd been listening to my father's word choices my whole life, so it didn't even take me that long to translate *sidekick* to *psychic*.

Carol gave me a look that clearly said *jump in anytime.*

"Sidekick or not," I said, "that ad could be perceived as a little bit creepy." I reached for more ammunition. "Plus, what if somebody takes you up on it? It's not like we actually have a free mattress kicking around. We had everything we're not planning to use hauled off to the Take It or Leave It at the dump."

Our father took a slug of beer, put the can back down on the scarred pine tabletop.

"I'm no gobermouch," he said, "so I don't like to meddle in other people's business. But once we get rid of the mattress she's sleeping on, I think it would open up the door to Polly moving into the man cavern with me. You'd be surprised at how much room they give you on those round beds."

I sat down at my regular seat at the table with a thud. "Dad, don't even joke about that. You can't take Polly's mattress away from her. And she is not, I repeat *not*, moving in with you."

Our dad ran one hand through his mane of white hair. "It's the baby I'm thinking of. That baby needs a good Irish daddy to lay eyes on when it's born. Somebody to help burp it and change its nappies."

"Nappies?" Carol said. "Who the hell says nappies in this country? It's not like you changed a single diaper when any of us were growing up. And the only time you helped us burp was when you let us take a sip of your beer when Mom wasn't looking."

Our Dad shook his head. "Don't be a snoutband, honey. If I'm looking for someone to argue with me, I can spend the day on my laptopper cruisin' the internut."

"Perfect," I said. "We'll help you update your profile on all the online dating sites. Before you know it, your dance card is going to be so full you'll forget all about Polly. It's really sweet of you to worry about her, Dad, but she'll be fine. I'm taking good care of her, and all the other teachers are looking out for her, too."

Our father drained his beer, held the empty can out to Carol.

Carol started to argue, shrugged, got up to get him another beer.

"Good girl," our dad said to Carol. He turned back to me. "Here's the rub—our Polly can't just up and have a baby by herself. She needs one of those Lacoste coaches."

"Lamaze," I said.

Our father took a long sip of his new beer. "Upon further reflection, in a pinch I might have wrangled a nappy or three back in the day."

"Okay, so let's do the math," Carol said. "With six of us, that's a helluva lot of nappies you didn't wrangle."

Our father threaded his hands behind his head, arched his back in a catlike stretch. When he finished, he unzipped his pink Bark & Roll Forever fleece halfway.

"Well, then," he said, "let's just say it's a chance to do it all over again and make things right."

"Dad," I said.

He went in for the kill. "I talked to your mother last night. Sure as God made little green apples, she thinks it's the right thing to do."

. . . . .

The kitchen door swung open again. If this kept up, we were going to have to consider adding a revolving door to the renovation list.

An orange and red sugar maple leaf skittered across the speckled linoleum floor. Polly and Johnny came in right behind the leaf. Polly was laughing, her head thrown back and her freckles camouflaged by her bright pink cheeks. Johnny was laughing, too, which was definitely a first since he'd descended on us.

My father was already on his feet. "*There* she is. What can I get you to drink, darlin'?"

"Seriously?" Carol said.

"No thanks, I'm all set, Dad," Johnny said. I couldn't be sure, but it seemed like he might have shrugged off his profound pouting long enough to attempt a joke. Not a particularly good one, but still.

Polly held up her water bottle. "I'm all set, too, thanks."

"Casserole's in the oven," I said. "Turkey tetrazzini or paparazzi or something like that."

Nobody laughed at my joke either.

Our Dad crossed the kitchen floor to Polly, grabbed her by the hand and twirled her around, water bottle and all. "How about I take you out for a nice meal instead, darlin'?"

"Back off, Dad," Johnny said. "Poppy and I just finished grabbing subs at Maria's."

"Poppy?" Carol said.

"Yeah, Poppy," Johnny said. "You wanna make something out of it?"

Polly's cheeks were seriously red now. "I think I'm just going to go up to my room now." She was almost out of the kitchen before she added, "Have a nice night, everybody."

Our father watched Polly disappear. Johnny glared at our father. John hadn't returned from the cat room. I smelled tragedy. And heartbreak. I just wasn't sure whose.

"So . . ." I said.

My sister Carol grabbed me by the sleeve, pulled me out of the kitchen.

"Ouch," I said as she pushed me into the hallway. "That pinches."

She dragged me about halfway up the stairs until we reached the step that, after years of childhood trial and error, we'd all discovered was low enough to spy on the floor below but high enough to keep the conversation private.

Dozens of family photographs hung in the hallway, gallery-like, flanking the staircase. A sepia wedding photo of my parents, Dad's arm draped across Mom's shoulders like a mantle, optimistic smiles on their faces. A color portrait of all six children taken on this very staircase: the three girls seated together on one step in identical pleated skirts and round-collared white blouses, the three boys a couple of steps higher in matching jackets and ties, their knees digging into our backs.

Six high school senior pictures in a long, staggered row. Snapshots of Christmas. Easter. Birthday parties. Summer vacations. Wedding photos. I'd taken down Kevin's and my wedding picture the day our divorce had become final in a ceremony that involved my father's biggest hammer and the sound of breaking glass while my family cheered me on. Just after John and I bought the house, I'd finally gotten around to printing out a selfie I'd taken of John and me and taping it up in the empty space.

Carol followed my glance. "Jeez Louise, get a real picture, will you? Like maybe taken by a professional photographer when you two actually get around to marrying each other."

"Not your beeswax," I said. "I hope you didn't drag me all the way up here for a photo consult."

"Sarah, Sarah, Sarah," Carol said.

"That's my name, don't wear it out," I said.

Carol leaned forward and looked around, then twisted her head to look up the stairs.

"Get her out of here," she hissed. "Immediately. If not sooner."

"Poppy? I mean, Polly?" I whispered. I looked around to make sure no one was sneaking up on us.

"Of course, Polly." Carol let out a puff of air. "Dad and Johnny are both crazy about her. If we don't get her out of here, eventually they're going to go all Shakespeare and challenge each other to a duel or something. And if Dad wins, don't kid yourself that we won't be the ones changing those nappies. I mean, diapers."

Twenty

I didn't have an exact count for the number of times I'd stood up to my sister Carol in my lifetime, but it had to be in the single digits.

"If Dad and Johnny want to make fools of themselves, that's their problem." I took a deep breath. "But it's John's and my house now, so Polly's staying. And if you don't like it, you know where the door is— don't let it hit your butt on the way out."

Carol reached over and punched me in the shoulder, like a one-person fist bump, only painful.

"Ouch," I said.

"It's about time you grew a pair," she said.

"Thanks," I said. "I think."

"Okay, then, if Polly's staying, we've got to get both Dad and Johnny romantically entangled elsewhere so they'll stop fawning all over her."

I nodded.

"Dad's easy," Carol said. "We take down that awful ad in the local paper, ramp up his internet presence, maybe even help him throw a holiday housewarming party in his new man cave."

I nodded some more. It was enough to know I'd grown a pair—I could let Carol take it from here.

"Jump in anytime," Carol said.

So much for that theory. "Um, sounds good. I don't know what we should do about Johnny. He hasn't told me anything about what happened between him and Kim."

Carol shook her head. "Michael and Billy were completely useless. They didn't even try to get the scoop out of him. I thought Johnny would be calling me so much he'd be melting my phone by now, like Michael did when he and Phoebe were falling apart, but I haven't heard a word from him."

"So, what do we do?"

Carol leaned forward like a coach on the bleachers at some game. She rested her forearms on her thighs.

"Okay," she said. "We drag Johnny out to the trailer. And we don't let up on him until he tells us everything. Once we find out what's going on, we take it from there. We'll bring Dad with us so we can keep an eye on him, too."

"Go team," I said. I reached over to give Carol a real fist bump.

Her knuckles touched mine, and then she walked her index and middle fingers away from me.

"*What* was that?" I said.

She grinned. "It's called the Michael Jackson. Ian and Trevor showed it to me yesterday after school. Even Siobhan thought it was cool, and Maeve picked it up like a pro."

I slipped into teacher mode. "Maeve has terrific fine-motor control for a three-year-old."

"Thanks," Carol said. "She also has terrific aptitude for swearing like a sailor, so it's kind of a wash."

I fist-bumped Carol again, and then we both moonwalked our fingers away from each other.

"Holy moly," I said. "That's the coolest thing ever. I always wanted to be able to moonwalk."

We heard a thump and then another one. Christine burst into the hallway from the direction of the kitchen.

"Help," she yelled. "Dad and Johnny are trying to kill each other."

"That was fast," Carol said. We pushed ourselves up to a standing position.

"I can't believe you were having a staircase meeting without me," Christine said as we all ran to the kitchen.

Our father and our brother were rolling around on the kitchen floor like two overgrown puppies.

"Stop," I yelled.

"Like that's going to work," Carol said.

"One . . . two . . . three . . ." I tried. Counting always worked on preschoolers.

"Do you have a squirt gun?" Carol said.

"Sorry," I said. "Fresh out."

"Do you want me to run home for one?" Christine said.

"No time," Carol said.

Johnny and our dad hit a kitchen chair. It keeled over on top of them. They kept rolling, the chair thumping along with them.

Carol turned on the kitchen faucet, filled an empty beer bottle with water.

Then she poured it all over both of them.

. . . . .

"That was a work shirt," Johnny said once we were seated at the tiny dinette. "You better wash and iron it for me."

"Talk to Carol," I said. "She's the one who baptized you with a beer bottle. And you're lucky we didn't let you and Dad murder each other."

As soon as I dragged him out to the trailer, Johnny had changed into a long-sleeve T-shirt and a pair of sweatpants in the tiny bathroom. Judging by the stuff strewn all over the place, I was pretty sure he'd relocated from the living room sofa and was sleeping here now.

After she'd doused them with water, Carol had escorted our dad up to his man cave. While she was yanking him out of the kitchen, he shook the water off his thick white hair like a polar bear. "Did you see that?" he yelled. "I had him arse over teakettle. You can't blame a fellow for being a legend in his own time, can you now?"

"I was totally winning," Johnny said now. "And I wasn't even trying that hard."

"I'll fight you with one paw tied behind my back," I said in my best Cowardly Lion impersonation.

Johnny ignored me.

A flashback bubbled up to the surface. "Hey," I said. "Do you remember when I had the mumps and you told me I looked like a fat chipmunk and gave me a piece of Bazooka bubblegum so you could laugh at me? That was so mean."

"Get over yourself," my brother said. "We *all* had the mumps, and we all looked like fat chipmunks. Remember, Mom and Dad made us breathe all over each other and share a root beer popsicle so they wouldn't have to go through the mumps six times? You should be thanking me that I gave you a piece of my bubblegum."

"It hurt to chew," I said. "A lot."

"Poor you," Johnny said.

I looked out the trailer window, hoping for some backup. Christine had gone off with Carol and our dad. But I knew she'd show up here soon, afraid of missing something. She'd probably go back and forth, dividing her time between the man cave and the trailer, the way some people divide their time between houses in New York and Key West.

"Wait." I gave Johnny a long look. "What happened to the hippie talk? And your man bun?"

Johnny ran a hand through his thick brown hair, which was already giving way to our dad's snowy white. Of the six of us, Johnny probably looked the most like our dad, Michael like our mom. The rest of us were hybrids.

"I thought maybe I could try being somebody else," Johnny said to the tabletop. "Since being myself hasn't been working out so hot."

"Well," I said, "at least the hippie thing was relatively original. You didn't embarrass yourself by going off and buying a midlife Porsche you can't afford or anything. So, what was the rest of the fantasy? You were going to hitchhike out to the west coast and start a rock 'n' roll camp for baby boomers?"

"Hazelnuts," he said. "I was thinking I could start a hazelnut farm and come up with a healthy, sugar-free version of Nutella. And make a fortune, but in a good way."

I shook my head. "That's nuts."

"Hardy har har," my brother said. He was talking to the tabletop again.

"Any other genius ideas, Nutella?" I said.

"If you're so smart, you figure out what I should do, Sherlock," he said.

Clearly this conversation was going nowhere fast. I knew I'd have to report to Carol, so I figured I'd better cut to the chase.

"What happened with Kim?" I said softly.

My brother lifted his head up, slowly, like it weighed a ton. When he shifted around, the vinyl-covered dinette cushion squeaked like a whoopee cushion. I didn't even make a crack, like telling him to say excuse me.

"She left me for someone else," he said. "This dude she works with. She used to call him her work husband. I never thought anything of it. He took her skiing in Colorado for Thanksgiving. He invited the boys to go with them. And they went."

"Ouch," I said.

"Yeah," he said. "Ouch. She wasn't even there when I went home to pick up my car. Whatever happened to loyalty? And trust? And till death do us part?"

"Do you want her back?" I asked.

He closed his eyes. "I can't stop thinking about the Las Vegas shooting. One of the guards said that when it was over and they'd rescued everybody they could, somebody turned out the lights in the venue. There were bodies everywhere. And then the cellphones started ringing and ringing, lighting up like stars, over and over again. And nobody was answering, because they were all dead."

He opened his eyes, rubbed tears off his cheeks with the back of his hand. "With no disrespect to those poor people, that's how I feel. Like I can't answer. Because I'm dead."

"But you're *not* dead," I said. "I know you're really hurting, but imagine what any of those people would give for even one more day to try to figure out their lives."

A gust of wind rattled the teeny window over the dinette table. Johnny stood up, pulled two old wool army blankets off the bed, handed me one.

I put the blanket on my lap, tucked my hands and feet under. "If I have one regret about Kevin and me . . ." I paused as I realized I was about to say this for the second time today. I mean, really, what kind of crazy world was this? Was it just a matter of time before I had to have this conversation with everybody?

It was the only advice I had, so I went with it. "My one regret is that when things were first falling apart, I didn't try harder to save my marriage."

"It takes two to save a marriage," Johnny said.

"Yeah," I said. "But one of you has to be the bigger person and get the ball rolling."

He looked up, not exactly at me, but not at the tabletop either. "What should I do?"

Ask Carol, I wanted to say. Carol would know.

I dove in anyway. "Talk to Kim. Call her up." As soon as it came out of my mouth, I realized I probably hadn't said *call her up* since high school. Apparently the *up* had gone away like so many other things, when I wasn't paying attention.

Johnny was back to staring at the tabletop.

I reached for something encouraging. "Who knows? By now maybe her work husband has turned out to have almost as many irritating little habits as her regular husband."

He squinted up at me without quite lifting his head. "Thanks. I needed that."

"You know what I mean. If they've known each other all this time, they'll probably fast-forward through the happy horseshit stage. I'm just guessing, but how exciting can it be once the thing between them is no longer forbidden fruit?"

Johnny considered this. "I don't think you can use happy horseshit and forbidden fruit together. It's a mixed metaphor."

"Of course you can," I said, "if they're two separate sentences."

We looked at each other over the trailer dinette, our faces about two feet away from each other, our army blankets touching. I wanted to keep arguing with him. About mixed metaphors, mangled clichés, dangling participles, misplaced modifiers, the Oxford comma—anything I could come up with that would eventually lead to me kicking him in the shins. Or pulling his hair.

I took the high road. "Have flowers delivered to Kim, along with a beautiful note that says you'd like to meet her for dinner to try to get things right. Because whatever happens, for the rest of your lives, even though they're practically grown now, you'll always be the parents of two awesome sons together."

Johnny was still looking at me. I realized this was essentially the same advice I'd given to Michael when his marriage was on the rocks. Michael's marriage was back on track, so there was always the chance that I'd get advice-lucky twice.

"And call your kids," I said. "Even if they act like it's no big deal at their ages, it is. So keep talking to them and let them know you love them and that you and Kim are trying to work this out."

He actually nodded.

"And back off from Polly. She's pregnant, she's vulnerable, and she doesn't need any drama."

"She's funny," he said, "and she listens to me. I like being around her."

"Back off anyway," I said.

He sighed. "Anything else while you're running my life?"

"Yeah. When you take Kim out for dinner, don't wear the hemp hat."

Twenty-one

We were sitting cross-legged on our classroom circle. We'd managed to get the kids positioned so they were each facing a partner. Polly and I faced each other so we could demonstrate.

Preschool students love repetition. If they enjoy an activity, or a song, or a book, they'll do or sing or listen to it over and over again, day in and day out.

But even though the kids would have been fine either way, I hoped the extra focus of a new activity would take my mind off things. By the time I'd made it back to the cat room last night, John's eyes were closed under the amber glow of the borrowed nightlight. His breathing was deep and slow and seamless, like someone who was either a perfect sleeper or pretending to be asleep.

"Goodnight room," I'd whispered. "Goodnight moon. Goodnight cats and dog and boyfriend acting like a goon."

John's breathing stayed the same, which didn't mean a thing. This morning, I'd woken up to an empty bed and a note on the kitchen counter saying that he was driving in to Boston for a work meeting. Before he left, he'd fed all the animals and checked it off on his stupid Excel spreadsheet.

"Sarah," Polly said, bringing me back to circle time.

"Right," I said. "High five." Polly and I gave each other a gentle high five like we'd rehearsed.

"High five," the kids said as they imitated us like perfect preschool parrots.

"Fist bump," I said. Polly and I kept our fist bump gentle, too, and the kids followed suit.

"Michael Jackson," I said. Polly and I fist bumped, then moonwalked our index and middle fingers away from each other.

The kids giggled. They yelled "Michael Jackson," whether or not they had any idea who that was, and moonwalked away from one another.

"Jellyfish," I said. Polly and I fist bumped, then opened our hands and pulled them back and up at an angle, again and again, like we were jellyfish swimming through the ocean. The kids laughed and did the same.

"Snowman," I said. When Polly came in to fist bump me, I brought one fist down on top of her fist and my other fist up from below, making the perfect three-fisted snowman.

"Snowman," the kids yelled. The made snowmen over and over again, most four-fisted instead of three, laughing hilariously.

The kids began making up their own fist bumps now, spontaneously, enthusiastically. That was one of the biggest joys of teaching: to spark the students' creatively, then sit back and watch it soar.

"Airplane," Gulliver yelled. He and Juliette fist bumped, then stuck their arms out to the sides and rocked back and forth. I took a moment to appreciate how far Gulliver had come from hurling himself off the dismissal benches and throwing things at his mother not so long ago.

"Barbie," Pandora yelled. She and Celine fist bumped, then flipped their hair and batted their eyelashes at each other.

From our little storage area, a cellphone rang.

"Cellphone," Morgan yelled. She fist bumped the air, then tilted her head and held her open palm to her ear. Suddenly all the kids were imitating Morgan.

"Sorry," Polly said. "I guess I forgot to turn off my phone."

"Answer it," I said. "I'll get them started on their individual work."

As Polly walked away, I twisted around until I was facing the center of the circle with my legs straight out in front of me. Waited for the kids to do the same. I took a deep breath in as I reached my hands up over my head. When the kids caught up, I exhaled slowly as I reached forward and touched my toes. I held the stretch to signal that we were transitioning from one activity to the next.

"I mean it," we heard Polly say. "Don't call me."

"I mean it," Juliette said. "Don't call me." She did an air fist bump, then shook her finger at an imaginary caller.

"I mean it," the other kids said one after another. "Don't call me." They did air fist bumps, shook their stubby fingers.

And of course, that's the fist bump that stuck. I jumped up and began redirecting the kids, herding them off to puzzles and letter tracing and counting games and the water table. But they were still punching their fists in the air, shaking their fingers and saying, "I mean it. Don't call me."

Polly came out of the storage area. She stood there for a moment watching, her freckles jumping out as the color drained from her cheeks.

I made peace signs with both hands, our classroom signal to stop talking, stop everything.

The kids froze, made peace signs, too.

Polly ran from the room, blocking her face from our students so they wouldn't see her tears.

. . . . .

One of the last of the fall leaves twirled and fluttered as it fell to the ground. The sky was getting darker and the air colder at this hour every day. No snow yet, but it was hovering just out of reach, ready to pounce. I rubbed my hands together to warm them up.

I wrapped the ancient orangey-brown suede jacket with the long suede fringe I'd found in the front closet a little tighter. Wondered if I could hold out a little longer before I broke down and started searching through the mountain of boxes for my winter coats.

"Why don't you take off," I said. Our final student had been picked up, and Polly and I were alone on the dismissal bench. "Ethan and I had a pre-meeting yesterday before the official committee meeting today. I think we're in good shape, and I can always fill you in at home on anything you miss."

Polly forced a smile. "Thanks, but I'm really looking forward to the meeting."

"Okay," I said. "Then how about you be the co-chair, and I'll go crawl into bed and pull the covers over my head."

Polly laughed, but we both knew that was fake, too.

"I don't mean to pry," I said, "but let me know if you need to talk or anything." The truth was that a part of me was dying to know what was going on. Another part of me really didn't want to think about the fact that the person on the other end of that phone call might be related to me.

Polly and I joined the rest of the holiday performance planning committee in our classroom. We all sat on kiddie chairs around the long rectangular table. I automatically reached down to feel how much of my hips and thighs were spilling over the sides of the seat, a little test I always did to make sure I'd notice if they started to spread at an alarming rate. So far, so good.

As if on cue, Lorna tore open a bag of peanut butter cups and dumped them out on the table top.

"Bless you," Gloria said.

"Are those gluten free?" June asked.

"Of course they are," Lorna said. "They were in the 75%-off Halloween candy section at CVS. All the good stuff with gluten is gone by now."

"Don't listen to her, honey," Gloria said.

We peeled the foil wrappers off our peanut butter cups. June took a tiny bite of hers, then wrapped it up again. I contemplated doing that, too, realized it wouldn't actually make me young and beautiful like June, popped the whole thing in my mouth.

"So," I said. "Ethan and I met yesterday. I think we have enough ideas to start reaching out to the individual classroom teachers. One performance per classroom, plus some extras for the third-year students, no solos no matter how extraordinarily gifted any of the kids' parents think they are. If the teachers have their own ideas for their class performance, we can help them with those, or they can use one of our ideas, or we can come up with something together."

Everybody nodded. Ethan reached for another peanut butter cup, so everybody else did, too. June took a tiny bite of that one as well, then wrapped it back up again. I'd never really noticed when she was my assistant, but maybe she did that with everything she ate all day long. It was kind of genius in its own way. But I'd rather eat or not eat, instead of bouncing back and forth between the two.

"What I was thinking," I said, "is that it might be better if we had some kind of story that pulled the whole performance together."

"That's a good idea," Polly and Ethan said at the exact same time.

"Owe me a Coke," they both said. They smiled at each other, looked away. Polly's cheeks turned pink.

Ethan looked at me. "What were you thinking?"

I shrugged. "Tell me if this is stupid, but what if we have a couple of the kids dressed up as a cute little dog and a cat, or we have a couple of dogs and cats, and they don't have a home."

June's big blue eyes teared up. "That's so sad."

Lorna rolled her eyes. Gloria elbowed Lorna.

"Anyway," I said, "they go around the world, watching all the multicultural performances along the way, looking for a place to stay, and at the end they find homes."

"That's good," Ethan said. "Having an overarching narrative structure will raise the bar. Every performance is better if it tells a story."

"Plus," June said, "maybe it will inspire some of the families to think about adopting a pet. Adopting Wrinkles from the Marshbury Animal Shelter was like the most incredible thing I've ever done in my entire life. She's my best friend."

I flashed back to my not-so-long ago dating days when I'd borrowed June's adorable adopted shar pei-Lab cross puppy. Essentially Wrinkles was bait for meeting this guy who'd adopted a puppy named Creases from the same litter. Wrinkles and Creases were perfect together—the guy and me, not so much.

I thought about John and his stupid designer dog fantasy. Put that out of my mind, too.

"Maybe," Polly said, "we could ask the shelter to bring some adoptable dogs and cats to the performance—"

"That's a great idea," I said. "Or even pictures of adoptable dogs and cats to hang up, if we can't get approval for the real thing."

"We just won't ask," Lorna said. "We'll say we thought somebody else on the committee was in charge of getting permission." Lorna crossed her arms in front of her and pointed her index fingers in opposite directions.

We all imitated her, crossing our arms and pointing at each other.

"By the time our bitch of a boss pitches a hissy fit," Lorna said, "we'll be practically out the door for vacation."

I nodded as I tried to imagine it going that easily.

Ethan looked at me. "We need a title to put on the program, right? Any thoughts?"

A wave of shyness broke over me. It was so hard to put yourself out there creatively, even in front of teaching colleagues you liked, who were friends, even when it was something as small in the scheme of things as a preschool performance.

I took a deep breath. "I was thinking maybe we could call it *A Howliday Tail*. You know, H-O-W-L and T-A-I-L."

There was dead silence. An embarrassing dead silence.

And then everybody started howling like coyotes under a full moon.

"I'd say that's unanimous," Ethan said. "Four paws up for *A Howliday Tail.*"

Twenty-two

By the time I got home, Joe and his crew were gone for the day. The absence of hammers and nail guns was heavenly, a soothing hush all its own.

In my head, Simon and Garfunkel serenaded me with "The Sound of Silence" as I crept softly up the stairs to check out the progress.

John was standing in our future master suite, running his hand over the new drywall.

"Looks good," I said.

"We're getting there," John said. "Joe says he'll definitely have us moved in before Christmas."

"That would be great. Listen, I'm really sorry we haven't been getting along."

John shrugged. "Some experts say that renovations can cause even more stress for couples than having children."

My eyes teared up. "And then there's lack of having children. Do *some experts* say where that falls on the stress-ometer?"

John closed the distance between us, wrapped his arms around me. "Sorry. I didn't mean to bring it up."

"That's okay," I said. "I have to admit, right now I'm having a hard time remembering what we're even mad at each other or not mad at each other about. There's just so much noise around here that even when it stops I can't hear myself think."

"I hear you," John said.

"See," I said, "I can't even tell if that was a joke."

We christened our almost-sanctuary with a kiss.

"Joe left us some choices to make for him by tomorrow," John said when we came up for air.

So we sat on the still-to-be refinished old maple floor of what would be soon be our master bedroom. We shuffled through paint sample cards like we were playing poker. The soft greige colors called out to us both: Canyon Echo and Gray Owl and Big Chill and Agreeable Gray. In the end we chose Agreeable Gray, probably as much for the sentiment as the color.

We turned to the trim colors, each of us grabbing a bunch of sample cards and fanning them out.

"Do you have any whites?" I said.

"Go fish," John said.

I smiled. "I've got White Dove, Linen White, White on White, Cotton Balls. This is so overwhelming. Ooh, how about Simply White?"

"I like the sound of that," John said. "And to tell you the truth, I can't really tell the difference—they all look white to me."

Joe's crew had salvaged some of the wooden lathe strips when the walls were knocked down. They'd cleaned up the lathe enough to wrap the bathroom walls in it like narrow shiplap. It was still pretty rough, so Joe wanted to paint it. We decided on Simply White for that, too.

"Well, that simplifies things," I said.

We both went right for the same tile sample for the shower. It was called Coastal Dew, a gorgeous tumbled edge frosted glass elongated subway tile that looked like seafoam green sea glass.

For the bottom of the shower, we chose a mosaic tile made from individual beach pebbles attached to a mesh square. Just to be sure we were making the right choice, John put the sample on the floor, took off his shoes and stepped on it with both feet.

"Perfect," he said. "It'll feel like a foot massage every time we step into the shower."

"If you take off your socks," I said, "I bet it'll feel even better. You don't step into the ocean like that, do you?"

John slid his feet back into his shoes. "You're not accusing me of being a nerd, are you?"

"Only in the sexiest way," I said.

For the rest of the bathroom floor, we chose a porcelain tile that looked like weathered driftwood planks, but also had hints of the maple tone of the wood on our bedroom floor.

"It's perfect," I said. "It looks almost like real driftwood."

John checked the notes he'd made on his phone. "Okay, we're not out of the woods yet. We still have to decide whether we want them to install the tiles in staggered or stacked lines."

"Gentleman's choice," I said, since I had no idea what he was talking about.

"I think staggered would be more in keeping with the age of the house, you know, like a brick walkway. Stacked might be a bit too modern." John pulled up some photos on his phone to show me.

"Done," I said. "Is that all?"

John pulled up an online catalogue on his phone. "I told Joe we want to splurge for the frameless shower door, but we still have to choose a tub and a vanity and fixtures. And pick an exhaust fan as well as a style for the recessed lights. And we also have to decide whether we want a chandelier or a paddle fan in the bedroom."

"Paddle fan," I said. "Sleeping under a paddle fan is like being on vacation, almost as if a tropical breeze is blowing through the room. The white noise is a bonus, too."

John kept scrolling through pictures. "What if I were to tell you I'm a chandelier guy? Something sleek and industrial . . ."

I sighed dramatically. "You being a chandelier guy would be a total deal breaker. We'd have to divide the bedroom down the middle, put a paddle fan on my side, a chandelier on yours."

"Nice to know we can always find a compromise. Fortunately, I like paddle fans, too. Which one?"

"Overload, overload." I leaned over, began scrolling through about a zillion paddle fans. "Too many choices. Plus, it's hard to pick things out without actually seeing them."

John checked his phone for the time. "How about we jump in the car. I think we have just enough time to hit the kitchen and bath supply store out by the highway, as well as Lowe's and Home Depot, and then circle out to Ikea if we haven't found what we're looking for, and then we can loop back home from there."

"Didn't you already drive to Boston and back today?"

John shrugged. "It's either that or guess from the online pictures. Or trust Joe to pick out everything for us."

"I don't think we can trust Joe," I said. "Think about it—he picked my sister Christine."

John shook his head. "If anybody else ever said something like that about Christine, you'd take them out."

"Exactly," I said. "Your point?"

John took Horatio out to pee, while I filled the food dishes, carried them into the cat room. We zapped some leftover casserole from last night and chowed it down.

"Should I put a fresh casserole in the oven for everyone else?" I asked.

"I can't believe our lives have come to this," John said. "An endless stream of casseroles."

"We're under construction," I said. "The last thing we need is cooking stress on top of renovation stress. I think you need to work on your casserole gratitude."

"Casserole gratitude," John said. "I think that might be an oxymoron."

I flipped the outside light on, peeked out through the panes in the kitchen door. John's and my cars were the only ones in the driveway.

"Oh, well," I said. "If anybody's hungry when they get home, they know where the casseroles are."

Most of the traffic was coming toward us, so we twisted and turned through the backroads to the highway in record time. I found a classic rock radio station on John's Acura and cranked up the volume. The DJ was playing the early Beatles, youthful optimistic songs that always made me feel practically youthful and optimistic, too.

John and I sang along to "Lucy in the Sky with Diamonds," "She Loves You," "Michelle."

I kicked off my shoes. I put my stockinged feet on John's dashboard and let the heat warm my toes. John reached over and put one hand on my thigh. We sang along to "Norwegian Wood" and "Love Me Do." We both knew all the words to all the songs, even the ones you'd think we would have forgotten by now.

Remember this, I thought.

. . . . .

We wandered the aisles in store after store. John checked things off his list as we found them. If they were small, we threw them in our cart. If they were big, we made arrangements to have them delivered.

"This is fun," I said. "It's like a cross between a scavenger hunt and a date."

We stopped at a freestanding tub, modern but cozy as a hug, white as snow. It was called Romance.

"That's it," John said.

"Agreed," I said. "But you don't think we're just picking it because it's called Romance, do you?"

John swung his arm around my shoulders. "Tub names don't sway me. I'd choose this bathtub even if it was called Catastrophe."

I leaned my head against his shoulder. "Good to know."

Finally, we'd found everything but the bathroom vanity.

"They're just all so cookie cutter," I said.

"Sounds like Ikea it is then," John said. "You can't beat it for good, cheap modern design. A nod to classic and midcentury, while still embodying that clean Scandinavian esthetic."

"Bold but not impertinent," I said in my best wine snob voice.

"Fruit-forward with notes of grilled M&Ms," John said in his best wine snob voice.

"Forget the bathroom vanity," I said. "I'd even go for a glass of that Two-Buck Chuck we leave out for my dad right now." We'd been displaying decoy bottles of wine to keep my dad from drinking all of John's good wine for a while now. Sometimes it worked. Mostly my father drank the good stuff and left the decoy bottles for John and me.

We put away visions of wine and headed for Ikea, where not so long ago we'd bought a sleek modern bed and a comfy latex mattress to replace the ancient twin beds my sister and I had slept on.

We parked the car, took the Ikea escalator up. We stood in front of a bed exactly like the new one we had at home.

"Maybe we could just sleep here," I said. "I mean, it's close enough to our bed, right? And those sheets look clean."

But we soldiered on. We remembered that soon we'd be able to ditch the rickety piles of books we'd been using for night tables. Instead of buying tables that matched the new bed, we bought metal tables, with clean funky lines and openings in the back of the drawers to create hidden cord charging stations.

We followed the maze that was Ikea, zig-zagging through the minimalist displays, past the wardrobes, the dining room furniture, the office stuff.

"I always forget how disoriented I get in this place," I said.

"The better to make us spend our money," John said. "Keep the customer lost inside for as long as you can, circling past things they suddenly realize they can't live without. It's actually pretty brilliant."

I yawned. "Brilliant if you don't have to work tomorrow."

Eventually we came to the land of bathroom vanities. We both immediately headed for the perfect one. It was old-fashioned and modern at the same time, wall-mounted but with simple legs in the front.

"Kind of like a mullet," I said. "You know, business in the front, party in the back."

"How did we end up with a running joke about mullets?" John said.

I shrugged. "Be happy that we don't have to try to knock down any more walls with one."

The vanity was the perfect shade of gray to coordinate with everything we'd just picked out for our new bathroom. It had double built-in white porcelain sinks and a matching backsplash, plus soft-close drawers that pulled out fully and had lots of room for storage. We chose retro-feel faucets, a modern throwback to the kind that used to have an *H* and a *C* to turn on the hot and cold water separately.

"I knew you'd love those faucets," John said. "They're perfect for a preschool teacher."

"Yeah," I said. "They'll look amazing with the gigantic *ABC*s I'm planning stencil all over the bathroom wall."

John looked scared.

"Kidding," I said. "I get enough practice on my letters at school. Anyway, it's going to be a great bathroom, unique but not so over-the-top that it will hurt the resale."

"Resale?" John said. He rubbed his index finger back and forth across his lower lip. "Why would you bring up resale?"

I shrugged. "I don't know. I guess because that's what they always say on HGTV."

CHAPTER

Twenty-three

Even though we had to stand in line forever to get to the register, our purchases were such a meant-to-be that all the Ikea boxes fit into the trunk of John's car. We wound our way back home, Christmas lights twinkling at us from way too many of the houses we passed.

"I am not going to feel guilty if we don't get any lights or decorations up this year," I said. "We're under construction."

John turned to smile at me. "If we don't get to it this year, we'll do it next year. We have plenty of time."

The classic rock radio station switched to Christmas songs. Elvis Presley's "Blue Christmas." Brenda Lee's "Rockin' Round the Christmas Tree." Bruce Springsteen's "Santa Claus is Coming to Town."

John and I sang along with them all, until Eva Cassidy's soul-soothing version of "Silent Night" began to play. We stopped singing and just listened to the purity of her voice, the simplicity of her guitar.

"Her voice always gives me goosebumps," I said when the song ended. "There's something so magical about it. I felt that way before I knew her story. But can you imagine dying at thirty-three, virtually unknown, and then being discovered a couple years later?"

"At least she spent her life doing what she loved," John said.

"That's true. I remember the first time I heard her singing 'Fields of Gold' on the radio. I actually pulled off the road just to listen."

"I'd never even heard of Eva Cassidy before I met you." John put on his blinker, pulled over to the side of the road, pulled up his Eva Cassidy playlist.

"See," I said. "Whatever happens, you can thank me for that."

John stared straight ahead for a moment. Then he put his blinker on and we were back on the road again.

Eva was singing "Autumn Leaves" as we crunched over the crushed mussel shell driveway. We pulled in behind the pink ice cream truck, my trusty old Honda Civic, Polly's car, Johnny's car.

We sat there until it ended, the old sad song about missing someone most of all when autumn leaves begin to fall. Under the light outside the kitchen door, a few dry leaves twirled to the ground as if their movements were choreographed to the song.

I took in the big old white elephant of a house. The massive dumpster on the side lawn. The turquoise and white canned ham trailer out back, just visible under the stars.

John turned off the radio, then the heat, then the ignition. He leaned over and gave me a kiss. "I love you."

"I love you, too," I said.

He kept his hand on my shoulder. "We'll have to do date night more often. Maybe even upgrade it from a plumbing supply store to dinner and a movie next time."

I rested my hand on his hand. "Do you ever worry that we might have made a huge mistake buying this house? I'm having the hardest time picturing how we're going to get through this whole renovation and come out the other side of it still getting along. And even if we do get through it, my family is still going to be my family, you know? And they're always going to be around."

John's car door opened with a click. "If you didn't want to buy this house, you owed it to us to say that. There were plenty of other paths we could have taken."

"All I meant was—"

John's door clicked closed again. His back was ramrod straight. "I know exactly what you meant. Every time things get the least bit challenging, you're looking for an out. House, partner, whatever. I think the real problem is that you're not fully committed to the house. Or to me."

"Where did *that* come from?"

John looked at me. "And I quote 'Whatever happens, you can thank me for that.'"

The good vibes of a moment ago were completely gone. It was like as soon as the radio stopped playing, we'd crash-landed on a new planet.

"I am fully committed," I said as I kicked the car door open. "To sleeping on the couch."

. . . . .

Okay, so sleeping on the living room couch was not my most genius move. It was definitely a step up from the plaid couch in the cat room, but not a big step. Decades of crumbs were quite possibly sleeping there with me, tucked between the cushions, just out of reach of the infrequent pass of a vacuum cleaner.

It was even possible that a hamster might have taken up residence deep within the upholstery, since when we were growing up one had tragically escaped in the living room, never to be heard from again. Her named was Hamburger, which we all thought was a hilarious name for a hamster, and she was golden and adorable and loved to climb into shirt pockets. After we'd torn the house apart looking for Hamburger to no avail, my brothers and sisters and I had continued to leave out tiny pieces of her favorite foods for years— sunflower seeds, carrots, broccoli—the remains of which might all be sharing the living room couch with me now, too.

Although by this point in time, it definitely would have to be one of Hamburger's descendants sharing the couch with me. Which would have to mean that Hamburger met a mate once she escaped. Maybe she got lucky at PerfectHamsterMatch.com? I hoped so.

I rolled over, pulled the frayed sheets and scratchy blanket I'd grabbed from the upstairs linen closet up a little higher. I'd fed the cats while John was in the bathroom, given Horatio a treat, grabbed my sleep T-shirt off the mattress on the floor. I'd moved fast and managed to avoid bumping into John on my way to the living room.

I rolled over again, tried to force myself to relax enough to fall sleep. I heard a door close softly upstairs. I waited for the sound of the wood floors creaking as Polly walked along the hallway to the upstairs bathroom.

Instead, I heard footsteps coming softly down the stairs. One person. Wearing shoes. Definitely a man.

Not my business, I said to myself.

The footsteps continued along the center hallway and into the kitchen.

Not my business, I said to myself. *Not my business, not my business.*

The kitchen door opened, then closed softly.

I counted to ten. Then I counted backwards from ten. Then I counted to ten in French and in Spanish, which was about the sum total of my proficiency in both languages.

I couldn't take it anymore. I jumped up, wrapped the afghan around my shoulders, sprinted through the hallway to the kitchen.

By the time I opened the kitchen door, there was nothing out there but darkness.

. . . . .

Conflict always makes me hungry. I hate that. I mean, why couldn't I be one of those delicate flowers who forget to eat and begin to waste away the minute they hit a few bumps in the road?

I decided that was the least of my problems, so I stopped to pick up breakfast on the way to work. Morning Glories is just short of hip, a delightfully overgrown hodgepodge of sun-streaked greenery, white lattice, and round button tables with mismatched iron chairs. The coffee is strong and the baked goods fresh and scrumptious.

The early morning take-out line would be backed up from the counter to the door soon, but for once in my life I was early.

The woman who took my order had shoe polish-black hair and a pretty smile. She was wearing a bright blue Morning Glories T-shirt and a nametag that said JANEY.

I ordered a large coffee plus a spinach and brie breakfast sandwich. I briefly considered doubling the order and swinging by to drop off breakfast for John. Maybe we could cut to the chase and get this stupid fight over with.

So much for the notion that with sleep comes clarity. Not only had I woken up exactly as confused about why we were fighting as when I went to sleep, but now my neck hurt. And I'd spent most of the night dreaming about giant hamsters clomping down the stairs.

In the end, I stayed with my single order. Maybe sometimes it's a good idea to give the other person a little space. Let him come to you. Maybe once we got through all the construction and our heads cleared, we'd be fine.

"Are you sure I can't get you anything else?" Janey said as she handed me the takeout bag.

"Why?" I said. "Do you think I should get something else?"

She laughed. "Not unless you want it, honey. Take it from me, never do anything just because the other person wants you to. Life's too short to spend it chasing other people's fancies."

"You're absolutely right," I said. "Thank you for that."

She tucked an extra napkin into my bag. "And make sure you tell that daddy of yours that Janey had a terrific time with him the other night and that I'll drop off that casserole I promised him soon."

"Will do," I said, like I'd said dozens of times before to strange women.

"That ad of his about the mattress just cracked me right up. Billy Boy Hurlihy is one hot ticket."

"Mmm," I said. "He's something all right." Cars were pulling into the parking lot. In a minute Janey would be so busy she'd forget all about me.

"When push comes to shove," she said, "at the end of the day what you remember is how much you laughed with someone."

I considered asking to borrow her pen so I could write that down.

I took my time eating breakfast in my car in the Morning Glories parking lot. Then I took my time driving to school. Even with all that taking my time, mine was the only car in the Bayberry parking lot when I pulled in. I emptied my takeout bag in one of the outdoor trash barrels and wandered around the school grounds, filling it back up again with the last of the bright gold and orange and red autumn leaves.

"Good morning," Polly said when she joined me in the classroom. She dropped her teacher bag to the floor, began shrugging off her coat.

"Morning," I said. "Hey, I just have to ask. Is anybody bothering you?"

Polly froze. Her cheeks turned pink. Her coat hung from her arms like wings.

"What do mean?" she said finally.

"You know," I said. "My father? My brother Johnny? Any other testosterone-laden relatives I might have forgotten about?"

She slipped all the way out of her coat, brushed one hand in front of her face. "Of course not. Your dad and brother are both fantastic. And really sweet to me."

I watched her for signs that she was lying, but she was looking right at me. No fidgeting, no looking off to the side, no shaking her head, no covering her throat or her heart. Even her blush was gone.

"Okay then," I said. "Let me know if you need anything, okay?"

"You, too," Polly said.

Morning took on its usual hum as the students trickled in. Jackets on hooks, backpacks in cubbies. Wooden puzzles and matching games spread across a table or on a mat rolled out on the floor. Some of the kids jumping right in to work, others wandering around as they finished waking up.

After circle time, Polly and I made leaf people with the kids. We used slotted wooden clothespins for the bodies, the original old-fashioned clothespins without any springs, the kind my grandmothers used to use to hang their laundry out to dry.

We squirted dabs of acrylic paint in paper cups and let the kids dip Q-tips in the paint to make faces on the top end of the clothespins. We made hats out of tiny acorn caps. Created bright autumn clothing from the leaves and glued the clothes to the clothespins with paste made from flour and water. Wrapped jute string around and around the leaf clothing to make belts. Glued on yarn, and more jute, for hair. Twisted pipe cleaners around the clothespins for arms. Snipped smaller pieces of a pipe cleaner to make crowns. Turned tiny bits of cotton balls into beards.

Polly looked up from the leaf person she was making.

"I could do this all day," she said.

"I know, right?" I cut a tiny piece of jute, knotted the ends together to make a necklace. "Wouldn't it be awesome to just stay in the land of the leaf people,

where the biggest thing you have to worry about is
whether or not you look good in fall colors?"

Twenty-four

After our students went home for the day, Ethan and I sat across from each other in the teachers' room, going over our notes for the holiday performance.

"I can't believe how fast we have to pull this thing together," he said. "It feels like it was just Thanksgiving five minutes ago."

"I know," I said. "But the good news is that the performance is the kickoff to vacation, so we wouldn't want it to happen any later, because this way we're off from mid-December until the Monday after New Year's Day. And the other good news is that preschoolers are always cute when they perform, even when they screw things up. Sometimes especially when they screw things up."

"Okay, let me make sure I've got this right. Essentially, there are two dogs and two cats—"

"Played by the hammiest, most overly theatrical third-year students we've got," I said. "It's one of those things they're born with—sometimes it's a pain in the neck, but it comes in handy every once in a while."

Ethan nodded. "And they're traveling around the world, taking in the sights as they look for a place to live."

I reached for my umpteenth cup of coffee of the day. "Right, and they're also time traveling in a way, too, which allows us to do a loose timeline of the history of dance, starting with the cave people dance. I'll write little snippets for the dogs and cats to take turns saying before each of the dance numbers."

Ethan looked up from sketching. "Should I make some big paper mâché clubs for the cave kids dance?"

"Ha. Do you want to get us both fired? There's no way the kids would be able to hold them for an entire dance without clubbing each other. We'll wrap some animal print fabric around the cave kids to get the idea across. Then from there we'll go right into "Walk Like an Egyptian" and then can let the teachers pick and choose from the Charleston, the Macarena, the Irish Step Dance, the Polynesian Puili dance, and the Tarantella from Italy."

"Impressive," Ethan said.

"Time will tell," I said. "The dance steps are all pretty simple—lots of knee bending and hip wiggling. But preschoolers love to dance, and if they're having fun, hopefully the audience will, too. Okay, then from there, we jump right into the holiday stuff. "Dance of the Sugar Plum Puppies", "Deck the Halls with Boughs of Catnip."

"Guaranteed crowd pleasers," Ethan said.

"Then all the kids will come on stage and sing and dance to Woodie Guthrie's 'Hanukkah Dance' followed by 'If You're Happy and You Know It, Kwanza's Here.' And then the teachers will join the kids on stage. We'll all dance around to 'Jingle Bell Rock' and 'Rockin' Around the Christmas Tree,' and then our grand finale will be "We Wish You a Happy Howliday and a Bark-Filled New Year."

Ethan was sketching frantically.

I took a deep breath. "And then the kids playing the dogs and the cats will yell 'home sweet home' and run off to their parents in the audience. I'm not sure it quite holds up in terms of plot, but it will get the idea across in a preschool kind of way."

"I like it," Ethan said. "And then we'll have the adoptable animals from the shelter front and center during refreshments, and maybe some of them will get lucky."

"Yeah," I said. "Let's hope. And let's also hope that your godmother doesn't kill us both. I mean, she can only fire me, but she can disown you, too."

Ethan shrugged. "She'll get over it." He slid his sketchbook over to me. "Okay, this is what I'm thinking of in terms of sets. Nothing fancy, but enough of a visual to help the kids and the audience get the feel of each number."

"Amazing," I said. "You're so talented."

Ethan smiled his surfer boy smile. "Right back at you. Having the kind of creativity that allows you to pull something like this together in a fun, age-appropriate way is a big deal. And Polly has told me about how you can rewrite lyrics to any song at the drop of a hat. You should think about packaging materials for other preschool teachers."

"Really?" I said.

"Yeah, really. And if you want to brainstorm about ways we could include a set design component, I'd be up for that."

"Really?" I said. Apparently *really* was the only word I still remembered how to say.

Ethan laughed. "Think about it. Maybe we can discuss it over the holiday break."

"Sure." I looked at him carefully, trying to figure out if he had an ulterior motive. Maybe Ethan was only pretending he wanted to brainstorm with me so he could legitimately spend time at my house, where Polly just happened to be living.

"Hey," I said. "I just have to ask you this. Were you at my house last night?"

Ethan looked right at me. No fidgeting, no looking off to the side, no shaking his sun-streaked hair.

"No, why?" he said. "Is Polly okay?"

. . . . .

I'd just finished woofing down a bowl of unlabeled casserole that tasted bizarrely of chicken pot pie, like comfort food dipped in a different comfort food. I'd put the rest of it back in the oven and turned the oven down, so that anybody else who showed up could dig in when they felt like it. If there was anything left, I'd probably zap some more for breakfast. Being in a construction zone was a great excuse to let my food standards dip even lower than they already were.

I'd also fed the cats. Now I was sitting with all four kittens in my lap while Pebbles cleaned up the leftovers from their dishes. John and Horatio must have been off having their own adventure, since Horatio wasn't waiting around for a treat and John's car hadn't been in the driveway when I'd pulled in.

The door to the cat room opened. Oreo leaped off my lap and made a run for the door. I made a run for Oreo. Squiggy and Catsby spilled off my lap and bounced around on the sofa. Sunshine held on for dear life.

"Holy cats," Carol said as she walked right in. "Find a home for some of these felines, will you?"

I scooped up Oreo just in the nick of time. "They have a home," I said as I unhooked Sunshine's claws from my pant leg. "But, wow, they're growing up so fast, it's getting harder and harder to keep them in this room. As soon as Joe and his guys are gone, we're going to have to give them some more space. Maybe set up some baby gates or something to keep them safe. You don't have any extras, do you?"

"Take my baby gates, please," Carol said. "Maeve was scaling them before she could even walk, so they're certainly not going to contain her at the ripe old age of three. Dennis actually caught her knocking on the neighbor's door yesterday when he was coming home from work. She told him she ran away because our house was boring."

Carol's daughter Maeve and Christine's daughter Sydney had been born months apart. They'd both just missed the preschool cutoff this year, but their Bayberry applications had been on file practically since birth. This wasn't even that unusual. Quite a few parents made cellphone calls from the delivery room to put down a deposit to reserve their infant's eventual Bayberry space.

I knew my sisters would each write letters requesting me as their child's teacher next year. I was fine with that, since it never hurt for a teacher to appear to be in demand. But if Kate Stone caught on to the fact that we were related, which she probably would, their requests would never fly.

When my wasband's new wife had requested me as a teacher for their twins, I'd nixed that placement. But I was torn about having my nieces in my classroom next year. On the one hand, Maeve was a handful, and Sydney was a quick study and picked up everything Maeve did, so they were essentially double trouble. On the other hand, I loved my nieces, and as much as my sisters could drive me crazy, I'd been dealing with them my whole life, so they were definitely the devils I knew. A new set of parents might drive me even crazier, plus I'd have to be nice to them because we weren't related.

"So," Carol was saying when I tuned back in. "Are Dad and Johnny keeping their mitts off each other?"

I shrugged. "I haven't noticed any more punches flying."

Carol picked up a couple of kittens and sat down on the couch. "I don't get the Polly attraction. I mean, what's up with that?"

I picked up the other two kittens. "She's smart and sweet and funny and adorable. Dad's attracted to pretty much all women, and Johnny's lonely and vulnerable. What's not to get?"

Carol shrugged. "I don't remember strange men falling all over me when I was pregnant. I felt like Shamu. I'm pretty sure I even looked like Shamu."

"Maybe," I said, "nobody fell all over you because you just didn't run into the right killer whale."

"Thanks." Carol handed her cats to me. "Anyway, I'm happy to report that Dad has had a date every night this week. I made him take down that tacky free mattress to a good home ad, but I have to tell you, it's still working for him. Print ads don't die—I bet it's still hanging on the refrigerator of every woman in Marshbury in his dating demographic."

Carol stopped talking long enough to check her phone for the time.

"Well," I said, "I guess as long as it keeps Dad out of trouble—"

"Okay, I don't have all night. What kind of progress have you made with Johnny?"

"Johnny?" I said.

Carol shook her head. "Yes, Johnny. Remember? The hippie brother living out back in the trailer?"

"What a coincidence," I said, "I was just on my way to check on him when you showed up."

By the time Carol dragged me outside and in the direction of the trailer, my sister Christine's car was crunching over the crushed mussel shell driveway.

"Unbelievable," I said. "If this keeps up, we're going to have to seriously consider putting in a parking lot."

Carol and I both immediately started to sing, "They paved paradise and put in a parking lot" in our best Joni Mitchell imitations, which I had to admit left a lot to be desired.

"Pinch, poke, owe me a Coke," we both said.

"Grow up," Carol said as she pinched me.

"Ouch," I said as I poked her.

Our younger sister slammed her car door and caught up with us. "What are you doing here?" Christine said.

"Um, I live here?" I said.

"Fine," Christine said. "But I'm meeting Johnny in the trailer."

She made a dash for the canned ham trailer, tried to pull the door closed behind her.

Carol and I looked at each other, shook our heads.

We caught up and grabbed the trailer's little metal door handle and pulled. Christine was no match for our combined force.

Johnny was just coming out of the teensy shower, a towel wrapped around his waist.

"Jesus," he said. "Knock, why don't you."

"Put on some clothes, why don't you," Carol said.

"That was actually the plan," Christine said. "I'm helping him decide what to wear to dinner with Kim."

All three sisters swung into action. Christine picked out a shirt, I found a decent pair of pants. Johnny disappeared into the tiny bathroom and came out dressed. Carol gelled his hair. Johnny must have stopped for a haircut on the way home from work, because I was happy to see that a man bun was no longer a possibility. I thought I could still smell the faint scent of patchouli, but maybe the scent had just lodged itself in the trailer, or in my memory banks.

Johnny did a slow turn so we could make sure he looked okay. We all gave him two thumbs up.

"Ohmigod," Christine said. "Do you remember in high school when all the boys used to stand in front of the library and rate the girls as they walked by?"

"I remember," Carol said. "That was so demoralizing."

"Me, too," I said. I looked right at my brother. "You gave me a minus eleven one time. My own brother."

"Hey," Johnny said. "I was just trying to survive. We all were."

"Survive this," I said as I flashed my brother the bird.

He flashed me the same finger.

"Trying to survive is no excuse," I said. "You should have been on my side, and you weren't."

"Listen," Johnny said. "I get that you're having some sort of decades delayed breakthrough or something, but all I want to do is work things out with Kim. So back off, okay?"

"You back off," I said.

"Kids, kids, kids," Carol said. "Okay, how did Kim sound when you talked to her?"

"Me?" Johnny said.

Carol blew out a puff of air. "Well, I hope somebody else didn't call her for you. Remember when you made me ask out that girl for you in eighth grade?"

"I didn't call her," Johnny said softly. "I texted."

"How romantic," Carol said.

"Do you think you guys could come with me?" Johnny said. "Maybe sit outside in the car for moral support?"

"I'll do it," Christine said. "After all, I was supposed to be the one helping you get ready, and these two butted right in. No offense."

"None taken," Carol said. "I'll even let you ride in my minivan."

"Shotgun," Johnny said.

CHAPTER

Twenty-five

Carol crunched over the crushed mussel shells as she backed her minivan out of our old/my new driveway.

"Swing by Mikey's house and pick him up, okay?" Johnny said.

"Seriously?" Carol said.

"Yeah," Johnny said. "I texted him earlier. I figured he'd be a good person to have with us. He's been through it, ya know?"

"I've been through it, too," I said.

Johnny twisted around in the front seat so he could look at me. "Yeah, but it worked out for him."

"Ohmigod," I said. "I can't believe you just said that." I skimmed over the fact that John and I weren't exactly speaking to each other. "It totally worked out for me—John and I are really happy together. You could even say we're crushing it."

"People who say they're crushing it," Carol said, "are rarely crushing it. It's like people who post sappy things to their spouses on Facebook about how much they love them. I mean, give me a break—they're in the next room. If you've got something sappy to say, put your phone down, get up off your butt, and go say it."

"I don't post sappy things to John on Facebook," I said. I made a mental note to check to be sure that was true.

"Well," Christine said. "At least you finally got rid of Kevin. What an asshole."

"Sasshole," Carol said. "And yeah, Kevin was a total prick."

"Why is prick okay," Christine said, "and asshole isn't?"

"Swear rules," Carol said. "I don't make 'em up."

"Why is it," I said, "that the whole ten years I was married to my wasband, none of you ever said anything bad about him?"

"Why state the obvious," Carol said.

"We're classy like that," Christine said. "I mean, why bother to rub it in when you were stuck with him. Plus, it's not like any of the other guys you were with before Kevin were all that hot either."

"Oh, and Joe is such a prize," I said.

"Watch it," Christine said, "or you'll be looking for another contractor."

"I love Joe," I said.

Carol pulled into Michael's driveway, beeped.

"Whoa," Christine said. "Holy déjà vu. I just had an out-of-body flashback to high school. Remember when we used to get in trouble whenever someone beeped for us in the driveway? We'd have to run out and bring whoever it was in?"

"I'm not asking you, I'm telling you." I tried to imitate my mother, but the truth was I'd lost the sound of her voice soon after she died.

"Don't make me go out there," Carol said.

"As long as you live under my roof," Johnny said, "you live by my rules."

"Don't use that tone with me, Missy," Christine said.

"Mom wasn't that embarrassing," Carol said, "but Dad—"

"Don't do anything I wouldn't do!" we all boomed together.

"The sad thing is," Carol said, "that I've used every single one of those with Siobhan. I can't help myself— they just come flying out of my mouth."

The door opened. Michael and Billy Jr. jogged toward the minivan, cut in front of the headlights, stopped just long enough to shake their rear ends in our direction.

"I texted Billy, too," Johnny said. "I didn't want him to feel left out."

Carol pushed a button and the minivan's power side door slid open.

"Hey." Michael waved his hand toward the rear of the van like he was directing traffic. "Way back, you two."

"Not going to happen," Christine said. "We were here first."

"The rate of serious accidents," Billy Jr. said, "is only half in the third seat compared to the middle seat."

"I like to live dangerously," I said. As soon as I said it, I hoped I hadn't just jinxed myself. Although it would serve John right. He'd sleep sitting up in a chair by the side of my hospital bed for months on end, wishing he'd been nicer to me. I'd be pale but beautiful, my injuries life threatening but not cosmetic.

"Hurry up and shut the door," Carol said. "I'm freezing."

"We can't be heating the whole outdoors," the rest of us said.

I tilted my seat forward. Michael and Billy Jr. squished themselves into the way back seat, their knees digging into Christine's and my backs through our seat.

"Dad would kill us if he knew we were all riding around together," I said. "He'd think we were partying without him."

"We could just say we were out shopping for his Christmas presents," Michael said.

"Which reminds me," Carol said, "I just ordered his presents online. I'll text everybody the amount you owe."

"Why didn't we get a vote?" Christine said.

"You did," Carol said. "But you didn't use it, so I took it back again. Okay, where to?"

"Driftwood," Johnny said. "Word on the street is they have a righteous new vibe, man."

"Uh, uh, uh," I said. "You dropped the hippie act, remember?"

Johnny shrugged. "It's just that when I get nervous, it gives me a persona to grab on to."

"You used to chew on your shirt when you got nervous," Billy Jr. said. "Remember? You'd make these big puddles?"

"Awkwardsauce," Christine said.

"I was like five," Johnny said. "Cut me some slack."

Nobody said anything, which was our way of cutting him some slack.

Johnny broke the silence. "If you want to help me out, a few words of decent advice might be good right about now."

"I already told you what to do," I said. "And I quote—Have flowers delivered to Kim, along with a beautiful note that says you'd like to meet her for dinner to try to get things right. Because whatever happens, for the rest of your lives, even though they're practically grown now, you'll always be the parents of two awesome sons together."

Michael flicked his finger against the back of my head. "That sounds so familiar."

"Ouch," I said. "Hey, at least *you* listened."

"I texted Kim some of that stuff," Johnny said. "I've been texting back and forth with the boys, too. And we still have time to grab flowers on the way, right?"

"Sure," Carol said. "At the grocery store." A minute or two later she put on her blinker and screeched into the Stop & Shop parking lot. I was closest to the door so I jumped out. Christine jumped out right behind me, held out her hand for Johnny's credit card.

The floral section was ablaze with red poinsettias.

"Look," I said as I pointed to a small bouquet of yellow roses tucked in a corner of the floral case.

"Perfect," Christine said. "Given the situation, yellow roses are a lot safer than red roses.

"Yeah," I said. "They're also a big step up from all those bouquets with the Santa picks and the pinecones covered in spray snow."

I grabbed the roses. Christine yanked a yellow ribbon off a sympathy bouquet and tied it around the roses. We raced through a self-checkout kiosk, jogged back out to Carol's minivan.

I gave the roses to Johnny. Christine handed him his credit card.

"So give us the action plan," Carol said as we rolled across the parking lot.

"Action plan?" Johnny said. "Me?"

"Yeah, you," Michael said. "Do we have to do everything for you?"

"Oh, please," Carol said. "We had to fly to Savannah with you when you messed up your marriage. At least Johnny's keeping it local."

"Whatever you do," I said, "don't start a fight. And if Kim tries to start one, do not engage." As I heard the words come out of my mouth, it hit me that I might possibly be a lot better at giving other people advice than I was at taking my own advice.

"Agreed," Carol said. "Just hand Kim the flowers and tell her how great it is to see her and how beautiful she looks."

"Right," Christine said. "Even if she looks like shit. I mean, if she looks like shit, that might actually be a good sign."

"Ask her how she's doing," Carol said. "And keep her talking. Don't try to fix anything. Just listen to her. Do that mirroring thing—you know, where you repeat what she says back to her in your own words, so she knows you heard her."

"I don't get it," Johnny said. "I thought the point was to try to fix this." He sighed, slammed his head back against headrest. "What the hell do women want anyway?"

CHAPTER

Twenty-six

"The million-dollar question," Billy Jr. said.

"I think it's probably up to a million and a half by now," Michael said.

"It's not that complicated, knuckleheads," Carol said. "Women want to be heard."

"Caring," Christine said. "We want you to care enough to try to make our lives a little bit easier."

"Blind loyalty," I said. "We want you to be crazy about us, even though that may or may not make any rational sense whatsoever."

Carol pulled into Driftwood's parking lot, found a space way in the back. We were a couple of seaside towns away from Marshbury, about halfway between Johnny and Kim's house and the canned ham trailer. Driftwood looked like its name—reclaimed wood siding weathered to a salty gray inside and out, a wall of floor-to-ceiling windows overlooking the harbor. The food was fishing boat to table, even this time of year. The clientele was a mix of upscale seasonal washashores, which we used to call summer bums back when we were kids, and more downscale townies splurging to celebrate a special occasion. The restaurant was understatedly expensive, the kind of place you'd meet someone to try to work things out if you were taking it seriously.

"Good choice," Christine said. "This is definitely a makeup restaurant."

"As opposed to a make out restaurant," Michael said. "You know, high end."

"Back to the action plan," Carol said. "I mean, how long do we have to sit out here?"

"I didn't really think that part through," Johnny said. "I only got as far as thinking it would be good to have you guys here for reinforcement."

"I say we go in and wait at the bar," Billy Jr. said. "Maybe order a beer and some appetizers. We'll be discreet."

We all cracked up.

"Yeah," Christine said. "Like Kim won't recognize the sound of our laughter. I don't think she was all that crazy about it even when you guys were getting along."

"How about this," Carol said. "We'll wait out here for about fifteen minutes—"

"Or as long as we can take it," Billy Jr. said. "That beer somebody mentioned is sounding good."

"And then," Carol said, "we'll drive down the street to Jake's Seafood. But one glass of wine and I'm out of there—I'll still have to drive everybody back to their houses. When you're done, ask Kim to take you home. Tell her you had a Lyft driver drop you off."

"What if she says no?" Johnny said.

Carol shook her head. "Hmm. Maybe this time around you could actually get a Lyft driver?"

Johnny turned his head to face Carol. From where I sat, I could only see his profile, but even that looked pathetic.

"Fine," Carol said. "Call me. If I'm still on the road, I might consider circling back."

Johnny checked his phone. "Six more minutes and I'll start walking in. I don't want to be too early."

"One question," Christine said. "What do you want to happen? You do want to get back together with Kim, right? I mean, even after . . ." When she let the sentence trail off, we all mentally added *the work husband*.

Johnny blew out a blast of air. "I always thought the two of us were pretty much soul to soul, you know? Until we weren't. It's like you wake up every day and you have it all. But you forget that you have it. And then one day you don't have it anymore. Bam. Blindsided."

"It's a shit ton of work," Michael said, "but you can get it back."

"Maybe two perfectly good people can stop fitting together," Johnny said. "Maybe Kim was just the brave one who figured it out first."

"So then you try to take what you learned to your next relationship," I said. "Which is also a shit ton of work."

"I'm scared to death of getting it wrong," Johnny said. "And I hate myself for being afraid."

"You'll hate yourself more if you don't even try," I said softly.

"Yeah," Billy Jr. said, "You have to go for it. If Dad were here, he'd be quoting Robert Frost and telling you that the only way out is through."

"And then he'd try to convince us Robert Frost was Irish," Carol said, "instead of Scottish and English. Or American."

"We're all afraid," Christine said, "Even me sometimes. And nobody's perfect—"

"Not even you," Carol said. "Which, by the way, is like the world's greatest understatement."

"What I was going to say," Christine said, "is that basically we're all winging it."

Johnny nodded. He started flapping his elbows like a bird. Tentatively at first, and then he picked up speed. The rest of us copied him, one after another, until we'd turned into a motley flock of seabirds flapping away in the dark in a minivan.

"Come on, bro, get your butt in there and make us proud," Michael said.

Johnny opened his door, climbed out. When he ran his hand through the lock of hair that had fallen into his face, he looked just like our dad. My eyes teared up.

"He has a good swagger when he walks," Carol said. "Like I might be a nice guy, but don't mess with me."

"Dad taught him that swagger," Billy Jr. said. "Right after he taught it to me."

Michael tapped me on the shoulder. "Open the door fast. I need to tell him something."

I slid the door open. Michael jumped out.

In the blink of an eye, Michael opened the front door, hopped in the front seat, shut the door again and locked it.

"Ohmigod," I said. "You can't do that."

"I just did," Michael said.

"No way," I said. "You know how it works—when somebody gets out, we rotate to the front. That means, I get shotgun, Christine gets my seat, you—"

Michael cupped his hand behind his ear. "Sorry, I don't speak loser."

We all sat there in the parking lot, the minivan's heat blasting, stars twinkling in the sky over us. On the other side of the parking lot, a trio of gulls were dive-bombing a dumpster under the soft glow of a streetlight, flapping their wings like they were copying us. The moon was almost full. Either that or it had just been full and I'd completely missed it.

"You want to hear loser?" I said. "I just realized that I might have married Kevin because I didn't think anybody else would ever ask me."

The minivan was quiet for so long that I started to wonder whether I'd actually said it out loud.

"Well, at least that explains it," Michael finally said.

Everybody laughed. I held off for as long as I could, then I joined in.

"Gee whiz," I said. "Thanks for the sympathy."

"You don't need our sympathy," Carol said. "You just need to not screw things up with John."

"I wouldn't dream of it," I said.

"Screw's not a swear?" Christine said. "How is screw not a swear?"

"Would you knock it off with the swear quizzes?" Carol said.

"Yeah, holy heck, Chris," Billy Jr. said.

"Fork you," Christine said.

"What do you think is going to happen in there?" I said. "With Johnny?"

"I think Kim might be over him," Carol said.

"Then why did we send him in there?" Christine said. "To tell you the truth, I was never that crazy about Kim."

"It's a fact of life," Carol said, "that sometimes our siblings will marry people we can't stand. If it works out, we keep our mouths shut. If it looks like it's not going to work out, we give them the minimum amount of truth to get the job done."

"Right," I said. "You guys are so gentle with your truth telling."

"One, two, three, fifteen," Billy Jr. said. "Okay, time's up—let's go."

. . . . .

When Carol pulled the minivan into the parking lot at Jake's Seafood, the first thing we saw was the pink Bark & Roll Forever ice cream truck.

"Surprise, surprise," I said. "Dad sure gets around, doesn't he?"

"I told you," Carol said, "I'm making sure he has a date every night. There's no way in hell I'm changing diapers for the offspring of some embarrassingly young stepmother."

"What?" Christine said.

"I don't want to know about it," Michael said.

"Ditto," Billy Jr. said.

"Carol's just being delusional," I said. "But if Dad's inside with a date, maybe we should find another place to get a drink. You know, so we don't get in the way of his razzle dazzling."

"Too bad we're not in Savannah," Michael said. "They have an open container law there. You know, it's legal to walk around with your drinks. Now there's a civilized custom."

"Yeah," Carol said. "Except that you can't drink in your car, and since we're actually in Massachusetts, it's thirty degrees out in that parking lot if we're lucky."

"Dream killer," Michael said.

"I think we should just go in," Billy Jr. said. "We can sit in the bar. Dad won't even notice us. He'll be too busy making applesauce with some baby cakes."

"You sound just like him," Christine said.

"How about this," I said. "I'll run in and make sure the coast is clear. And check to see if there are any seats left at the bar. And also make sure Dad's not with one of his bad old girlfriends."

"If it's Dolly, run," Michael said.

"Or Sweepstakes Sally," Christine said.

"Now you're scaring me," I said. "Maybe somebody better come in with me."

"Dad's less likely to spot just one of us," Carol said. "You'll be fine. I'll pull right up by the front door and keep the engine running. We can always high tail it back to Marshbury and get a drink at High Tide if we have to."

"Whatever," I said. I tried to slam the side door behind me for emphasis, but it had some kind of anti-slam feature, like the vehicular equivalent of a soft-close kitchen drawer. What was the world coming to when you couldn't even slam a minivan door anymore?

"Hey," Michael was saying as the door shut. "Is that my favorite jacket from high school?"

I ignored him. The long suede fringe on the jacket swung back and forth as I walked away. I could see my breath in the frigid air, so I pulled the jacket tighter. Maybe my father was inside with his bosses, the Bark & Roll Forever ladies, having their own little holiday party. If so, we could all hang out. I loved spending time with them—they were hip and ageless and hilarious and gave me hope that by the time I got to be their age, I might actually have my act together. Plus, I could ask them about the best way to get Pebbles and the cats acclimated to the rest of the house.

I pulled the restaurant's heavy door open, walked through the lobby and glanced into the half-empty bar. Nobody stopped me, so I rounded the corner to take a peek at the restaurant side.

My father was seated at a candlelit booth tucked away in a corner.

He was a holding hands with a woman across the heavy pine tabletop. He was leaning forward and lifting up the woman's chin with two fingers of his other hand. She was looking into his eyes. They were both smiling.

It was Polly.

Twenty-seven

The ceiling of the cat room was just visible in the faint glow of the nightlight. The cracks in the old plaster looked like the lines on the palm of a hand. I tilted the palm of my own hand until it caught enough light to compare the two. It was impossible to be sure in the almost dark, but I seemed to have an awful lot of downward lines branching out from my life line. Or maybe it was my heart line.

I reached over to the top of the rickety pile of books, turned off my alarm before its obnoxious buzz could make me feel even worse than I already did. My entire body ached, as if I was coming down with the flu and my immune system had kicked into overdrive to try to ward it off, even though it was way too late for that.

I barely remembered the rest of last night. I'd walked back out to Carol's minivan feeling numb right down to my toes. I was sure neither Polly nor my father had seen me—they'd only had eyes for each other.

Carol had pushed the button to open the side door for me. A burst of hot air hit me in the face, like getting burned twice.

I faked a smile. "High Tide it is. Dad's sitting at the bar in there with some aging hot tamale, and even if we were crazy enough to want to join them, the bar is packed and there aren't any seats left."

"Casting the line and getting ready to reel her in, huh?" Billy Jr. said.

"Hoping for a little backseat bingo in the ice cream truck later on," Michael said.

"Eww, thank you for those lovely images," Carol said. "But at least Dad's back on track with his dating again. I knew I just needed to give him a nudge to get the momentum going."

Carol took the beach road back to Marshbury, the minivan twisting and turning along with the jagged coastline. Even under the stars, the ocean was a gloomy black. There must have been music playing, but I couldn't hear it over the sound of the waves crashing in my head.

"I wonder how Johnny's doing," Christine said.

"He hasn't called or texted yet," Michael said. "That's a good sign."

"Or a bad sign," Carol said.

I waited until we were a few blocks away from the house. "Hey, do you mind dropping me off? I have to get up really early tomorrow."

"Ha-ha," Christine said.

"Surely you jest," Billy Jr. said.

I had this crazy urge to open the minivan door and leap. We weren't going that fast, and I'd seen it done a million times in the movies. Like in *Crazy, Stupid, Love* when Steve Carell's character tells Julianne Moore's character *If you keep talking I'm going to get out of the car.* You just jump and roll.

Carol must have read my mind, because she clicked the locks on all the doors. Everybody but me burst out laughing.

We sat at a tall pub table in the bar at High Tide. The server had gone to high school with some of us, so she got our drinks right away.

We held up our glasses. "To Johnny," we said.

"Sláinte," we roared.

Christine put her wine glass down. "If it doesn't work out, we can turn Kim into a drinking game. You know, every time someone says her name, we have to drink."

"Kim," Michael said.

"Not yet," Carol said. "She has to earn it."

The thing about a big family is that when you're quiet they're usually too busy talking to notice. I didn't even try to follow the conversation, just let it swirl around me.

I should have been relieved that my sisters and brothers didn't know that Polly and our dad were on a date. Together. I hated that Carol had been right. I couldn't believe Polly would do that to me. I couldn't believe I'd invited her to stay in our house. I couldn't believe I'd hired her in the first place.

At least the pink ice cream truck wasn't in the driveway when Carol dropped me off. When I let myself in through the kitchen door, the smell of seriously crispy casserole greeted me.

"Perfect," I said. I turned off the oven, grabbed a potholder and plopped the casserole on top of the stove, peeled back the foil. I spent a moment considering whether or not it might still function for breakfast in a pinch.

While I waited for the casserole to cool enough to put in the refrigerator, just in case, I tiptoed up to check on the renovations, desperate for some good news.

Pink, the plastic flamingo I'd last seen stuck into the pot outside the entrance to the mudroom and my father's new man cave beyond, was leaning back against the wall beside Polly's bedroom door, the bedroom that had once belonged to my parents. If I still had any doubt at all that those were my father's footsteps I'd heard coming down the stairs in the middle of the night, they were gone. *Gross,* I wanted to yell at the top of my lungs, like I was still back in high school.

I turned around and walked downstairs again without even bothering to check on John's and my new sanctuary-to-be. The magic was gone. It was a really stupid idea to move in here. None of this would have happened if John and I had just bought another house. Any other house.

I put the casserole in the fridge. I filled dishes for the cats, grabbed a treat for Horatio.

John was asleep. Or pretending to be. At the rate we were going, if the cats and I moved out, he probably wouldn't even notice.

I slithered out of my clothes, pulled on my sleeping T-shirt, slid under the covers of the mattress on the floor.

"'Twas the night before tomorrow," I whispered, "and all through the house, more than one person, is acting like a louse."

I tossed and turned all night. I pulled the covers off John. He yanked them back. I dreamed about diapers— cloth diapers, disposable diapers, pull-ups, easy ups, diapers made out of clouds and marshmallows. I dreamed about boxes and boxes of diapers under the Christmas tree. I dreamed that we finally found Hamburger, our long-lost hamster, and she needed her diaper changed, too. I pulled the covers off John again. He yanked them back.

Somehow I made it through the night, only to wake up to have to face another day.

John rolled over beside me, swung his legs over the side of the mattress, pushed himself up to a standing position.

There were a million things I could have said to him. *Good morning. I love you. You'll never guess what happened. We need to talk.*

But I didn't say a word. And neither did he.

By the time I got out of the shower, he was off taking Horatio for a walk.

By the time they got back from wherever they'd gone, I'd already left for school.

I wondered, just for a moment, if this was how it had started with Johnny and Kim. And then I wondered if that's how it had started with John and his ex-wife. With Kevin and me.

. . . . .

"I get eight presents for Hanukkah," Pandora said at circle time. "And my Barbie gets eight presents for Hanukkah, too."

"The three wise men," Josiah said, "brought coconut oil and guacamole and a sheep for the table."

"Angel Gabriel," Jaden said, "used to be the tooth fairy. He's happier now."

"My nana," Ember said, "says it takes all kinds of kinds."

"My daddy," Celine said, "says the commute is a bear."

"What kind of bear?" Morgan said.

"An orange teddy bear," Juliette said.

"Do you know what I want for Christmas?" Depp said. "Everything, baby."

Polly rested her hand on her baby bump, caught my eye, smiled.

I looked away.

We got the kids settled in with their individual work. Griffin staggered over to the reading boat. He pulled a book off the shelf, held it high over his head.

"I can't read!" he yelled.

I crossed the room to him. "It's okay," I whispered. "You're only three, honey. You don't have to read yet."

He traded the book for a pillow, curled up and fell asleep.

Polly sidled up to me. "Everything, baby," she said. She sounded exactly like Depp.

"Excuse me," I said as I walked away.

After lunch, Ethan and I opened the door between our classrooms so that June and Polly could help each other keep an eye on our full-day students. Then we went classroom to classroom so the other Bayberry students could rehearse their holiday performance numbers for us.

"I have to admit I was a little bit worried," Ethan said, "but they're really coming along. And just in the nick of time. I can't believe we're on the homestretch."

"It won't be perfect by any means," I said, "but I think cute is a definite possibility."

Ethan smiled, his teeth sparkling like a tooth-whitening ad. "If there's one thing I've learned over the last few years, it's that nothing is ever perfect. Even when it looks like it from the outside."

The "Dance of the Sugar Plum Puppies" was adorable. Ethan and I fist bumped each other as we walked down the hallway to the next classroom. "Deck the Halls with Boughs of Catnip" was possibly even cuter.

"How'd it go?" Polly said when I got back to my classroom a few minutes before dismissal. She was glowing like she always was now. It was exhausting.

I shrugged, took a long sip from my water bottle.

Polly tucked her hair behind her ears. "Is something wrong, Sarah?"

"Nope," I said.

"Are you okay?" she said.

"Fine," I said.

"Are you sure?"

"Yes."

"Really?"

"I *said* I'm fine," I said without making eye contact.

Our classroom telephone rang. This rarely happened anymore, since for better or worse the parents all had my cellphone number and email address now. The retro ring was a blast from the past, a dinosaur. Someday our classroom phone would be gone completely, off to join the AV carts, the mimeograph machines, the dot matrix paper, the fax machines, the rolodexes, the manual typewriters, the hand-stamped due date cards for library books.

"Polly," the office manager's disembodied voice said through the tinny speaker. "Phone call for you."

Polly wrinkled her nose, crossed the room to the phone. The beige phone was so old that it even had a curly cord, the kind I used to love to twirl around my finger as I talked, plus a non-remote voicemail system that I had to keep reminding myself to check every once in a while.

Polly picked up the receiver, whispered hello so she didn't distract the kids from their work.

Her freckles jumped out as the color drained from her face. Then her whole face turned red.

"How did you get this number?" she whispered.

She angled her body to face the wall.

"No means no," she said. "I mean it. Stay away from me."

I gathered up the kids and brought them out to their cubbies to start getting ready for dismissal. Papers in backpacks, jackets zipped up, hats on heads, mittens on hands.

"Do you have a minute, Sarah?" Polly asked when she came out to join us.

I smiled sweetly. "Actually I don't, but you might want to try my father."

Twenty-eight

There's an old quote about how holding onto anger is like drinking poison and expecting the other person to die. It's been attributed to everyone from Buddha to Alcoholics Anonymous to Nelson Mandela.

It doesn't really matter who said it first. It's true. Anger filled every inch of me, like the spray insulation that expands with a *whoosh* to seal off all the cracks. I couldn't breathe. And the worst thing about it was that when the negativity rushed in, it pushed all the joy right out.

Polly and I sat at separate ends of our dismissal bench. Once most of the kids had been picked up, Ethan moved over and sat down beside Polly. The two of them talked softly, their heads close together. Ethan rested one hand on Polly's shoulder for an instant, and then it was gone.

We were down to our final pickup. Gulliver's mom pulled up in her mammoth SUV, last but not even late, which was big progress. Polly rocked forward and pushed herself to a standing position, reached out a hand to Gulliver. The two of them walked over to the SUV, Polly opened the back door, gave Gulliver a boost as he climbed in, smiled and waved to Gulliver's mom, shut the door.

A movement caught my eye. Or maybe I simply felt a disturbance in the force field.

Bayberry had a larger parking lot below the school, but the dismissal line snaked up the hill and around a portion of a smaller parking lot, essentially a single row of spaces edged by trees on one side. About halfway down the length of the row, a man leaned back against a pine tree, one foot resting on the bumper of a white car. The car was nondescript, generic.

The man was anything but. He was tall and lean and elegant. He was dressed in jeans, a T-shirt, a hipster black leather jacket, but he somehow managed to look like he'd just changed out of his James Bond tuxedo. He had dark hair with hints of caramel, velvety skin the color of coffee with heavy cream. Even from this distance, his eyes glittered a Caribbean blue-green that couldn't possibly be real. Outside of Hollywood, he was the most spectacular looking man I'd ever seen. Maybe even inside of Hollywood.

I realized I was staring. Possibly even panting a bit.

But the man didn't notice. Because he was looking right past me at Polly. I turned to watch her, too, as she slowly walked across the dismissal area on her way back to our classroom. Her winter coat was open, her arms crossed protectively over her baby.

I glanced back at the man again, then walked casually over to sit on the bench next to Ethan.

"Don't look now, but see that guy over there?" I said.

Ethan looked.

"Do you know who he is?"

Ethan stood up. "I'll take care of it. Go talk to Polly."

. . . . .

Polly was sitting at the kiddie table in our classroom, tears streaming down her cheeks.

"I am so, so sorry," I said. "If you want to date my father, it's none of my business. You're both consenting adults, and it's none of my business, and as long as you don't make them change too many diapers, the rest of my family will come around eventually. Did I already say that it's none of my business?"

Polly wiped her eyes with the back of one hand.

I handed her a tissue, because that's what preschool teachers do. I sat down across from her.

"*What?*" Polly said after she finished blowing her nose.

"My father," I said. "I saw you two together at Jake's Seafood last night. And I heard him coming downstairs from your room the other night. Not that it's any of my business."

"*That's* what you're mad at me about?" Polly said.

I shrugged. "Not mad. Exactly."

Polly rested her arms on the table, her head on her arms. "So if things worked out between your dad and me," she mumbled to the tabletop, "that means that technically I could ground you, right?"

I squinted at her.

She lifted her head off the table, started to laugh. "Are you insane? After all you've done for me? Everything in my life seemed so dark and hopeless. You gave me a job, took me in when my rental got flooded. Why in the world would I mess that up by dating your dad?"

I looked at her some more.

"He likes to keep me company. He talks about your mom, and tells me about all of you when you were babies. How you were bald as cue balls, except for Billy Jr."

"Michael," I said.

"And he worries about me getting enough to eat. That's why we went out for fish and chips last night."

I stood up, walked over to our whiteboard, grabbed a purple marker.

"Never assume," I said as I wrote ASSUME in huge letters on the board.

I circled the first three letters. "It makes an ass."

I made big circles around the U and then the ME.

"Out of you and me," I said. "Although in this case, it probably just made an ass out of one of us."

"Ohmigod," Polly said. "That was one of my favorite episodes of *The Odd Couple*. Remember, the one about ticket scalping, and Felix asked to use the blackboard in the courtroom? I couldn't believe he actually said ass on TV—it was such a big deal back then."

"*Benny Hill* did an assume sketch, too," I said. "We had a huge family fight about which show stole it from the other one. My father swore up and down that they both stole it from *Abbott and Costello*. From then on, anytime anyone assumed anything at our house, everybody would start writing all over the place and doing their assume bits, and eventually all hell would break lose."

Polly smiled. "I can't even imagine how amazing it would be to be a part of a family like yours."

I shrugged. "It's loud. And occasionally obnoxious. No, that's a lie. More than occasionally obnoxious."

"But the unconditional love you all have. That's gold. I'd give anything to give that to this baby." Polly patted her belly. "I have to tell you, the first time your dad asked me to marry him—"

"*What?*" I said. The poison was back.

"I said we weren't dating," Polly said. "I didn't say he didn't ask me to marry him."

"I'm not sure the distinction is quite as significant for me as it is for you," I said.

"Sorry," Polly said. "He just wants to make sure the baby and I are all right."

"It seems to me," I said, "that there are plenty of other people around who could take care of that."

"I'm fine," Polly said. "I'm perfectly capable of taking care of this baby by myself. And I'm certainly not looking for a sugar daddy, if that's what you're thinking."

Ethan knocked on the doorframe, walked into our classroom. I was still standing in front of the white-board, holding the purple marker.

"Wow," he said. "Your kids are way ahead of ours in terms of spelling words. We're still working on cow."

"Funny," I said.

Ethan nodded at the board. "That was actually one of my favorite bits on *The Odd Couple.*"

"Mine, too," Polly said. Polly and Ethan gave each other that look that always made me feel a little bit left out, like they had their own separate world.

"So what happened with the guy?" I asked Ethan. "Who was he?"

"Guy?" Polly said.

Ethan walked over to the kiddie table, sat down beside Polly.

"He was here," Ethan said. "Your ex-husband. At dismissal."

Polly's cheeks turned bright red, then the color drained out of her face, leaving only the polka dots of her freckles behind.

"Holy crap," Polly said. "How the hell did he find out where I work?"

"He probably tracked you through your cell," Ethan said. "It's not that hard."

Polly wiped her nose with the soggy tissue. I handed her a fresh one.

"Thanks," she said. "He kept calling and texting me to say that he was going to be in Boston on business and he wanted to see me. I told him to leave me alone, and then I stopped answering."

Polly looked over at our classroom phone. "And then he called me here. He knows where I work. Ohmigod, what am I going to do?" She looked down at the unmistakable swell of her belly.

"I took care of it," Ethan said. "I told him, Galen, that the baby's mine."

Apparently I wasn't the only one who knew Polly's secret—that her ex was the father of her baby.

"Really?" Polly said.

Ethan nodded. "He's staying at The Inn at Marshbury Harbor. We're picking him up for dinner at 7."

"We?" Polly said. "As in you and me?"

"Seems like," Ethan said.

"How's that going to fly with your girlfriend?" I asked, because it seemed like somebody should.

"I'll get back to you on that," Ethan said.

"You don't need to do this," Polly said. "I'll figure out something else."

"It's done," Ethan said.

Crisis or no crisis, the holiday performance must go on, so the three of us headed to the all-purpose room.

Ethan began hanging a backdrop he'd made out of a painted drop cloth. Polly and I sat cross-legged on the floor on the other side of the room, hot glue gunning dog bones to plastic headbands for the "Dance of the Sugarplum Puppies."

"So," I said. "Would it be inappropriate for me to mention that your wasband is unusually hot?"

"Ha," Polly said. "Usually the first thing people say is *what* is he?"

I picked up a red plastic headband. "I'm embarrassed to say that might have been my second question."

"Galen's a little bit of everything," Polly said. "Ethiopian grandfather and Norwegian grandmother. Scottish-Hawaiian great grandmother on the Ethiopian side. Or something like that. I could never keep it straight. Either that or he kept changing it—his idea of truth was always pretty malleable. He's crazy exotic looking though, isn't he? It's like a genetic fluke. Those turquoise eyes are real, too, by the way. I was sure they were contacts until I started staying over at his place and rummaged through his bathroom."

"So that was the attraction?" I said. "His exotic good looks?"

Polly reached for a green plastic headband. "No. I mean, it's hard to miss that, but he's just one of those people who makes everybody he meets feel like they're the most interesting person in the entire world. He's got that laser focus, you know? When I met him, it was like he melted my soul. Although in hindsight, it might possibly have been another body part."

"Ha," I said. "Don't feel bad. The kids get their body parts mixed up sometimes, too."

"He's like this big, beautiful spider who keeps weaving everyone into his web with flattery. We worked together. He was married. I knew better, but I got pulled in anyway. And then he did the same thing to me with wife number three. People, even strangers, have been falling all over him his whole life. I mean, you have to stand in line to have a crush on him. When he has us, he doesn't want us anymore, and we're just another one of the long trail of crazy bitches trying to get him back. But once we lose interest, he always knows. And then he wants us back."

"Wow," I said. "I just remembered when you told me who the father was, you said something like he's an asshole, but he's got great genes."

Polly shook her head. "Pretty superficial, huh? I guess I thought he might be a better risk than the luck of the draw at the sperm bank. And maybe a part of me thought I deserved something after all the years I spent being sucked in to his relentless need for attention and drama."

I globbed some hot glue on a dog bone. "You might not want to hear this, but you said you wanted a family for your baby, and it occurs to me that you've already got one. Didn't you say your ex has three kids with his first wife, and one with the second?"

"At last count," Polly said. "But, no way. My baby will have unconditional love and stability and absolutely no drama. Which by definition means no Galen."

"So you don't think he even has the right to know?"

Polly shook her head. "Galen only cares about Galen. His only interest in this baby would be as leverage over me. He's a bad idea that feels good for a while, but he always, always lets you down. You can't hang your heart on charm, you know?"

"At some point," I said, "you might have to face the fact that you're depriving your child of not just a father but some pretty exotic step siblings."

"Maybe way, way down the road," Polly said. "When and if I'm sure she or he is old enough to handle it."

"Maybe that makes sense," I said. "Like how old?"

"I don't know," Polly said. "But at least thirty-one."

Twenty-nine

It was long past sunset and the last light had disappeared, but because it was New England in December, it wasn't even 5 P.M. yet. Ethan, Polly and I walked out to the parking lot under the yellow glow of the outdoor lights. Crispy leaves swirled around our feet. I shivered in the cold air, wrapped my suede jacket around me tighter.

Polly's head was swinging back and forth as she scanned the shadowy edges of the parking lot.

"It's okay," I said. "I already checked. He's not out here."

Ethan put his arm around Polly's shoulders. "I think you should leave your car here and ride with one of us. Just to be on the safe side."

"Don't be ridiculous," Polly said. "I wouldn't give him the satisfaction."

"Okay," I said. "Then how about you go first, and I'll follow right behind you."

Polly nodded. I realized we'd all been whispering.

Ethan took his arm back, shrugged. "I'll pick you up about ten minutes before seven."

Polly wound slowly through the backroads of Marshbury. I stayed tight on her tail, as if her ex might come out of nowhere and try to wedge his car between ours. Flecks of snow dotted the windshield, then disappeared as if they'd never been there. Just a hint of winter weather to come, not even enough to bother flicking on the windshield wipers.

When I turned on the radio, David Lee Roth's version of "Just a Gigolo" blasted out, the perfect tribute to Polly's wasband. I hoped the song was playing in Polly's car, too, and she was laughing and singing along with me, a duet stretched between two cars. I flashed on being a kid and playing telephone between two paper cups attached to each other with a string pulled tight, decided to try it out with the kids at school one of these days.

An animal darted into the space between Polly and me. I hit my brakes. Before I got a good look, whatever it was turned around and took off into the woods. Maybe a coyote or a possum or a half-grown fawn. I hoped it wasn't the scruffy little dog, on its way to the beach to scavenge for dinner at the Christmas tree.

There was a full house in the driveway when Polly and I crunched our cars over the crushed mussel shells.

John's car. Johnny's car. Joe's truck. A white work van. The pink ice cream truck.

A generic white sedan.

My breath caught in my throat as I pulled in behind the white car. Under the glare of my headlights, I could see a bar code sticker on the rear window—easy scanning for a quick pick up or return. No dealer frame with a catchy saying around the license plate. Definitely a rental car. Empty.

"Polly," I whisper-yelled as I jumped out of my car.

Polly stopped, turned to face me.

"That's his rental car," I said. "Galen's," I added as if she might have any doubt who I was talking about.

"How did he find out where I live?" she said.

I shook my head. I had this crazy feeling I'd seen this before on an old television show, and if I could just remember which show, I'd know exactly what to do next. *The Rockford Files? Cagney & Lacey? Murder, She Wrote?*

My second thought was to call Carol. Carol would know what to do. Carol knew everything. After decades of lapsed Catholicism, it was the one miracle I still believed in. But Carol would probably be so busy getting dinner ready for her four kids that she wouldn't answer. Or she'd yell at me.

My final thought was my least preferred option: I was going to have to come up with a plan myself.

"Okay," I said. "Go to the trailer, and stay in there with Johnny until I find out what's going on. I'll text you when it's safe to come to the house."

"I'm not afraid of him," Polly said.

"That's good," I said. "Because this is really creepy, and I'm afraid enough for both of us. Now, go."

When I pushed open the kitchen door, Galen was sitting at the scratched pine trestle table with my father. A bottle of John's fancy pants wine was on the table between them, and both of their glasses were full. The two decoy bottles John and I had left on the counter were still sitting there.

My father held up his glass in my direction. "Well, now, look what the cat dragged in. Meet my lovely daughter Carol."

"Sarah," I said. I dropped my teacher bag to the floor, slid out of my suede jacket and threw it over the back of my chair.

"Just making sure you're awake, Sarry girl," my father said, "just making sure you're awake. Say hello to Gaelic. With a nice Irish name like that, I knew we'd be fast friends the minute I bumped into him on Main Street."

I glared at Polly's wasband, just so he'd know I was on to him. He must have driven by the house last night or this morning, seen the cars in the driveway. Maybe he'd picked out my father as the weakest link, followed the pink ice cream truck to fake a coincidental meeting.

When Polly's ex smiled at me, his teeth were even more blindingly white than Ethan's. And those Caribbean eyes were mesmerizing. They couldn't possibly be real. Maybe he'd had some kind of sparkly turquoise lens implant.

"It's Galen," I said. "You do know he's Polly's ex-husband, right, Dad?"

"I most certainly do," my father said. "As our Alfred Lord Tennyson was wont to say, 'I hold it true, whate'er befall;/ I feel it, when I sorrow most;/ 'Tis better to have loved and lost/ Than never to have loved at all.' All by way of saying I was just telling Gaelic here better luck next time. And filling him in about the little lady's and my upcoming nuptials. Given that we're in the family way and all."

I backed up so I was standing out of Galen's line of vision, made a cut sign with my finger across my throat, mouthed *Ix-nay on the baby daddy talk.*

My father ignored me. He threaded his fingers behind his head, leaned back in his chair. "Just when you think love is behind you, you find it again. It's richer. More satisfying. Like a fine wine." He unthreaded his fingers and took a long sip of John's wine.

Galen rolled John's wine around in his glass, took a measured sip.

My father ran a hand through his white mane. "Make sure you leave your address, flutter bum, so the missus and I can pop a birth announcement in the mail to you."

Galen pulled his phone from his pocket, started searching. "Hmm. It says here that flutter bum actually means a good-looking boy."

"Don't let it go to your head," my father said. "One of the biggest surprises in life is that flutter bummery doesn't last forever."

I wasn't sure exactly what was going on, so I couldn't quite think of anything to contribute.

"Casserole, anyone?" I said. I turned on the oven, grabbed the top foil-wrapped rectangle from the pile in the freezer, shoved it the oven.

"All my girls are good cooks," my father said. "Thank the good Lord."

The kitchen door swung open and a gust of cold air blew in along with a few dry leaves. Johnny and Polly followed, Johnny's arm draped protectively around Polly's shoulder.

"Somebody was supposed to wait for a text," I said.

"What are you doing here, Galen?" Polly said. "I told you, stay out of my life."

Johnny reached his hand out to Galen. "Johnny Hurlihy. Poppy's fiancé."

Johnny and Galen shook.

"*What?*" Polly said.

"It's okay, babe." Johnny patted Polly gently on her baby bump. "I think our secret's pretty much out there by now anyway."

My father shoved his chair back, lurched to his feet. "Get your hands off my Miss Polly."

Johnny stepped in front of Polly. "She's not yours, Dad. You've got underwear older than her, for Chrissakes."

Galen looked back and forth between Johnny and my dad as if he were watching a slow game of pickleball.

My father got nose-to-nose with Johnny. "This is my house, sonny boy, and I make the rules. One, you don't take the Lord's name in vain. B, you don't talk smack about my underwear. And four, you keep your thieving mitts off my Polly."

"Can I get anybody a drink?" I tried. "Wine? Beer? Tea?"

My father threw the first punch. I pulled Polly out of the way. Johnny tackled my father. A chair went over, then thudded along as they dragged it with them.

"Stop," Polly yelled, like that was going to work.

"Anything I can do to help?" Galen said.

"Sure," I said. "Go for it."

Galen stood, took off the hipster leather jacket he was still wearing, held it out to Polly.

"Ha," Polly said. "Like that's ever going to happen again."

Galen shrugged, put his jacket on the back of his chair. He leaned over my dad and Johnny, looking for a place to get a handhold.

My father grabbed Galen around the ankles, yanked.

Galen fell on top of my father and Johnny. Johnny grabbed Galen around the neck.

"This is why we can't have nice things," I said.

We heard a knock on the kitchen door.

"Sorry to be so early," Ethan said as he walked in. "I just wanted to make sure everything was all right."

Ethan noticed the pig pile, recognized Galen.

"Get off them, you piece of crap," Ethan yelled as he reached for Galen.

"I don't like the cut of your jib," my father said. He grabbed Ethan's legs and pulled.

Polly's baby's three wannabe fathers, plus the real one, rolled around on the speckled linoleum floor like a litter of supersized puppies. One of Galen's shoes went flying across the kitchen. It was a beautiful shoe with a red lacquered sole. Even I could tell it was expensive.

"Christian Louboutin," Polly whispered. "I mean, he's always late with his child support payments, but he buys freakin' designer shoes?"

We jumped back as the clump of bodies rolled in our direction. There weren't a lot of punches flying, maybe because it was hard to tell whose fists belonged to whom in such close quarters. I heard the sound of fabric ripping.

"Thoughts?" Polly said.

"I have to warn you," I said. "Most of our holidays end up this way."

Polly shrugged. "Men. You can't live with 'em, and you keep forgetting to live without 'em."

We heard work boots clomping down the center staircase. Horatio bolted into the kitchen, barking ferociously and nipping at Galen's stockinged foot. Dogs can always tell the good guys from the bad guys.

"Hey," Galen yelled. "Get that ferocious mutt away from me."

"Did you hear that, big guy?" I said to Horatio. "He called you ferocious."

John and Joe were right behind Horatio.

Joe waved his nail gun. "What the hell kind of family did I marry into?"

"Wait," I said. I ran over to the kitchen sink and grabbed the kitchen sink sprayer.

"Good thinking," Joe said. "Fewer stitches that way."

John pulled Horatio out of the way. I turned the water on full blast and sprayed.

All four of Polly's suitors sputtered and rolled away from one another. They sat on the floor, shaking the water off like dogs who'd just finished a swim in the ocean.

John disappeared. He came back with four beach towels from the linen closet and passed them out.

"Is that my wine?" John said as he came over to stand beside me.

"Sorry," I said. "We'll hide it better next time."

John pointed. "Who's that guy?"

"Galen," I said. "Polly's ex."

Galen waved. John waved back. John and I looked at each other, looked away.

"So," I said to Polly. "Galen and I are going to have a little chat in the other room. How about you read your other three admirers the riot act while we're gone."

"Done," Polly said.

Thirty

Galen sat on a living room armchair and retied his fancy red-soled shoe. When he wrapped his beach towel around his neck, he managed to make it look almost like an ascot. Carly Simon immediately started singing "You're So Vain" to me in one of my favorite auditory hallucinations. I botched the lyrics I heard as I always did, substituting *your scarf it was an ascot* for *your scarf it was apricot*. Carly's version was more colorful, but I thought mine held up pretty well.

I took a moment to look around for signs of Hamburger before I sat on the couch across from Polly's ex.

Galen smiled his radioactive smile, focused in on me with his technicolor eyes. He was seductive, charismatic, almost likable even though I knew better. If he ran for office, he'd win in a heartbeat.

"Beautiful home you've got," he said. "The period details are incredible. Must be what, early 1900s?"

"1890," I said.

He had the kind of smile that lights up sad, lonely hearts. His attention was riveted on me, as if I were about to say something absolutely fascinating. And whatever came out of my mouth, he'd make me feel sexy and maybe almost beautiful by hanging on every word.

If I'd run into Polly's ex after my long empty marriage had finally disintegrated completely, once my family had pushed me, kicking and screaming, back out into the dating world, I would have been ripe for the picking. I would have fallen for him. Hook, line and sinker. The flatter. The flirt. The thrill of the hunt. It would have been all fun and games until I opened up my long-buried heart. And he stomped it.

I thought about the notebook I'd kept while I was trying to navigate the personal ads. A page for each of my dates, rated with hand-drawn stars and flags. So many red flags billowed across the tops of the pages that it looked like a sale at a car dealership.

Maxwell, the guy who said he looked a little bit like Hemingway. George from Hanover, who was looking for a relationship one day a month, no strings, no commitments. Ben, who grew his own alfalfa sprouts. The guy looking for a plus-sized Woman, that I'd briefly considered partly because I liked the way he capitalized Woman, but mostly because I could eat a lot. Ray Santia, the former almost hockey star I'd almost slept with.

Bob Connor, the parent of one of my students I shouldn't have slept with. His tousled curls, his green green eyes and twisted front tooth, his bad little boy allure. The way he'd charmed the pants off of me, literally. And then, *wham-bam-thank-you-ma'am*, it was as if once he'd slept with me, I no longer existed. There was simply one fewer name on the list of women he hadn't been with yet.

These guys were amateurs next to Polly's ex. But I'd figured out the Galen lesson already: If it looks too good to be true, it is.

Galen nodded as if even my silence was captivating. "You and Polly work together?"

"Yeah."

He smiled some more, the spider lounging back against his web like it was a hammock, knowing he could have me at any moment.

"I'd like to say thank you," I said, "for reminding me how lucky I am to have found a nice, normal guy who isn't flashy or smooth or perfect, but who really loves me and is almost always there for me."

Boom. Just like that the light went out behind those eyes. No more frivolities. Galen was completely over me. Restless already.

I could actually see him scrambling for a new angle. *What can I get here?*

Galen crossed his legs, leaned back to control the entire armchair. "Why don't we just do a non-invasive DNA prenatal paternity test since I'm here anyway. Not that I think there's any doubt, but maybe you could grab some samples from those clowns rolling around on the floor while you're at it."

"Good idea. I think we probably have enough alleged fathers to get a group rate." I smiled sweetly. "Don't you just love a bargain?"

We stared at each other. It was a face-off, a dominance game, and there was no way in hell I was letting him be the Alpha. We held our gaze for a second, maybe two. And then Polly's wasband blinked slowly, deliberately, and looked away, making it clear that it was his choice not to play anymore, and a disdainful one at that.

Silence stretched between us, a time-out to regroup.

"Whew," I said. "One more child support payment. How much fun would that be. Especially since I've heard that you have a slight tendency to be late on the multiple payments you're already making."

"Ha," he said. "Like she needs it. She did tell you about her trust fund, didn't she?"

Galen got all sincere again. "I hope she's paying you rent. The truth is our Polly has a slight tendency to play the victim, in case you haven't caught on to that."

I felt so greasy that I wanted to excuse myself and go take a quick shower.

"Doesn't matter," I said instead. "The law's the law. And I've got four more siblings like the one you just finished wrestling with on the kitchen floor, but stronger and meaner, and they're all Team Polly. They'd have a blast tracking you down and making sure you paid up. And Ethan, the surfer boy with the limp? He's got some serious rage issues—you should see the other guy."

Galen glared at me. Even if those turquoise eyes were real, he was a total fake.

His look changed to one of total boredom. "What do you want?"

"I want you to leave Polly alone. I want you to pretend you never met her, unless you hear from her telling you otherwise."

He considered this, nodded.

"And I want you to be there for the kids you do have. It's a lifetime commitment, and it really messes them up when you don't stick to it. I'm a preschool teacher, I know. I see it."

Galen checked his watch, which looked to me like a fake Rolex. "Do you think that dinner invitation is still on?"

I was just debating whether or not to invite him to stay for dinner so I could spit in his casserole when my father strolled into the living room.

"So this is where the slither meets the slime," my father said.

My dad's bushy white eyebrows were sticking out all over the place, like Santa gone wild. He had a Band-Aid over one of his knuckles and a long rip in the knee of his chinos. Other than that, he looked pretty good.

"Everything okay out there?" I said.

"Fine and dandy," my father said, "just fine and dandy. We make up fast in the Hurlihy clan. First one to throw a punch buys a round of subs at Maria's, so that's where I'm taking them in the ice cream trunk now. The plan is to see if we can burp the entire alphabet between here and the sub shop, like the boys and I used to do back in the day. Care to come along, flutter bum?"

"I'm going to take a hard pass on that," Polly's ex said.

"Well, Gaelic," my father said. "Then I'm afraid we're going to have to escort you and your little white rental car back to your hotel room."

"Just to make it clear," Galen said, "I'm only driving that car because the rental agency was out of sports cars."

. . . . .

Polly, John and I sat around the kitchen table, big plates of casserole in front of us. The animals had all been fed. The house was quiet. The kitchen floor was dry. The beach towels had finished their wash cycle and were bouncing around in the dryer.

"Just to make it clear," I said in my best Galen imitation, "the only reason I'm driving that little white car is that the rental agency was out of sports cars."

"He always has a story," Polly said. "Sorry about that," she added for like the eighth time.

"That bun in your unmarried oven is going to be one ridiculously cute baby though," I said.

"Thanks," Polly said. "I think. I'm banking on the fact that being a psychopath is more nurture than nature, and the baby will turn out fine."

"Those shoes of his with the red soles were pretty great," John said.

"What size are you?" Polly said. "Maybe I can sneak in and grab them while he's in the shower."

John and I laughed. I took a bite of casserole. The casseroles were all starting to blur, as if yesterday's casserole had stayed on my taste buds, along with the casserole from the day before that and the one before that. I could almost even imagine never eating another casserole again once things got back to normal.

"Well," I said. "He was everything I thought he'd be, and less."

"Exactly," Polly said. "He's an empty shell. What can I say? I got got. The struggle is real, y'all."

I reached for my seltzer. "He was certainly one cool customer, as my dad would say."

Polly took a bite of her casserole, a sip of her milk. "My parents left me a small trust fund. I'm just so grateful that they structured it in such a way that, as hard as he tried, he couldn't manage to get his hands on it. It killed him."

"Smart parents," John said.

"His first wife," Polly said, "told me he once rented out an apartment he didn't even own. It belonged to a neighbor who was away for a few months, and he knew where the key was. She said she found out and left him over that, but eventually he talked her into coming back."

"There's a technique called hoovering," John said, "that's used by narcissistic con artists to suck their victims back into relationships with them. Basically, they pretend they've changed and they can't live without you. It's named after the Hoover vacuum cleaner, both because the hoovering person not only desires to suck you back into the relationship, and because he or she will always ultimately treat you like dirt. I worked for a guy like that once. He kept trying to manipulate me into doing things that could land us both in jail."

"Wow," Polly said. "I'll never look at my vacuum cleaner the same way again. I wish I knew about this hoovering thing earlier—it might have saved me a few bad years."

I looked at John. "You never told me that story."

He shrugged. I shrugged. I'd completely forgotten why we were mad at each other.

"So," I said to Polly. "How did it go with the three faux fathers?" My preschool teacher's brain immediately kicked in. Despite myself, I started singing in my head to the tune of "Three Blind Mice." *Three faux fathers, three faux fathers, see how they run, see how they run. They all rolled over the kitchen floor—*"

"So sweet," Polly said. Tears came out of nowhere and cascaded down Polly's cheeks. She wiped them away, but not before one plopped on top of her casserole.

I handed her a paper napkin.

"Sorry," she said. "Hormones. I thanked them all for their kind attention, which I wish I could bottle and share with all the other pregnant women in the world. And then I told them to back off."

"How'd they take it?" I took another bite of casserole. For something almost completely unidentifiable, it was oddly addicting.

Polly smiled. "Your dad seems particularly concerned about the baby having a father's name on the birth certificate. I told him I already have one: Toby Continued."

"Ha," I said. "You're going to absolutely rock this baby. Pun intended."

Thirty-one

"Hi," I said as I walked into the cat room in my sleep T-shirt.

"Hi," John said. He was standing in the only available floor space holding a little red and blue plastic clicker. I looked back and forth between the mattress on the floor and the old plaid couch, decided to take a seat on the couch.

"Sit," John said. Horatio sat. John clicked the clicker and gave Horatio a dehydrated chicken treat.

"Ohmigod," I said, "Will you look at that?"

Pebbles and all four kittens were sitting on the floor over by the bookcase, waiting for treats.

"Maybe it's just a coincidence," John said. He gave the cats each a treat anyway.

"Sit," John said again. Horatio sat. The cats sat, too. John clicked the clicker and passed out treats all around.

John made a circle with one hand. Horatio walked around in a circle. Pebbles and the kittens did, too. John clicked and gave out more treats.

"Wow," he said. "I guess they've been paying attention all along. I've been doing short sessions with Horatio for a while now. Something to do while we're trying to stay out of the workmen's way."

"That's amazing," I said. "Maybe we can start posting YouTube videos and quit our jobs as soon as they're famous."

John sat on the floor beside Horatio and extended his legs in front of him. He tapped the floor on the other side of his legs. Horatio jumped over his legs. Oreo galloped over and half walked/half jumped over John's legs, too. The other cats looked like they wanted to, but stayed where they were.

John clicked and gave Horatio and Oreo each a treat.

"Aww," I said. "But I think the others should get treats, too, just for considering it."

"That will only confuse them," John said. "They need to associate the behavior with the reward."

"Fine," I said. "Then make them sit again, so they don't look so sad."

John did one more round of sitting, clicking, and treats, then he hid the treat bag out of sight in the closet. The kittens immediately ran over and started scratching at the door.

"It won't be long," John said, "before they figure out how to open doors."

I sighed. "I wish they'd stay kittens forever. And I wish you and I would stop being mad at each other."

John sighed, too, sat down beside me on the couch. "It's late."

"I know. But the longer we don't talk to each other, the more I get used to it and that scares me. And I honestly can't even remember what the whole thing is about anymore."

When John turned to look at me, the light hit his glasses. He had a big smudge across one lens, possibly ricochet from when I sprayed everybody down on the kitchen floor.

I reached over and slid his glasses off his face, polished them with the hem of my T-shirt, handed them back.

"Thanks," he said. "I think that's the most domestic thing I've ever seen you do."

I held out the hem of my T-shirt like a skirt. "See, before you know it I'll be wearing aprons with ruffles."

"I'd settle for a month without thirty days of casseroles," John said.

"30 days hath September," I chanted, "April, June and November. All the rest have 31, except when February is done. Because it only has 28 days I fear, and 29 in each leap year."

I cleared my throat. "Sorry. But may I point out that if you're sick of casseroles, you know where the grocery store is."

"And I'm perfectly happy to cook. I can understand your father's casseroles coming in handy while we're under construction, but lately I've been wondering whether you'd be just as happy living like this forever."

"Um," I said. "No. Yes. Maybe?"

"How about this? On Sundays we get a menu plan for the week. I do most of the cooking, and you can be sous chef and navigate the dishwasher."

"Sure," I said. "As long as we can cherry pick the best of the casseroles. I mean, why waste them? And a steady diet of cooking would get old fast, too."

John nodded. "Deal. And let's add dinner out once a week to the mix."

"Preferably out of town so we don't run into my family."

We knuckle bumped on it. I taught him the Michael Jackson and we knuckle bumped again.

"Thanks," he said. "I always wished I could moonwalk."

We sat there quietly while we decided whether to quit while we were ahead or keep going.

"We made this decision," John said. "These decisions. To build a life together, to buy this house. We can talk about improving things, but what I'm not okay with is the way as soon as things get the least bit challenging, you're ready to give up on us."

Tears surprised me by streaming down my cheeks. "I think," I whispered, "when things get tough, I might want to leave you before you can leave me."

John wiped my tears away. "I won't leave you. Ever. I'm in one hundred percent. And I'm an accountant, so you can count on that."

I laughed. "It's a good thing you're not a comedian, because that's a really bad joke. And I won't leave you either."

He leaned over and kissed me. "Good to hear."

"But sometimes when things get tough and I'm spinning, it has to be okay to share my feelings, you know? I don't need you to try to fix things. Or fix me. I just want you to listen. And maybe talk me down from the ledge."

"Intellectually I get all that. Stop trying to fix each other. Celebrate our differences. Be responsible for our own happiness."

"Love is patient, love is kind," I said.

"Love is blind," he said.

"You're a poet and you don't even know it," I said.

"Love means never having to say you're sorry," he said.

"Love hurts," I sang.

"Love the one you're with," he sang.

"Okay, where were we?" I said.

John shrugged. "Not trying to fix things is easier said than done. How about I'll work on it while you're working on your casserole withdrawal."

I nodded. "If you think about it, you have to be pretty damn lucky to have these problems. If we had bigger problems, we'd never get to them. This is the good life, you know? We've got it. Now we just have to not screw it up."

"Here-here," John said. We kissed, long and leisurely, like floating out to sea on a sunny summer day. Except that we were sitting on an ancient plaid couch in the cat room with five cats and one dog staring at us.

Horatio plopped down at John's feet. Sunshine and Squiggy crawled up on my lap. John and I both yawned.

"One more thing?" I said. "You know the scruffy dog on the beach? I can't get it out of my mind. What's if it's still running around loose? It could freeze to death. A coyote could get it."

"Or the Marshbury Animal Control officer could have caught it when I called and it has a good home by now."

"Maybe," I said. "But what's really bothering me is that you said you wanted a dog to be a companion for Horatio, but when a perfectly good dog crossed our path that was a great match for Horatio—"

"I love your big heart. But you can't take in every animal you see."

"But you're planning to get a dog anyway. I'm saying rather than throw money at a dog whose breed I can't even pronounce, let's fill the slot with one that no one else in the whole wide world but us might give a chance to."

John crossed his arms over his chest. "We can't just go around scooping up random dogs. And we certainly can't bring a strange dog into a house filled with other animals. First it has to be seen by a vet—"

"It could stay up in my dad's man cave until we're sure it's okay. Or out in the trailer with Johnny. They've both had their shots."

I thought it was a pretty good line, but John didn't even laugh. He just shook his head.

"I need to think about it," he said finally. "Speaking of Johnny, how did it go with his wife?"

"Smooth change of subject," I said. "And excellent question."

. . . . .

I knocked on the trailer door. Then I actually waited for Johnny to open it for me, which in our family passes for extreme civility.

"Hey," he said. He stepped back to let me in. He was holding an unopened beer bottle against one eye, which was well on its way to becoming a shiner.

"You okay?"

He nodded. "You know Dad. No decent punches at all, but he's got a mean right elbow."

We took seats at the tiny dinette. Johnny peeled the plastic wrap off an individual slice of processed cheese, stuffed it into his mouth.

"Eww," I said. "How can you eat that stuff?"

He shrugged. "I'm practicing being single."

"Thanks for pretending to be Polly's baby daddy," I said. "I'm sure she appreciated the gesture."

"You know me, act first, think later." Johnny spun the beer bottle around to find a colder spot, pressed it gently to his eye. "I like Poppy a lot. And given my current circumstances, being her wingman seemed like a better use of my time than, say, killing myself."

"Don't even joke about that."

"Don't worry. I talk big, but I've got no follow through." He put the beer down, ran his hand through his hair. "You know, I used to daydream that Kim was dying. Not painfully or anything."

"Perfectly normal. I used to daydream that I accidentally put Nair in Kevin's shampoo so his hair would fall out and he'd *think* he was dying. Actually, I might possibly have done it. Just once though."

"I'll file that one away in case I need it. Anyway, I guess I'm kind of relieved Kim shook things up first so I didn't have to. Also kind of pissed. Occasionally apoplectic even."

"Good high-end vocabulary word. How did it go with you and Kim at Driftwood?"

"Okay. I think she was expecting drama, but I stayed calm. She didn't mention the work husband and neither did I. I think she's living at our house alone though. We're going to spend Christmas with the kids there. Beyond that, I have no idea."

"It's a start," I said. "Hey, I'm sorry that I threw all that childhood stuff at you. I meant it, but I apologize for the timing."

I once read that evolutionary scientists say there's a biological explanation for the force of the sibling bond. Siblings share half of their genes, so that mutual connection and devotion is always lurking just below the surface, even when you lose it for a while.

Johnny reached over from the dinette and opened the postage stamp-sized refrigerator. He pulled out two water bottles, handed one to me.

"I'm sorry I treated you like that," he said. "I may not have always been the best brother, but I would have laid down my life for you in a second if anyone else messed with you. Still would."

"I appreciate that," I said. "And ditto."

When Johnny smiled, he looked just like our dad. "I'm sorry I just showed up here after not being around very much all these years."

I took a long gulp of water. Even if I was exhausted tomorrow, at least I wouldn't be dehydrated. "I always thought of you as the family escape artist, the one who got away."

"I guess I always knew you guys were there for me if I needed you." Johnny looked around the trailer. "Even if you wouldn't let me all the way into the house."

I laughed. "The second John and I move in to our new master suite, you can totally take over the cat room."

"Great." Johnny held his water bottle to his eye. "Not to get all mushy or anything, but hang onto that guy, okay? He really loves you. It's all over him."

Thirty-two

No matter how early you arrived at a Bayberry Holiday Performance, coats, purses, nannies, and the occasional baby in a carrier would already be sprawled across the best seats. These items were planted as place holders by families who were either entitled or sneaky, or perhaps a hybrid of the two. Or maybe it was just the preschool version of camping out to get the best seats at a rock concert. While their seats were being saved, sometimes the families milled around in the all-purpose room, chatting with other families or talking on their cellphones. Sometimes they had the audacity to go out for a quick bite.

The first row of seats was reserved for Kate Stone and the teachers who weren't on the holiday performance committee. In part, this was a gesture of respect. Mostly it was to keep them close enough to the stage to intervene at lightning speed if necessary. The reserved seats were individually marked with poster board signs. Just to be sure there was no room for misinterpretation, brightly colored yarn was wrapped around the entire section. A large RESERVED sign hung from the yarn enclosure.

Lorna shook her head, grabbed a winter coat and a designer purse that had invaded the reserved section to save two seats. Since the purse alone was probably worth more than a teacher's salary for an entire month, there was no doubt at all that the items didn't belong there. Lorna wound up, got ready to pitch them in the direction of the cheap seats.

Pandora's mother came running up and held out her hand. "Oh, well, it was worth a try." She gave Lorna and me a dazzling smile. "At least I didn't let Pandora drive her Barbie jeep in and park it in the back of the room, which is what she wanted to do."

"And you wonder why teachers drink," Lorna said, possibly a little too loudly, as Pandora's mother walked away.

I waved at two Bayberry graduates with younger siblings in tonight's performance who were passing out programs for us. I tried to guess how old they were now. Third grade? Fourth?

Ethan peeked out between the stage curtains. I checked my teacher's watch with the big analog face and nodded to him. Ethan disappeared again. Lorna and I walked to the back of the room. I flicked the light switches repeatedly. "Please silence all personal electronic devices, including laptops and cell phones," Lorna and I repeated over and over again like flight attendants.

The audience—parents and grands and siblings—chittered and chattered away as everybody took their seats.

I felt John's presence before I saw him. My heart actually skipped a beat when I picked him out in the back row, dressed in a charcoal gray suit and red tie. He looked handsome and intelligent and kind and everything you'd want the guy you were hoping to spend the rest of your life with to be. It had been his idea to come watch the performance. *I want to see you shine*, he'd said.

In all the years we were married, my wasband had never once come to a Bayberry performance. Although, of course, my life being my life, he was here now with his replacement wife to watch their twins perform. Not only that, but he was waving at me from his seat. I ignored him, smiled at John.

My dad and Johnny slid into the seats beside John. *Behave*, I mouthed to them. I wasn't even pissed that I knew they'd come more for Polly than for me.

Kate Stone and the teachers filled in the front row. They wound up the brightly colored yarn and piled up the poster board signs and handed it all to me like a neatly wrapped Christmas present.

"Thanks," I said.

"Break a leg," my bitch of a boss said.

"Not with our health insurance," Lorna mumbled as we walked away.

The Bayberry students were jammed into the green room, which was a long narrow room off the backstage area. They were sitting cross-legged on the floor with their assistant teachers.

Ethan and I smiled at everybody. "*Shhh*," we said as we put our fingers to our lips. The kids' eyes lit up as they put their fingers to their own lips and *shhh*-ed.

I walked the third-year students who were playing the two dogs and two cats to the short podium Ethan had made out of repurposed wood pallets, which we'd placed near the front of the stage and off to stage right. They'd stay there and recite their dialog as the song and dance numbers unfurled behind them.

Ethan joined us on stage. When he turned on the microphone attached to the podium, it made a noise like a fart. The students playing the dogs and cats completely lost it. The kids behind us in the green room joined in with an explosion of laughter that carried right out to the audience. The audience started laughing, too. In true preschool fashion, the kids who could fart on command began doing just that.

A putrid odor followed, like rotten eggs crossed with sour milk and tinged with the distinct smell of peanut butter, strong enough to clear a room. Polly tiptoed down the stairs on one side of the stage, holding Griffin by the hand, on the way to Griffin's cubby to find his change-of-clothing bag. Not only wasn't Griffin quite as toilet trained as his parents had led us to believe he was, but apparently he hadn't quite mastered farting on command either.

People were trying to hold their noses without being obvious. Griffin's mom scrunched down in her chair and covered her face with her program as Polly and Griffin passed. Griffin's dad videoed his son's walk of shame with his iPhone.

Everybody was laughing now, performers and audience alike. I wondered if we could get away with calling it a performance and taking our bows now.

Ethan and I each gave the dog and cats a thumbs up, then we walked behind the curtains, where Gloria had the students who were doing the cave kids dance all set up and ready to go.

"What a beautiful world," one of the cats said into the microphone. "If only I had a family to belong to."

"I know," one of the dogs said. "Let's travel through time and place and see if we can all find the perfect homes to live."

"That way we can enjoy all the magical celebrations along the way," the other cat said. "Starting with the first people in the history of the world ever to dance."

"I was supposed to say that part!" the other dog sobbed.

The audience erupted in laughter.

I figured if we opened the curtain fast it might look like it was supposed to be part of the performance. I nodded across the stage to Ethan and we both started pulling the ropes. June crawled out from the side of the curtain to make sure the crying dog was okay.

The cave kids dance was adorable. Lots of knee bending and low swinging arms and hopping around which might have looked a little more frog-like than caveman-like, if not for the animal print fabric wrapped around the dancers.

We moved on to Polly's and my class dance to "Walk Like an Egyptian." Our kids were all dressed in white T-shirts and sweats, except for Griffin whose back-up clothes happened to be red and black plaid, but that was fine. I mean, it was preschool not Broadway. Polly had made gold lamé bands to wrap around their foreheads, smaller serpent-like gold bands for their upper arms.

What our students lacked in finesse they made up for in enthusiasm. They sang along to the record as they bent and straightened their knees and made their pyramid hands go up and down. They formed a single file with minimal shoving. They yelled, "Walk like an Egyptian" at the top of their lungs as they walked through the back door of Ethan's awesome pyramid and out the front door. They took turns climbing up the little stepladder, with a hidden Polly holding their hands, and peering over the red bow on the top of the pyramid for their photo opp moment. When some of their parents guerilla-crawled across the floor with their video cameras and phones to get closer, they looked like wannabe Spielbergs taking a Cross-fit class.

Nobody fell. Nobody cried. Which in the preschool world is a raving success.

Polly leaned over and whispered, "Wow. Just wow. I could spend my whole life doing this."

"Great," I whispered. "Then you can be in charge of the next one."

The audience cheered and howled. The students sang and danced up a storm. Time flew. As soon as each class finished their number, the adults backstage scrambled to attach jingle bells to the kids' shoes with twist ties for our grand finale.

Finally, we were all on stage together. The teachers from the front row came up to join us, along with our bitch of a boss. Pandora's mother moved in to take over one of the front row seats. Several other people followed—parent see, parent do.

We sang and circled around to Woodie Guthrie's "Hanukkah Dance." Then Gloria brought out her ukulele to accompany us as we sang and clapped to "If You're Happy and You Know It, Kwanza's Here." The kids put those jingle bells to work with "Jingle Bell Rock." Ethan slid a green slipcover over his pyramid, and two of his students rolled it center stage and we all danced around it for "Rockin' Around the Christmas Tree." We brought down the house with "We Wish You a Happy Howliday and a Bark-Filled New Year."

"Home sweet home," the dogs and cats yelled, their arms stretched wide. They walked carefully down the stage stairs the way they'd rehearsed and then ran to their parents in the audience.

With perfect timing, the doors to the lobby opened. In walked the shelter dogs, big red bows around their collars, volunteers in Santa hats holding their leashes. Several other volunteers carried out cats in crates with big red bows on top. Everybody *oohed* and *aahed*.

I walked over to the mic. "We hope you enjoyed our howliday tail. And we hope you'll help these animals find their home sweet home, too. All the dogs and cats you see here, the non-preschool ones anyway, are available for adoption through the Marshbury Animal Shelter."

"Maybe some of the preschool ones, too," somebody yelled. Everybody laughed.

The rest of the kids marched down the stage stairs and made a beeline for their families. The families made a beeline for the dogs. My eyes teared up. Sometimes, in your own small way, you really can make a difference in this crazy, crazy world.

And then I saw the scruffy dog from the beach.

Time stopped. The heavens practically opened and the angels almost sang, like in those old religious holy cards my grandmothers used to send us tucked into our birthday cards along with a five-dollar bill.

It really was the scruffy dog, wagging its tail, surrounded by a circle of kids who were petting it. It had been bathed and brushed and had a big red bow around its neck. And yet somehow it was still undeniably scruffy.

I scanned the room looking for John, couldn't find him anywhere in the crowd.

I race-walked across the room, dodging and weaving around parents and kids, and wiggled my way in to get close to the scruffy dog. It seemed to recognize me, or maybe I just wanted to think so. I squatted down, scratched it behind the ears while it licked my face. "I'm so glad you're safe," I whispered.

"Hi," I said to the volunteer on the other side of the scruffy dog's leash. "Does this one have a home yet?"

The woman smiled, adjusted her Santa hat. "I'm happy to say they're all spoken for, and we even have waiting lists for most of them. Of course, all of our adoptions are contingent upon a home visit so we can be sure it's a good match."

"That's great," I said in a sad little voice I didn't even recognize.

I made sure all my students had found their families. Then I walked through the lobby and down the hallway to my classroom. I grabbed my coat and stood outside in the frigid air, leaning back against the building and staring up at the stars. At least it was a good night for stars.

I knew I should be happy for the scruffy dog. I knew I was completely overreacting, that I'd lost a dog and not a baby. But I still felt a hole in my heart, like I'd felt a hole month after month when I found out I wasn't pregnant after all, like I'd felt when my niece Siobhan lost the baby she was going to let John and me adopt. Loss is loss.

John came out of the school and walked toward me, his long overcoat buttoned up.

"You're amazing," he said when he got close. "Truly impressive performance," He whipped out a big bouquet of roses and baby's breath from behind his back. "Brava."

"Thanks." I tried to take in the deep, heady smell of the roses as I sniffed them, to appreciate the gesture, the thought behind it.

"So, we've got her."

"Polly?" I said. "She doesn't need a ride—she drove her own car."

John grinned. It was what my father would call a pie-eating grin, what my sisters and brothers would call a shit-eating grin. Or maybe it was like the proverbial cat who ate that poor canary.

"The scruffy dog," John said. "She's ours, as long as we pass the home visit tomorrow."

"Really?" I said.

"Really. I recognized her right away. I think she recognized me, too, although it could be that I just smell like Horatio."

I held the bouquet out to the side so I could lean in for a kiss.

A clump of kids walked by with their parents. The kids giggled. One of the parents made kissy sounds.

"Are you sure?" I said.

"One hundred percent," he said. "You were right."

I smiled. "The most important three words in any relationship."

John put his arm around me, and we walked toward our cars under a sky full of stars on the eve of winter break.

"Well, I'll be doggoned," I said.

Thirty-three

John and I spent the morning of Christmas Eve moving our things into our finished master suite. Every time I passed through the new door at the top of the big old house's center staircase, I locked and unlocked it a few times, just because I could.

Polly and Johnny helped us carry the king-size mattress up from the cat room. We flopped it onto the bedframe and nudged it around until the mattress and frame were lined up evenly.

Polly tucked her hair behind her ears. "I'd be happy to move down to the cat room. It'll give you guys more privacy up here."

"No way," I said. "That room is perfect for you and the baby. And there's plenty of separation up here."

"Too late anyway," Johnny said. "The cat room is mine. Unless you care to join me?"

Johnny grinned. Polly blushed. Who knew what would happen down the road? A part of me was dying to find out if Polly would end up with Johnny or Ethan or, ugh, even my dad. Another part of me was just hoping we could get through the holidays without anybody else punching anybody out.

We split up the garden shears and kitchen scissors, and the four of us walked around the yard cutting branches from blue spruce and white pine and holly and winterberry. We pulled out the dead plants and filled the pots by the entrances. I poked Pink the flamingo into the middle of the pot outside my dad's man cave to make sure everybody knew where we were celebrating Christmas Eve this year.

My father pulled into the driveway, the pink ice cream truck playing a tinny version of "Let it Snow," the back doors open and the trunk end of a massive Christmas tree sticking out.

"Better late than never," I said.

"Seventy-percent off," my dad said as he jumped out of the truck. "Who says it doesn't pay to wait until Christmas Eve to go tree shopping?"

John and Johnny helped him carry the tree into the man cave, while Polly and I found the ancient boxes of lights and ornaments in the basement.

We rolled up our sleeves and got to work decorating the tree. My mother had given each of the kids a special ornament marked with a dated name tag each year, making every Christmas a stroll down memory lane as we unwrapped the tissue paper that kept them safe. Most of my siblings had taken their ornaments to their adult homes. They'd also started the same tradition with their own kids. But my ornaments were still here, a testament to my late blooming.

I held up a round ornament, hollow and fragile, with a picture of Raggedy Ann skiing on it. A little gold tag said *Sarah, 1973* in my mother's handwriting.

John came over to stand beside me, and I showed it to him. "Next year," I said. "We'll have our own tree. And I'm not even going to think about how we're going to keep the cats from climbing it yet."

My family started arriving in waves. Chinese food had been our Christmas Eve tradition for a while now, so everybody dropped takeout food containers on my father's kitchen counter on the way in. Our dad cranked up his record player and Nat King Cole started singing "The Happiest Christmas Tree." He clapped his hands and the LED lights on his red round vinyl platform bed in the middle of the room flashed from red to orange to blue to purple. The lights on the Christmas tree in the corner glowed a more demure white.

We chowed down on Chinese takeout served on disposable plates with plastic forks. The adults ate standing up. The kids who didn't manage to grab one of the few chairs sat around the edge of the bed.

"Yum," John said as he speared a bite of beef and broccoli. "It's not casserole."

I noticed Polly chatting away with Carol and Christine. Already I could tell they were warming up to her, as if she were some new hybrid of family and friend, a member of the *framily*.

John disappeared after we finished eating and came back with the dogs.

"Hey, everybody," I said. "Meet Scruffy Dog. Isn't she the sweetest thing?"

"You can't call her Scruffy Dog," Carol said. "That's a ridiculous name for a dog."

"I like it," Christine said. "It's like the dog version of Phoebe's Smelly Cat on Friends.

"Anderson Pooper?" Billy Junior said.

"William Shakespaw?" our father said. "On second thought, make that O'Shakespaw."

"She's a girl dog," I said.

"What about Sandra Flea?" Michael said.

Our latest addition was rolling around on the floor with Horatio, happy as a clam and completely oblivious to the name controversy. John and I had bathed her and brushed her and put a bright red collar with a bow on her to match the one Horatio was wearing. But even though her fur was three shades lighter when she was clean, it was still a flyaway dishwater blond and she still looked scruffy.

"Scruffy Dog it is," I said. "It's the perfect name for her."

"Agreed," John said.

We sealed the deal with a Michael Jackson fist bump.

Tomorrow our dad would dress up like Santa and make the rounds to his grandkid's homes to deliver presents. But tonight, we lugged in my father's

Christmas presents from the various vehicles that had transported them over here: a massive TV, a new vinyl recliner with dual cup holders and a heated back massager, a 150-can beverage center mini-fridge. We helped him arrange them in his new man cave.

"You kiddos did all right," he said. "I guess I'll keep you around for another year."

John and I looked at each other. I was pretty sure we were both hoping we'd keep each other around for a lifetime.

. . . .

Be the first to hear about the next book in the Must Love Dogs series and stay in the loop for giveaways and insider extras at ClaireCook.com/newsletter/.

Sarah's Warm Winter Non-Casserole Howliday Salad

(that she absolutely plans to make one of these days)

1 head Romaine lettuce, chopped
1/4 head red cabbage, chopped
1 handful Kale - stems removed and chopped
1/2 cup red onion, finely chopped
2 cloves garlic, finely chopped
2 or 3 large sweet potatoes, peeled and cut into 1-inch cubes
2 tablespoons olive oil
Salt and pepper, to taste
1/2 cup pomegranate arils
1/2 cup dried cranberries
1/2 cup pecans
6 oz. goat cheese crumbles
1 package bacon
3 tablespoons apple cider vinegar
2 teaspoons Dijon mustard
3 tablespoons extra virgin olive oil
2 tablespoons reserved bacon drippings
Honey or maple syrup or stevia to taste
Salt and pepper to taste

Preheat oven to 400 degrees. Place sweet potatoes on a large baking sheet. Drizzle with olive oil and toss until well coated. Sprinkle with onion and garlic and season with salt and pepper. Arrange bacon on another baking sheet. Roast both for 20-30 minutes, stirring occasionally, until sweet potatoes are tender and bacon is crisp. Remove from oven. Add sweet potatoes to large bowl. Mix in pomegranate, cranberries, pecans, and goat cheese. Crumble bacon and add.

Add lettuce, cabbage and kale to bowl and toss gently. Whisk together vinegar, mustard, olive oil, sweetener, bacon drippings, and salt and pepper in small saucepan until warm. Drizzle over salad and enjoy immediately.

. . . . .

Claire

Thank you so much for reading *Must Love Dogs: A Howliday Tail,* Book 6 of the *Must Love Dogs* series! If you enjoyed it, I hope you'll take a moment to tell a friend or leave a short review online. I really appreciate your support!

Just in case you haven't read *The Wildwater Walking Club: Back on Track* yet, I've included an excerpt for you.

Happy Reading!

Excerpt
The Wildwater Walking Club: Back on Track

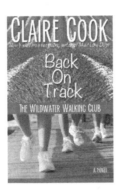

DAY 1
198 steps

· · · · ·

LAVENDER WATER

2 cups distilled water
2 ounces (4 tablespoons) isopropyl alcohol or vodka
15 drops lavender essential oil

*Mix all ingredients and pour into a glass container
you've sterilized by placing it in boiling water for 4 to 5
minutes. Fill a small spray bottle and shake before
spritzing sheets and pillowcases to release tension and
encourage calm.*

· · · · ·

313

On the one-year anniversary of the day I became redundant, I woke up between crisp white sheets I'd sprayed with a new batch of homemade lavender water before hanging them out to dry on my backyard clothesline. I took a moment to inhale the invigorating fragrance of fresh summer air mixed with the soothing caress of lavender.

"It's okay," I whispered to the dark blur of my ceiling. "I still have six months of base pay and benefits left. I don't need to panic. Yet."

As a positive affirmation designed to get my morning off on the right foot, even I knew it could use some work.

"Every day in every way I'm getting better all the time," I whispered.

I gave the sheets another reassuring sniff. "Amazing opportunities exist for me in every avenue of my life," I tried.

"Every little thing is going to be all right," I whisper-sang in my best Bob Marley imitation.

My best Bob Marley imitation wasn't much, so I lip-synched to an imaginary version of Bobby McFerrin's "Don't Worry, Be Happy" playing in my head.

I'd completely forgotten I wasn't alone until Rick rolled over in my bed. I chose to see this not as proof of my lack of focus on our relationship, but as evidence that I was getting comfortable in said relationship. I wiped an index finger across the corners of my lips in case I was getting so comfortable that I'd inadvertently drooled in my sleep. I cupped the palm of one hand and blew into it to assess my level of morning breath.

"Hey," I whispered.

A small screen glowed softly as he held his phone above us.

I got ready to pull the sheets over my head in case just-woke-up selfies were a new thing.

Rick swung both legs over the side of the bed and reached for his clothes. He put his phone down on the bedside table and pulled on his boxer briefs and jeans.

Rick and I had met at a series of small group outplacement counseling classes offered by a company called Fresh Horizons that had been a part of our buy-out packages. The classes had seemed helpful at the time, but I also had to admit that almost a year later, we were both still unemployed, or at least underemployed.

Before we'd taken our respective buyouts, I'd been a Senior Manager of Brand Identity at Balancing Act Shoes. Rick had been some kind of IT ethical hacking wizard at a company that helped financial institutions, as well as the occasional political party, identify their website vulnerabilities. Because the word *wizard* had actually been in his official job title, I always pictured him sitting at his computer behind a red velvet curtain, shirtless and wearing a pointy white wizard hat with Senior Overlord of Ethical Hacking emblazoned across the brim in gold letters. It was sexy, in a geeky kind of way.

You could say that Rick's and my former companies had unwittingly played cupid and brought us together. Or because we'd both taken buyouts, you could say that maybe like really did attract like. But then again, you could also say that two people as messed up as we were right now had absolutely no business attempting a relationship until they got their rebound career paths figured out.

A shadowy Rick slid into his flip-flops and yanked his T-shirt over his head.

"Hey," I said again. I was romantic like that. "What's up?"

He didn't seem to hear me. Maybe he was sleepwalking. Or at least sleepdressing.

Rick picked up his phone again and held it arm's distance away. He gazed at it as if it were some kind of magic orb. Or as if someone really important was on the other end, and he didn't want to chance losing his phone before he could take the call privately.

Then he flip-flopped out of the bedroom without even glancing in my direction. A long moment later, my front door clicked shut.

"This can't be good," I whispered.

. . . . .

I stood on my front steps and watched puffy white clouds and soft blue sky jostle for territory above picture perfect green trees. I swatted a mosquito.

I did a time check: 8:05. The deal was that if my walking partners hadn't joined me by now, I'd head out on our regular route without them. I'd start off slowly to give them a chance to catch up, in case one or both was running late instead of simply blowing me off.

I sat down on the top step and retied one of my laces. I was wearing a pair of the sneakers I'd bought just in the nick of time before my employee discount expired. This particular model was called the Walk On By. It was strictly a women's model, and I'd been part of the team that had positioned it as the shoe every woman needed to walk away from the things that were holding her back and toward the next exciting phase of her life. *Shed the Outgrown. Embrace Your Next Horizon. Walk On By.*

I'd logged lots of miles in these sneakers, but I wasn't sure I'd gotten much closer to that next exciting phase of my life.

After I'd been tricked into taking a buyout from Balancing Act Shoes and dumped by the guy who'd tricked me in one fell swoop, I'd wallowed for a while. But even rock bottom doesn't last forever, and eventually I was all wallowed out. At that point I'd somehow managed to get back up on my feet and start walking. Before long two of my neighbors, Tess and Rosie, joined me.

My house was the smallest of five houses built on the grounds of a working lavender farm when the owners decided to sell off some of their property. As my realtor had explained it to me, if you imagined a pie, the original house still owned half, and the five newer houses each had a pie-shaped slice of the other half.

Rosie lived directly behind me on the original lavender farm. I lived on the middle pie slice. Tess lived on a slightly larger slice next to me. The street Tess and I lived on was called Wildwater Way, although there was neither any noticeable wildness nor water in the immediate vicinity. The three of us called ourselves The Wildwater Walking Club, which was a little goofy, but so what.

I took a moment to retie my other shoelace, even though it didn't actually need it.

Walking solo today would make me feel virtuous. Perhaps even a tad superior. I'd head for the beach and fill my lungs with great big gulps of life-affirming salt air. I thought about how good I'd feel once I found my rhythm and the endorphins started to kick in. How I'd be strengthening my bones and muscles. Preventing heart disease, high blood pressure, type 2 diabetes. Improving my balance, my coordination, even my mood.

I extended my non-dominant wrist, the one wearing my Fitbit. I twisted my arm back and forth, and back and forth some more, for as long as I could take it.

My faux walk complete, I swore softly and went back to bed.

DAY 2
231 steps

I'm not going to think about Rick. I'm not going to think, period.

Apparently I'm not going to walk either.

Just when I thought I was doing so well.

DAY 3
54 steps
Why is it that my life is always two steps forward and one long pathetic slide back?

DAY 4
132 steps

I know what I'll do. I'll create a lavender ice cream flavor for Ben & Jerry. I'll call it Lavender Fields Forever. They'll love it. They'll love me. The three of us will live happily ever after.

But first I have to try all their other ice cream flavors. Research.

DAY 5
1179 steps

I contemplated the weeds in my garden as I circled my spoon around and around in a pint of Ben & Jerry's Hazed & Confused. Then I took a massive bite and let the hazelnut and chocolate iciness melt in my mouth while I checked my Fitbit. 38 steps without moving a foot. Not bad.

I contemplated the weeds some more. They appeared to be coexisting happily with all three varieties of my lavender—Grosso, Hidcote and Munstead. When Rosie had started my lavender garden for me, she'd told me that the trick to taking care of lavender is not to overlove it. Not much danger of that happening.

I stroked Grosso's foliage to release its feisty fragrance, which was laced with a hint of camphor. I loved its tall, brave, pointy stems and the way the whole plant stretched gracefully and unapologetically, not afraid to take its full space in the world. I widened my own stance and tried to access my inner Grosso.

I racked up 23 additional steps of ice cream-stirring mileage. I sighed a time or two, checked to see if sighing registered on my Fitbit. No such luck.

As soon as I heard Tess's car pulling into her driveway, I bent over and yanked a weed just so she wouldn't think I'd noticed her. I stayed low until the whirring sound of her garage door closing stopped.

Tess and I had been doing a lot of this kind of ignoring lately. Waiting until the other one brought in her mail before checking our own mailbox. Making sure the coast was clear before we headed out to our adjacent backyards. Rosie was easier to avoid since a buffer of woods separated us, but I was pretty sure Rosie and I had both pretended not to see each other at the grocery store late one afternoon.

Dodging one another had turned into almost as much of a workout as walking together every day had been.

When I was vertical again, I juggled the ice cream I was holding and spoon-fed myself some Chocolate Therapy. I tried to separate the taste of the chocolate ice cream from the tastes of the other ingredients, chocolate cookies and chocolate pudding. As if somehow this level of discernment might lead me to a deeper understanding of my life, or lack thereof.

One arm was freezing from hugging three pints of ice cream and the other was getting tired from all that twisting. I put the Ben & Jerry's down on a grassy spot while I switched my Fitbit to my other wrist.

I racked up some more mileage by twisting my fresh arm back and forth.

"Why, Noreen Kelly," Tess's voice said behind me.

I jumped.

"Are you actually cheating your Fitbit *and* eating ice cream for breakfast at the same time?"

I ignored her and pulled another weed.

Tess put on her reading glasses so she could get a closer look at the Ben & Jerry's on the ground. "Ooh, Empower Mint—I don't think I've tried that one yet."

Three chickens emerged from the wooded path that connected Rosie's and my properties. They cut across my backyard in a well-choreographed row. I was pretty sure they were making a beeline for my ice cream.

"Yikes," I yelled. "The Supremes."

"Rod Stewart's right behind them," Tess yelled.

I scooped up the Ben & Jerry's containers from the ground and held them over my head.

The hens surrounded us. Rod, their rooster, stood off to one side for reinforcement.

"Come on, you guys," Tess said. "Cluck off."

The chickens kept circling.

Even chicken decisions were beyond me right now. "What do you think?" I asked Tess. "Should I let them split one pint, and then you and I can have the other two? Although I'm pretty sure I've read that dairy is bad for chickens."

Tess shrugged. "And then there's always the issue of ice cream headaches."

"Good point. Although maybe we could just warn them to eat slowly."

"There you are," Rosie yelled as she jogged our way shaking a box of Kashi Good Friends. As soon as they heard the sound of their favorite cereal, The Supremes ditched Tess and me and Ben & Jerry and headed for their owner.

"I'll be right back," Rosie yelled, still shaking the cereal box. The Supremes followed her in a single file, Rod Stewart hot on their heels. "And thank you for not giving them any of that. Poultry diarrhea is not a pretty sight."

Tess and I looked at each other. "Eww," Tess said. "Thank you for that lovely image."

I nodded. "Yeah, I know. It's almost enough to make me throw away the rest of this ice cream."

And then I dug back into the Hazed and Confused.

"Hey," Tess said. "You're not going to hog all that to yourself, are you?"

"Oh, cluck off," I said.

. . . . .

Keep reading! Download your copy of *The Wildwater Walking Club: Back on Track* or order the paperback. Find out more at ClaireCook.com

Be the first to find out when the next book comes out, and stay in the look for giveaways and insider extras. Sign up for my newsletter at ClaireCook.com/newsletter.

Acknowledgments

It's so hard to believe that this is my 18th book. How can it be! If you have a buried dream, I hope you'll go for it, too. It really is never too late to shine on!

I'm so grateful to my incredible readers for giving me the gift of this midlife career and for allowing me to write the books I'd love to read. Thank you for cheering me on, sharing my books with your friends and family, and making me feel that we're all in this together.

A big thank you to my Facebook and Twitter followers for jumping in to be my research assistants time and again. The details you share are often surprising and always helpful.

Huge thanks to Ken Harvey, Jack and Pam Kramer, and Beth Hoffman for your huge hearts and sharp eyes and for helping me make this a better book. Your support means everything.

Thanks to Pebbles, Sunshine, Squiggy, The Great Catsby, and Oreo for feline inspiration. And to granddogs Coco and Kobe for canine inspiration.

Thanks and more thanks to Jake, Garet, and Kaden for always being there when I need you.

ABOUT CLAIRE

I wrote my first novel in my minivan at 45. At 50, I walked the red carpet at the Hollywood premiere of the adaptation of my second novel, *Must Love Dogs*, starring Diane Lane and John Cusack. I'm now the *New York Times* bestselling author of 18 books. If you have a buried dream, take it from me, it is NEVER too late!

I've reinvented myself once again by turning *Must Love Dogs* into a series and writing my first nonfiction books, *Never Too Late: Your Roadmap to Reinvention (without getting lost along the way)* and *Shine On: How To Grow Awesome Instead of Old*, in which I share everything I've learned on my own journey that might help you in yours.

I've also become a reinvention speaker, so if you know a group that's looking for a fun and inspiring speaker, I hope you'll send them in my direction. Here's the link: http://ClaireCook.com/speaking/. Thanks!

I was born in Virginia, and lived for many years in Scituate, Massachusetts, a beach town between Boston and Cape Cod. My husband and I have moved to the suburbs of Atlanta to be closer to our two adult kids, who actually want us around again!

I have the world's most fabulous readers and I'm forever grateful to all of you for giving me the gift of this career. Shine On!

xxxxxClaire

HANG OUT WITH ME!
ClaireCook.com
Facebook.com/ClaireCookauthorpage
Twitter.com/ClaireCookwrite
Pinterest.com/ClaireCookwrite
Instagram.com/ClaireCookwrite
Linkedin.com/in/ClaireCookwrite

Be the first to find out when my next book comes out and stay in the loop for giveaways and insider excerpts: ClaireCook.com/newsletter.

73749095R00200

Made in the USA
Lexington, KY
11 December 2017